TALLAPOOSA

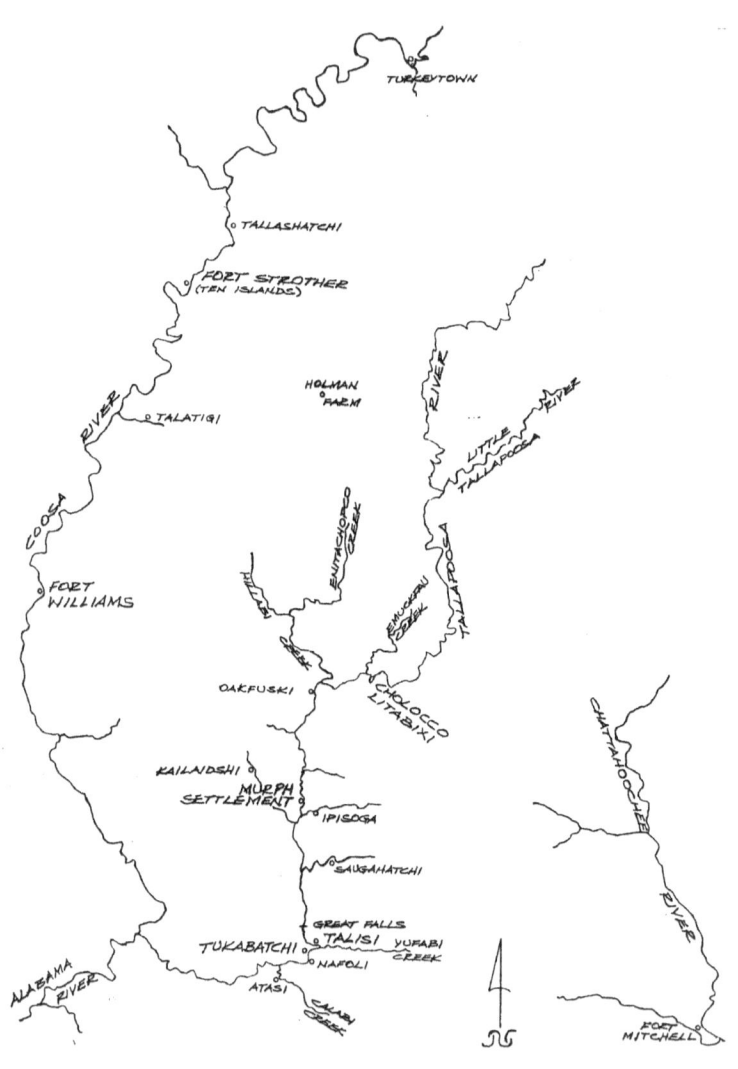

TALLAPOOSA RIVER REGION
MISSISSIPPI TERRITORY

Tallapoosa

A NOVEL

LARRY WILLIAMSON

NewSouth Books
Montgomery | Louisville

NewSouth Books
P.O. Box 1588
Montgomery, AL 36102

Library of Congress Cataloging-in-Publication Data
Williamson, Larry, 1938-
Tallapoosa : a novel / Larry Williamson.
p. cm.
ISBN-13: 978-1-60306-029-5 • ISBN-10: 1-60306-029-4
1. Tallapoosa River Valley (Ga. and Ala.)--Fiction. 2. United
States--History--1809-1817--Fiction. 3. Frontier and pioneer
life--Fiction. 4. Creek Indians--Wars--Fiction. I. Title.
PS3623.I57 T35 2001
813'.6--dc21

2001047240

Second Edition, 2007

Design by Randall Williams
Printed in the United States of America

ACKNOWLEDGMENTS

I must thank my legion of readers/critics. I was too stubborn to
accept all their advice, but the corrections and suggestions I did
use made the work much better. Thanks and hooray to Helen
Blackshear, W.C. Bryant, Dell Catherall, Joyce Franz, Dianne
Greene, Kurt Maurer, Catherine McLain, Pat Moran, Barb and
B.J. Taylor, Francis and Mary Alice Tucker, Gina Vaughn,
Murry Williamson, and Mrs. Wilton and her fifth graders at
Wrights Mill Road Elementary School. A special cheer for
Carolyn Buchanan, Norman Davis, Ora Maurer, Bill Robinson,
Dennis Hale, John Frandsen, Charlotte Miller, and all the other
creative talents from Mary Carol Moran's Novel Writers Work-
shop at Auburn University, and for Mary herself, the world's
greatest writing teacher. — L.W.

FOR MY MOTHER

LENA WILLIS WILLIAMSON

(1904-1997)

A MARVELOUS, HUMBLE LADY OF THE TALLAPOOSA

CHARACTER INDEX

Listed in order of first appearance.

‡ indicates historical characters.

* indicates characters who are mentioned in the story and are important to the historical events but don't actually appear in the book.

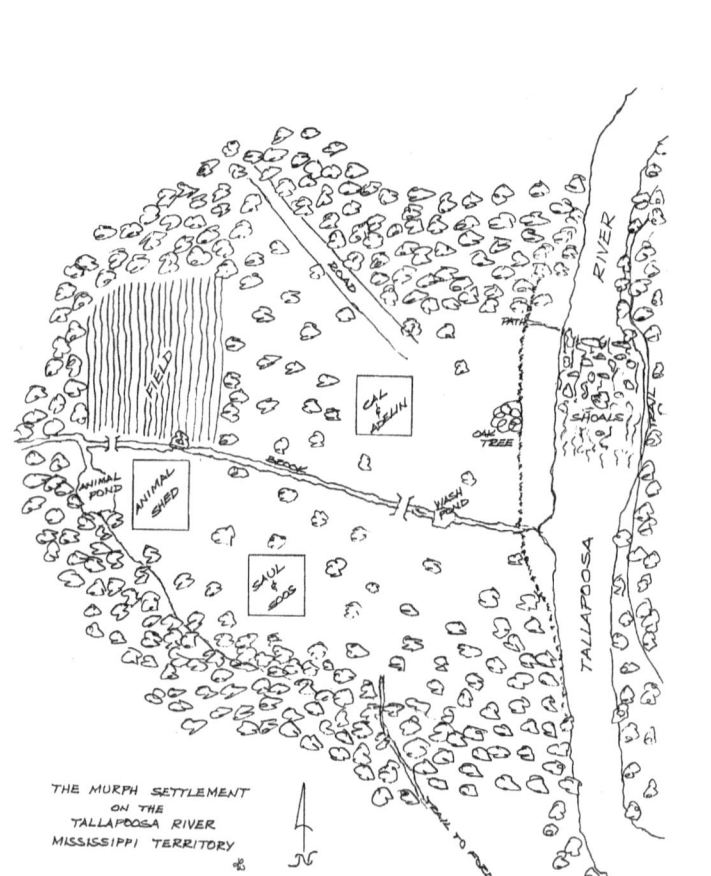

THE MURPH SETTLEMENT
ON THE
TALLAPOOSA RIVER
MISSISSIPPI TERRITORY

1

The Tallapoosa River, early October, 1813

The clap of a musket shot split the soft rumble of the river shoals.

In the cabin atop the bluff, Saul Murph splashed the dregs of his coffee into the banked hearth fire. "Damn! What's that?" He grabbed a musket, checked its charge, and handed it to his wife, Soosquana. "Stay here, Soos. Get over in the corner." He motioned to the cranny beside the fireplace and against the back wall.

Saul slung his pouch of powder and shot across his shoulder and reached for a second musket. At the door he listened, then peeked out. Hearing and seeing nothing, he slid from the cabin, crossed the porch, and sprinted to the giant oak at the edge of the bluff thirty yards away.

Another musket shot. Seconds later, another. Saul peered over the bluff in time to see lingering smoke from the last shot. It wafted above and behind five young Indians running from upriver along the opposite bank, at places splashing through the water's edge. Red Sticks.

Saul searched downriver to his right. A hundred yards ahead of the pack ran their prey, another young Creek, but not a Red Stick. The pursued man darted in and out of the forest, keeping a shield of trees at his back while he searched for the safest escape route. As he approached the bend of the river, he darted sharply left and raced up a steep ridge. A final shot missed as he disappeared over the top through a thicket of pines and hickories.

Saul knew the Red Sticks could not catch the man now. He probably had come from a downriver village, perhaps Ipisoga or Saugahatchi, and had wandered too far upriver while hunting. Or maybe he came up purposefully to create mischief.

The warriors, decorated with red body paint, had stopped directly below Saul, giving up the chase. They waved their prized muskets and bright red war clubs and screamed curses after the evader. As they wheeled to return upriver, one man glanced toward Saul and the wisp of smoke rising from the cabin's chimney. He scowled, then followed his companions.

A moment later, Saul tensed anew as the man screamed and ran back along the river bank and leaped onto the first boulder at the head of the shoals. He shook his club wildly above his head and skipped across several other rocks. His friends had taken his cue and followed him onto the slippery surfaces, stepping as agilely as he and echoing his curses and threats. They all stopped in the middle of the river, balanced precariously on crags inches above torrents rushing to a raging froth, and taunted the bluff above them. They cursed, screamed, waggled clubs and muskets. One aimed his piece, flint-lock at full cock, at a point above the bluff and pulled the trigger. The flint smashed against the strike and pan with a loud clatter, clearly heard even above the roiling water, but no explosion followed. The warrior had not reloaded since firing at the fleeing man. He roared at his joke.

After several minutes the youths tired of the exercise and hopped back across the boulders and lightly jumped to the bank. Again they started upriver, laughing and celebrating an imagined victory.

Saul relaxed his grip on the musket, fell back to rest on one hip, and allowed himself to breathe again. He suspected that the warriors had not seen him, but their interest frightened him. They knew he was there, he and his Indian wife and his brother Cal. They had been good neighbors atop their bluff for more than three years, since the spring of 1810. But now it was early October, 1813, and the Red Sticks were angry — angry at their more tolerant Upper Creek brothers from down the river, angry at the American agent Benjamin Hawkins and the Lower Creek villages on the Chattahoochee River he had won over, and certainly angry at the push of settlers from the north and east. Each new incident heightened tensions. Raids and counter-raids by both factions of the Creeks, some reliably reported and others rumored, had become more frequent. Once welcomed by their native neighbors as the only whites within days of travel, Saul and younger brother Cal had grown more vigilant and worried. They were now perceived by militants as precursors of a massive wave of hated invaders onto sacred tribal lands.

Americans called these Indians Creeks for their tendency to live on the banks of creeks and rivers. The natives rejected the name and instead proudly referred to themselves as Muskogis, the identity inherited from untold generations of ancestors. The spoken language was, therefore, Muskogean. English-speaking settlers and travelers found the language exceedingly difficult, perhaps because no tradition of writing existed.

All violence to date had been Indian against Indian, the Red Sticks who opposed white encroachment onto ancestral lands versus those Muskogis, especially of the Lower tribes, that seemed to condone it. The Red Sticks — so called for the red war clubs carried by the dissident warriors — resented the Indian agent Hawkins, who seemed to have most villages on the lower Tallapoosa under reasonable control. The more excitable of the militants followed the counsel of the great Shawnee leader Tecumseh, who prodded southern tribes to banish Americans from all Indian lands. The memory of Tecumseh's rage during his visit two autumns ago still drove them into frenzies. The threatened Creek civil war that had simmered since July could blow up any day and it could jeopardize white settlers. The Murphs felt the danger. They just wished to be allowed to remain at peace.

"Be glad when Cal gets back," Saul muttered. He chastised himself for being slow to start work this morning. At an hour past dawn, he should have been at the new cabin construction long ago. He spat forcefully and turned to cross the yard back to the cabin. He froze, startled. Across the way, at the edge of the clearing, stood a fully armed Red Stick.

2

Callister Murph cursed again, first to himself and then aloud. The wheel had gone wobbly right after he left Turkeytown yesterday at dawn.

"I'm sorry, George," he said to the mule pulling the two-wheel cart loaded with provisions, new tools, powder and shot, and miscellaneous goods to keep the little Murph compound going for the next year. "It ain't your fault. Hang on. We'll get the damned thing fixed at the Holman place."

Cal and George and Cal's horse, Tom, lagged a good half day behind schedule. Tom, tethered to the backboard, followed the cart while his master kicked at the cursed wheel. The condition of the faint, seldom-traveled road didn't help. The track beyond the Holman farm into the wilderness was even rougher and at places nonexistent, so the wheel had to be fixed or replaced. The farm lay nearly halfway to the Tallapoosa from Turkeytown, a Cherokee village on the upper Coosa River with a scattering of white settlers and a trading post. The Holmans had settled at the edge of the white man's reach into Indian lands. Only the Murphs had dared to venture farther and succeeded.

Getting the wheel repaired wasn't the only reason Cal wanted to reach the Holmans. Adelin awaited. He had admired her since he and big brother Saul met the Holman family when they first immigrated to the Tallapoosa three years ago. Adelin, at twenty-four, was three years older than Cal. Saul couldn't understand why younger sister Bess Marie, Cal's age and prettier than Adelin, had not caught Cal's eye. No, it had to be Adelin. Perhaps her rugged nature, her independence, her intelligence set her off. Cal didn't know why he preferred Adelin, but on his way to Turkeytown last week he had somehow summoned the fortitude to ask Daniel Holman for his daughter.

Holman had seemed stunned. "Son, you want to marry my daughter? Adelin?" He looked as if he should have added, " . . . and not Bess Marie?"

"Yes, sir."

"And what does she say?"

"I don't know, sir. I ain't asked her; I wanted to talk to you first. I hope she will have me. We talked a bit about it last year, that's all."

"Then let's call her and her mother in and see what they think."

Mr. Holman left to gather his family while his guest fidgeted. He found the girls and younger son Zack in the barn caring for Tom and George. His wife came in from the back-porch kitchen.

"Adelin," announced her father, "I believe young Mr. Murph has something he would like to ask you." He looked from his daughter to Cal, now frozen and ashen. "Cal?" Cal didn't move. "Cal?"

Cal shook loose great courage. "Uh, uh, Adelin," he stammered. He cleared his throat. "I was wondering if, I mean, I was asking your father, uh, ... Uh, aw hell, if you would like to go back to the Tallapoosa with me? I mean, as my, as my, uh, wife. Uh, would you? What, what do you think?" Cal exhaled.

Mrs. Holman and Bess Marie stared open-mouthed. Adelin stood expressionless. "Mr. Murph," she began, "I'm flattered. And honored." A long, excruciating pause. She finally smiled. "I will travel to the Tallapoosa with you." Bess Marie squealed. "As your wife."

So it was settled. The wedding would be ready for Cal on his return. Daniel would send with his daughter her good saddle horse, a dozen chickens, and anything else of use they could take. Cal had told the Holmans about Soosquana's coming baby and the new cabin they had built for her and Saul. Cal would get the old cabin. It would be Adelin's new home.

Mrs. Holman had insisted they take with them her best nanny goat as a gift to Soosquana. "That little mother-to-be needs lots of good goat's milk," she asserted. "And when the little one is born, there is nothing better. My three grew up strong on goat's milk."

Cal didn't know how Adelin really felt about him. He supposed she liked him well enough, though he was sure she didn't share his deep feelings. But he knew he had the advantage. The Holmans were stuck on the frontier and the girls' chances to find husbands were not great. They almost had to take the first offer. Also, Adelin's parents had to have been concerned that Adelin was twenty-four years old! She was almost beyond marrying age. Since Mr. and Mrs. Holman seemed to regard Cal with fondness, he congratulated himself that he was doing them a great favor.

That was the good part of Cal's journey. The bad part was that he would now have to tell the Holmans the wedding was off, or at least would have to be postponed. The news at Turkeytown had been gruesome, much worse than anything that had happened yet in the entire Mississippi Territory. In the south, whites had ambushed and killed a party of Creeks in late July. A month later, Indians attacked a white settlement called Fort Mims just north of the Mobile seaport and massacred more than two hundred fifty — possibly five hundred! — and kidnapped many women and children. Americans in the State of Tennessee were shocked and frightened. There was talk of the government sending regulars and volunteers down from Nashville through Big Spring, and from

Knoxville, to fight the Indians. Settlers around Turkeytown referred to the Creeks as savages, usually with a sneer or a forceful splatter of tobacco juice.

The Red Sticks on the Tallapoosa, already upset and near civil war over white settlers, would certainly become less tolerant of the likes of the Murphs on their lands. It was too dangerous for himself, Saul, and even Soosquana, and Cal refused to put Adelin in such peril. He was sure Mr. and Mrs. Holman would agree with him.

The Holman farm appeared through a slit in the forest. The opening became a clearing, then a wide meadow with plots of withered cornstalks and dying bean plants, stripped clean by the recent harvest. The cart's wheel had endured.

"Looka there," said Cal happily. "We made it, boys!"

Tom and George stepped with new energy when they saw the buildings. They already tasted oats. Cal smiled at Tom's soft whinny, but then his eagerness turned to dread. He had to explain the change of plans.

After supper would be ample time for bad news and serious discussion. The Holman siblings fed, swabbed, and curried George and Tom while Daniel Holman and Cal assessed the cranky wheel. The group finished unloading the cart just as Mrs. Holman sounded supper.

Cal gorged on roast pork, newly dug boiled potatoes, and cornbread. He would have asked for heaping seconds of everything even if he wasn't trying to delay his report to the Holmans. Several times he noticed both Adelin and Bess Marie studying him a little too closely, gauging his eating habits, he supposed.

Later, with everyone seated in the parlor, the family listened in horror to Cal's stories from Turkeytown. They had never heard of Burnt Corn Creek or Fort Mims, but knew there were settlers in the south of the Territory. That hostilities had accelerated shocked and concerned them. Tales of minor skirmishes were part of life on any frontier, and they were used to that. But to have major conflict possibly come their way was distressing.

No question that Adelin should not go with Cal.

"Shouldn't you and Saul leave?" asked Holman. "At least for a while?"

"I guess that would be wise. But no, we can't. We won't," Cal corrected. "We've made many friends among the Creeks and we like our little place. Soosquana comes from one of the main warrior villages down near the Creeks' tribal capital. Even most of the hotheads up the river know better than to harm her." Cal paused and searched each concerned face. "No, we won't run. I know Saul feels the same. We'll stay alert and keep our noses out of trouble."

"Well," sighed Daniel Holman, "I'm sure things will be calmed down when you come back through next year." He looked at his eldest daughter. "Adelin will still be here."

Adelin sat motionless for long seconds, then got up and walked from the room. Cal and Mr. Holman continued to talk of the situation, speculating on its seriousness, whether a military column might indeed march from up north, and if the Holman farm could be in danger. Rumors that the Creek Nation had allied with the British in the current conflict with the United States added to the peril. An encouraging point was that the major troubles so far had happened in the south of Alabama country, far removed from the east of the Territory. But growing anger on the upper Tallapoosa could not be ignored.

Adelin reappeared in the doorway. She looked from one person to another, fixing each with a brief stare. She stood tall, feet set wide, arms folded.

"Father. Mr. Murph," she announced in a strong, even voice. "I'm going."

3

The Executive Mansion, Washington, D.C., early October, 1813

"Ah, Mr. Armstrong. Come in. Sit down, please."

"Thank you, sir. You wished to see me, Mr. President?" John Armstrong, President James Madison's Secretary of War, strolled to the center of the Blue Room, the oval-shaped office of the President. After shaking hands with Mr. Madison, he flipped the tail of his dress coat up behind him and sat in the large, upholstered chair before Madison's desk. He cradled his felt flattop hat in his lap.

"To be sure, Mr. Armstrong—" President Madison sat down and leaned forward in his massive stuffed chair. The chair made the diminutive man look even smaller. "—We continue to receive dispatches from Nashville regarding the Creek Indian situation in Alabama country."

"I know, sir. I received still another from General Jackson yesterday pleading for invasion troops, and for authorization to invade."

"And I one from Governor Blount just this morning. He begs for the same things Jackson does. Been doing it for weeks. Now he informs me that the Tennessee legislature has authorized him to raise a militia of three thousand five hundred men and has budgeted three hundred thousand dollars to finance a campaign into Creek lands."

"Sir? They have no right outside their state borders."

"I know. I want to get your and Monroe's opinions on this. He should be here shortly. Tell me, John, what do you think of General Jackson?"

Armstrong had been a military man himself, as well as a United States senator and a diplomatic minister to France. Princeton educated, born in Pennsylvania, transplanted to New York, he was regarded as a bright man, a doer, but not very well liked, not even by Madison. But he was a competent Secretary of War.

"I've never met the man, sir," he began after a lengthy, thoughtful hesitation, "but I understand he's somewhat of a rogue. A most able military leader, but doesn't like to take orders."

"Yes, I know. His Natchez debacle pretty much defined the man. His defiance and his leadership." Madison chuckled at a personal remembrance. "He sure was a rebel during his short time in Congress. A real pain in the butt. He didn't like the city of Washington, that's certain, or many of its people or its ways."

A knock at the door interrupted. In walked James Monroe, President Madison's Secretary of State, a fellow Virginian, and his most trusted official confidant.

"Mr. President?"

"James. Come in. I need to consult with you and Mr. Armstrong about the Indian problem down south. You are aware, I trust, of recent developments?"

"Yes, sir. Unless you have something fresh."

"We do." Madison shared the latest dispatches with him.

"This could be dangerous," Monroe judged.

"I agree. I understand there have been a couple of isolated incidents, but nothing that would justify an invasion of the Territory."

"Until now," Armstrong jumped in, "most hostilities seem to have been confined to the Creeks fighting among themselves; Red

Sticks against those Indians that are more friendly to Americans."

"Red Sticks?" puzzled Madison.

"Those are the militants, the ones that hate us and have vowed to banish us from their regions. Fortunately for us, all Creeks don't sympathize with them, especially the Lower tribes along the Chattahoochee."

Monroe stroked his chin and wrinkled his forehead. "I don't know the strength or the disposition of the Creeks, but if Jackson gets them stirred up to the point that they actively throw in with the British, we could be in big trouble down there. We don't need Redcoats coming at us up through the State of Georgia or gaining free run of the Mississippi."

"Think it could come to that?" asked Madison.

"Could. Right now the British and Spanish have a presence around Pensacola, but don't seem to be that much of a threat."

Armstrong pitched in again. "The Creek Nation has the Tennessee and Ohio Valleys sealed off from the Gulf of Mexico. If that barrier is breached by the Creeks offering the British clear passage up the Alabama and Chattahoochee river systems, well, that would open a whole new front for us. We can't cover our ass everywhere as it is."

"Hmmm. Surely Blount and Jackson know that," Madison said. "What do you think they are up to?"

"Simple, sir," offered Monroe. "Not to disparage their motives, but a few things are pretty well known." He looked at the President as if seeking permission to disparage.

"Go on."

"Well, sir, a lot of settlers are flooding west and south. They have to have some place to go. Creek lands have been called by some the richest land on the continent not yet settled. You can imagine the speculation if our treaties with the Creeks are circumvented. Too,

Blount's big planters in Tennessee want access to the Gulf so they can ship their goods out of Mobile. As we are shielded from the British by the Creeks, so are Blount's producers blocked from Mobile."

"Also," added Armstrong, "Jackson, as you know, has been lobbying for a regular army commission and for command of the forces that are eventually going to have to defend New Orleans. I believe he thinks a glorious campaign against a pagan, pro-British Indian force will achieve his goals."

"What about the Georgia and Mississippi Territory militias?"

"Well, sir, General John Floyd commands the Georgia militia. He cooperates closely with the Indian agent down there that has been educating the Creeks—with a certain degree of success with many of them, I must say. General Ferdinand Claiborne, as you know, sir, is monitoring the south of the Mississippi Territory with his Mississippi militia and some regulars. He's providing protection where he can for settlers in the region where the recent troubles occurred. I'm certain that he intends to go no farther north than he has to. Both Floyd and Claiborne seem to be holding true so far, staying well within their boundaries. Governor Blount and General Jackson will exhibit grave disregard if they invade from Tennessee without orders."

"Sir," interrupted Monroe, "if I may say so, it looks like a pure land grab to me. We have treaties with the Creeks. We have no call to go in there, nor does the Tennessee militia. And the settlers that are there are obligated to behave themselves."

"Gentlemen," said Madison, "I agree with most of your assessments. And I certainly appreciate your insights. You both are very wise." He paused. "Now, the big question. What can we do about it? What should be our course of action?"

4

"Safe?" asked the Red Stick.

"Oh, thank God, it's you," sighed Saul. He relaxed. "You scared me for a moment."

"Safe?" repeated Pokkataw in English. While he knew more English than his friends Saul and Cal Murph knew Muskogean, he tended to speak in one- and two-word sentences. Somehow, with gestures, he always made literal sense.

"Yes, thank you. Guess those boys were just out for an early morning romp. Playing games with each other."

"No games. Danger. Angry. Careful."

"Yeah. I know. We are watching ourselves. And thanks for checking on us."

"Soosquana?" He always used her full name.

"Soos is fine. A little queasy at times, but that's normal. Six months along now. She's tough, though. You know that."

The two walked to the porch. Soosquana stood in the doorway, still holding the musket. She greeted Pokkataw in Muskogean. He smiled broadly as they spilled into an animated conversation. He rambled freely and happily; no clipped sentences in his native language. Saul picked up little of the exchange, but knew they talked about the baby when Soosquana rubbed her belly and gingerly placed Pokkataw's palm against it.

Pokkataw turned his attention back to Saul, and his language back to semi-English. "Cal?"

"Cal left for Turkeytown eight days ago to replenish our stores. We have most of the crops in except some potatoes and squash and a few other things. I can handle that, so this is a good time of year for him to go."

"Cabin?" Pokkataw pointed south across the yard to a grove of pine saplings surrounding a new split-log cabin.

"About to move in. Soos really likes it. More room, an extra window, better heat. That's really good for when the baby gets here. Cal will take this place for himself."

"Him wife? Indian? Like Soosquana?"

"I don't think so. Not for a while anyway. I think he's kinda sweet on the daughter of a farmer we know back along the track to Turkeytown. A nice family from back in the west of Virginia near where we come from. We didn't know them, though, till we came down here from Big Spring and found their place along the trail. They had already been there about five years."

"Farmer sell?"

"Sell? Sell what?"

"Wife. Cal."

"Oh no. No, the farmer doesn't have to sell his daughter to Cal. All Cal has to do is ask the girl."

Pokkataw's face wrinkled in puzzlement. "Ask girl? Not father?"

"Well, him, too. At least sometimes. But the one that has to be convinced is the girl." Saul laughed at Pokkataw's frown. "What strange ways we Americans have, hey?"

"Girl come?"

"No. Certainly not. No girl like that would ever come this far into the woods."

The men had walked slowly north along the bluff to the edge of the forest where began the path down to the river. It dropped steeply and was pocked with stones, from fist size to small boulders. Safe enough for humans stepping lightly, but perilous for horses. A ford a quarter-mile south could be reached from the bluff by a horseman needing to cross the river.

At the bottom of the path lay a canoe, out of the water and tied to the base of a pine tree.

Pokkataw pointed. "Canoe."

"Eh?"

"Not safe. Steal."

They descended the trail to the river. Another canoe lay forty yards downriver, also on the bank and in plain view. The river shoals spanned the distance. One canoe was usually used above the shoals, the other below. Exposed as they were, the band of hotheads could have stolen or damaged them earlier if they were of a mind.

"Hide," suggested Pokkataw. "From warriors."

The men moved the boats farther from the water's edge into the brush. They assured themselves they could not be seen from the river, certainly not from the opposite bank by travelers on foot.

Pokkataw bade Saul goodbye with a renewed pledge of peace. He set off upriver toward his small warrior village near the mouth of Hillabi Creek. The several Indian towns along that stream still resisted the call to violence of their brothers elsewhere on the Tallapoosa. Fortunately for the Murphs, so did most nearby villages and half of those to the immediate south, on past the great falls and the council capital of Tukabatchi, where the river bends to the west. Past there, Saul knew nothing of the mood of the Creeks that inhabited the land south and west.

Saul returned to the cabin. Soosquana swept imaginary trash from the doorway with a brush broom. Saul could tell she was a little shaken, though she tried hard to hide it.

"Will Muskogis fight each other?" she asked. Her concern was clearly for her family and friends in Talisi town, across the river from Tukabatchi below the great falls. "I not want them to fight."

"I don't either, Soos," said Saul as he returned both muskets and his pouch to their corner. He checked again the readiness of each weapon before he stacked them in their niche. They had to be instantly usable for any emergency. His fears increased daily that such might be inevitable. "There have already been some small troubles. At least both sides have left us alone so far, but some of Pokkataw's Red Stick friends certainly don't like us."

Saul began his morning chores, but the crisis among the Upper Creeks nagged at him. He thought of Talisi and Tukabatchi. They lay on the flat shores of the Tallapoosa just below the great falls, which represents the fall line between the Appalachian foothills and the coastal plain. The chiefs of the Muskogi Nation gathered regularly for talks beneath the Great Council Oak on the sacred grounds of Tukabatchi. Talisi, the most important of several warrior towns in the vicinity, sat directly opposite Tukabatchi on the eastern bank, at the mouth of Yufabi Creek.

Saul and Cal had visited the two Creek towns twice, the first time in the autumn of 1810, a few months after settling at their compound. Pokkataw had already befriended them and he escorted them south and sponsored their visit. The Murphs found the Muskogis gracious and generous.

At Talisi, the party met a warrior leader named Naupti, the half brother of the elderly village chief. He and his three sturdy sons greeted them warmly. One of his daughters, a beauty of about twenty, stood in the doorway of their house. Saul stared at her, then forced a smile. She smiled back.

"Who is she?" Saul begged of Pokkataw.

"Daughter warrior. Uncle chief."

"Can you find out more?"

Saul found an excuse to come back around later in the day, hoping to see the girl again. She was there; Saul learned afterward she had watched the visitors constantly and was as fascinated as he. She understood a little English, having listened to the U.S. government Indian agents that visited regularly, but could speak none, or at least didn't. She only smiled and nodded her head. Saul had to leave a few minutes later and the girl held out her hand. She had learned the white man's custom of shaking hands. Saul gingerly took the hand, held it too long, didn't want to let go.

"Her Soosquana," Pokkataw told him on the way home.

The entire journey back, Saul treasured his right hand that had touched the beautiful maiden's. He looked at it magically and massaged the consecrated fingers with the thumb. He would talk of her often in the ensuing months, especially when Pokkataw visited.

The next year Tecumseh came to the Tallapoosa. The Shawnee chief from the Great Lakes envisioned a Confederacy of Indian Nations and traveled through Choctaw and Upper Creek lands recruiting allies. He hoped to unite the Muskogi villages at a Great Council at Tukabatchi and at a gathering of warriors at Talisi. He made many converts, especially among younger, impatient warriors opposing the Civilization Program of Agent Benjamin Hawkins. However, the wise chiefs of most of the lower Tallapoosa towns rejected Tecumseh's militarism, as did all the leaders of the Lower Muskogis along the Chattahoochee River.

Soosquana would tell the story many times of how Tecumseh spoke for hours, ranting about the invasion of the white man into sacred tribal lands, whipping his converts into angry mania. How, at the conclusion of his speech, his Shawnee warrior companions leaped to their feet with terrifying screams and threw themselves into a maddening, prolonged war dance that frightened every warrior and elder present. Then, when the chiefs decided against his Confederacy despite such rhetoric and antics, how irate he became.

"Because of the treachery and cowardice of these tribal chiefs," he threatened, "I must return to the land of the Shawnee unfulfilled. When I arrive, I will stamp my foot with such force I will cause the entire earth to shake!"

Tecumseh and his associates had toured the Muskogi towns all along the river for weeks afterward, convincing many. When he left, some of his Shawnee brethren, led by a mystical prophet named Seekabo, remained to solidify his influence. The Upper Creeks had been feuding since, village against village, and often among warriors of the same village.

It had been too dangerous to travel downriver the entire next year. But by the spring of 1812 relative calm had returned to the region and, one bright day, Pokkataw appeared at the Murph compound.

"Soosquana. Yours," he said proudly.

"What?"

"Soosquana. You marry."

"I'm to marry her? I don't understand. Who says?"

"Father. Naupti. Uncle chief. Good medicine."

"Good medicine, huh? And what if I don't want to get married?"

Cal, laughing, sat down against a tree. "Looks like you have no choice, big brother. You wouldn't want to make the chiefs mad, would you? Besides, admit it, that's the best news you've had since we were down there. You haven't thought of much since."

So the Murphs' second visit to Talisi town began. They had walked the first time, a distance of twenty miles or more. This trip they and Pokkataw floated down the river in two canoes. Three long islands, parallel with each other and with the flow of the current, guarded the falls. Just short of the islands, the travelers pulled into a cove fed by a branch about a quarter-mile above the falls, on the east side. From there they hiked the remaining four miles—down the steep slopes, across a small creek to the flat plain and on to Talisi.

Saul and his willing bride were married the next morning in an elegant ceremony, very little of which was understood by Saul and Cal. Pokkataw attempted to explain most of it later. What Pokkataw didn't explain but was all too evident by scowls on the faces of many of the warriors, was that everyone did not approve. Clear to all, however, was that Naupti was pleased to give his eldest daughter what she most desired.

The men and Saul's happy new wife started north early that afternoon so they would arrive at the compound before dark. For a time, Cal would sleep outside near the animals' shelter while Saul became acquainted with his wonderful Soosquana. A week later, after they partitioned off a small section of the cabin for his sleeping accommodations, Cal moved back in.

Soosquana adjusted magnificently. She practiced the English she already knew and added to it, speaking it well in a brief time. She attempted to improve the brothers' command of Muskogean, but with little success.

Saul loved her every bit as much as he had thought he would. Cal liked having a woman around the compound. He and his new sister-in-law quickly developed a great fondness for each other.

"Best thing I've ever done," Saul mused aloud, talking to himself. He looked up from his work. Soosquana stood smiling at him from an open shutter of their new cabin.

5

The Holman farm, early October, 1813

Cal, Daniel Holman, and Zack worked in the Holman barn at first light. They decided the faulty wheel couldn't be trusted to carry the loaded cart over another fifty miles of rugged trail. They replaced it with a spare wheel the Holmans kept in the barn for emergencies. Daniel thought he could rebuild Cal's wheel later and use it as his spare.

By midmorning, they were ready for the wedding. Mrs. Holman and Daniel made another weak attempt to dissuade Adelin, but she had decided. Guilt gnawed at Cal since he knew he should be more forceful, if not outright adamant. But he admired Adelin more than ever for her resolution. He could resist her no better than could her parents.

Mr. Holman would perform the ceremony. He produced a document hand-lettered on coarse thick paper that gave him proper authority. Zack would stand up for Cal, Bess Marie for Adelin.

Both girls entered the parlor in bright, starched frocks. Adelin's straight auburn hair flowed down her back. Cal skipped a couple of breaths. He had never seen either sister wear anything but britches of coarse spun cotton, wool, or buckskin. Adelin glided to Cal's side and lightly attached both hands to his forearm. Cal squirmed. Sweat oozed from his forehead.

Mr. Holman began. "My friend Judge Ozment Phipps back in Virginia made me a marrying judge before we left home. He figured I might need it someday, having daughters and all, and so here we are." He cleared his throat, making a big show of it. "Judge Phipps told me what words to say, too, in a marrying situation."

"Get on with it, Father," coached Adelin.

"Uh, yes. So I will." Another quick cough. "Callister Murph, do you want to marry this girl?"

"Woman, Father," Bess Marie corrected.

"Callister, do you want this woman?"

"Ye . . . , yes, sir. I sure do." Cal tried to smile.

"So. Very well. And Adelin Anna Holman, do you want this fellow, Cal Murph, for a husband?"

Adelin looked up into Cal's eyes. "Yes, Father."

"Well, I reckon you're married then," Daniel concluded. He angled his chin upward, pleased and proud of himself and of his daughter. Bess Marie clapped with delight.

Cal had again contracted paralysis; he had turned into a statue, unable to move. Adelin laughed, grabbed him by the shoulders, and tiptoed to kiss her bashful new husband gingerly on the lips.

Shortly before noon, after a big dinner of beef stew and blackeyed peas, the party made ready to travel. Somehow, room had been found on the cart and on the flanks of the two horses for the added baggage. The twelve chickens making the trip fretted in three cages strapped atop Tom's rump. The goat would walk behind the cart, looped to the backboard by her halter rope.

Adelin, back in her thick cotton trousers, cotton shirt, and vest and riding leggings of buckskin, sat astride her pale buff mare with its black mane and tail. Her own musket hung from the saddle. Cal had no doubt she knew how to use it.

Adelin leaned down to kiss each member of her family one last time. Mrs. Holman wiped away tears. Cal reached from his perch aboard Tom to again shake Daniel Holman's hand.

"We'll see you in about a year," Cal tried to say cheerily. "Don't worry. We'll be fine."

"I know, son," said Daniel. "Take care of my girl. God bless."

Less than a mile into the bush, the track disappeared; only faint traces of it would occasionally reemerge for short distances. Cal knew the way, but the miles passed slowly and carefully. It would take a full two days to reach the Tallapoosa, possibly three with such a pack.

Over rougher stretches, and at other times to unburden the horses, Cal and Adelin dismounted, tied them to the cart alongside the goat, and walked together, leading George the mule and the wagon behind them. Those intervals provided opportunities for delicious conversation.

"Why do you call your horse Okra?" inquired Cal.

Adelin giggled. "That's a good story. When I was a little girl, I hated okra. The vegetable, that is. Still do. Well, my mother promised me that when I grew up I would love okra. When I got this horse, she reminded me of it. She said that since I still wouldn't eat the stuff and I did love my horse, I should name her Okra. That way her promise would be fulfilled. Isn't that crazy?"

"It is a strange way to name a horse."

"You should hear the names of some of our other animals. Now you tell me why Tom and George are who they are."

"That's easy. George is President George Washington and Tom is President Thomas Jefferson."

"I see. Makes sense."

"And Saul's horse is named James, after . . . "

"After Mr. Madison! Very good."

"All those fellows are from Virginia, too."

Across two more ridges, Cal's curiosity resurfaced. "How good are you with that thing back there?"

"What thing?"

"Your musket. Are you a good shot?"

"I'll just have to show you sometime." She pointed to her vest and leggings. "I brought down the big buck that these skins came from. I don't lie," she laughed. "A big buck!"

"Well, now, I am impressed."

Adelin asked about the compound, and about the river, and about Soosquana. She wanted to know everything. That she was excited about reaching her new home and asked so many questions made Cal happy.

An hour before sundown, they halted at a small rushing creek and made camp under a big willow tree. Adelin walked to the edge of the stream and scooped a few handfuls of clear, cool water to drink. She stood and rotated slowly, turning completely around twice.

"This is beautiful, Mr. Murph!" she exclaimed. "This whole country is beautiful."

"You have to stop calling me Mr. Murph, Adelin. I'm Cal."

"Yes, I know. Cal. I think I can get used to that." She looked at him with wide eyes and a light smile. "But you can call me Mrs. Murph any time you please."

The two busied themselves caring for the animals. They unsaddled, unhitched, and unloaded. They fed and watered each beast, including the chickens, then swabbed and rubbed clean George, the two horses, and the goat. Cal kindled a small campfire with a flint and a pinch of gunpowder. They prepared a supper of dried beef, beans, and hard bread, and ate while watching the sun sink from a cloudless sky.

As dusk faded to dark and the fire withered, night creatures tuned up the music of the forest. An owl hooted through the chatter of a thousand crickets. A small animal, perhaps a raccoon, scurried through the brush near the burbling stream. Far away, the screams of angry contenders, species unknown, split the air. Probably frisky males fighting over a lady fair.

Cal and Adelin talked a while longer, until a three-quarter moon and millions of stars reached full luminescence.

Adelin arose, retrieved a bundle from the cart, and carried it to a grassy clearing away from the overhang of the willow. She spread a heavy blanket over a thick layer of pine straw she had gathered earlier, and sat down on its edge. Cal watched closely as she removed her buckskin vest.

"Come sit beside me, Cal," she invited as she unlaced her leggings.

That night, under that gorgeous, mild October sky, Adelin Holman Murph taught Callister Murph things she did not know she knew, and learned beautiful lessons herself. She and Cal would forever remember that clearing, that willow tree, that wonderful brook, and the nocturnal serenade of an Alabama forest.

6

"Now you must fight! The whites will overrun your lands!" Seekabo, the prophet Tecumseh left behind when the Shawnee chief returned to the Great Lakes country, screamed his angry impatience. "The Muskogi cannot trust the invaders further."

Hopoithle Miko, the wise aged chief of Talisi town, spoke with a firm, even voice. "Muskogis do not wish to fight. But we will not give more land to the white government."

"Then you will have to fight!" insisted Seekabo. "They will take your land if you do not. The news from the Tensaw River, and before that from the creek the whites call Burnt Corn, proves it. Many of your brothers have been killed already. And now with the death of Tecumseh, the intruders will march without fear over the Muskogi and over the Shawnee if we are not bold!"

Seekabo and his small band of Shawnee brethren, accompanied by Red Stick converts, had toured the Muskogi Nation since Tecumseh's visit late in 1811. They had arrived in Talisi that afternoon in mourning paint and with grieving hearts.

"Words have flown swiftly to us from our land of the Shawnee," announced Seekabo to Hopoithle Miko immediately upon arrival, "telling of the death of our great leader Tecumseh. He fell in glory on the Thames River near Fort Detroit fighting the Americans. We come to you first with this news, wise chief of Talisi, as you are the leader of the Muskogi's strongest warrior town. We implore you now to join the fight against all invaders of lands to the west and south. We will perish, all of us, Shawnee, Muskogi, Oneida, Choctaw, Seminole, Cherokee, Sauk, Chickasaw, all of us, if we do not become one against those who would have our land and slaughter our deer and destroy our forests!"

Hopoithle Miko was the head chief of Talisi, on the east bank of the Tallapoosa opposite Tukabatchi, the capital of all the Muskogis, Upper and Lower tribes. He had once welcomed Benjamin Hawkins and his assistants and his Civilization Program, as had most of the villages on the lower Tallapoosa. He had participated with enthusiasm, interested in this alternate culture and economy, not as a lifestyle for himself and his people but as a matter of understanding his new neighbors. He had traveled to Washington and played an important role in negotiating with the American President, Thomas Jefferson, a treaty of peace and understanding.

As recently as 1805, Hopoithle Miko favored the concession of all Muskogi land between the Oconee and Ocmulgee Rivers to the State of Georgia, assured that white settlers would come no farther and that remaining Muskogi hunting grounds would be respected. But when settlers immediately flooded westward across the Ocmulgee and continued to hunt in Indian forests, Hopoithle Miko had finally lost all trust for American promises. He had been transformed from Agent Hawkins's best conduit for the Civilization Program to one of the most influential enemies of the white man's culture.

Hopoithle Miko now hated Benjamin Hawkins. He constantly groused his resentment of the arrogant designs of the Indian agent to any ally who would listen. Ever encouraging any dissent, especially from so prominent a leader as Hopoithle Miko, were the shamans and the prophets, interpreters of the Spirits and guided by the supreme Muskogi Spirit, Essaugetuh Emissee, the Maker of Breath. These mystics were major catalysts of tension between the Upper Muskogi Red Sticks on one side of the current conflict, and the Lower Muskogi and pacifist Upper tribesmen on the other.

"No!" he reluctantly answered Seekabo's demand. "I am truly saddened by news of Tecumseh's death and mourn with you. He was a noble champion of the Shawnee and a conscience for all our peoples. But we cannot fight the white man. We will have to, I concede, if they come to us with larceny and malice. We will not run, but we dare not provoke them. Muskogi warriors have little chance against the whites' superior numbers and superior weapons."

"That is why we must unite as one! That is what Tecumseh taught us! That is what the Spirits implore. We are protected by the Maker of Breath, so as joined Nations we cannot be defeated."

The debate raged all afternoon, the same debate that had stormed up and down the Tallapoosa and divided the Upper Muskogis since Tecumseh's visit nearly two years earlier. The argument continued in the fading twilight as Hopoithle Miko and his elder advisers and warrior leaders strolled along the river's edge with Seekabo and his Shawnee and Red Stick confederates. Across the river the cookfires of Tukabatchi winked at them.

"You know that I do not trust Hawkins," Hopoithle Miko patiently insisted again. "His government and his people have betrayed the Muskogis too often. I have dealt with them for many years, hoping that we could live in peace and that our land and our ways would be respected."

"You trusted them to keep their promises, over and over. You have seen what they do each time."

"Yes. We have been true, but I know now that they do not keep their word."

"We will not make those mistakes again," spoke Naupti, Hopoithle Miko's half brother.

"But the white settlers still come and you do not stop them."

"You speak truthfully," conceded Naupti. "Whites now crowd the river they call Flint and have outposts on the Chattahoochee."

"And a military fort on the near bank of the Chattahoochee," interjected Suanji, an angry young Red Stick from Kailaidshi, the village from which Seekabo operated. "It is but a day's easy walk distance. And yet you do not challenge the white man?"

"We challenge him when he comes to take our villages!"

"He has already come!" stormed Suanji. "Those lands are ours! We give nothing else!"

"We leave affairs of the Chattahoochee to the Cowetas and the Cussetas. The towns of the Lower Muskogis do not welcome our counsel," said Hopoithle Miko.

"But yet you fight against the Lower tribes," argued Seekabo. "Why do you not attack the whites? The Lower villages belong on the Chattahoochee. White settlements do not!"

"You do not understand. I have resisted the white government's intrusions for many years. Agent Hawkins demands the right to build two roads through the heart of Muskogi lands, and free passage of the American military. I said no. I said no to Mr. Jefferson eight years ago when he requested the same. From the north, Tennessee prizes trade roads and free navigation of the Coosa and the Alabama to reach the great ships at Mobile with their trade goods. My friends, the chiefs of the Coosa tribes, say no. We will forever say no."

"Those things cannot be permitted," agreed Suanji. "They would destroy our hunting grounds and corrupt our people."

"We do not disagree," said Naupti. "But we do not share your view that all whites are evil. My eldest daughter has taken a good white man as her husband. He and his people respect us. We will fight as hard as you against those who do not."

Seekabo turned away. He stood for a long time with closed eyes and clenched fists. "My brothers," he finally started, again spitting anger, "you are wrong to hope further for peace on the terms of the white government or on the good will of their settlers. Though the body of Tecumseh has been killed by American soldiers in the northern war, his mighty spirit lives eternally here among his Muskogi brothers. His mother was birthed on the banks of the Tallapoosa. Though he and his brother, Tenskwatawa, the master of the prophets, led the great Shawnee tribesmen, he never forgot his Muskogi ancestry. Now that he is dead, his spirit cries out more than ever for victory over the aggressions of the white nation. I speak for Tecumseh and for Tenskwatawa and for all the shamans of the Muskogis and the Shawnees. I implore you to abandon your caution, fight for your people, and reclaim your sacred homelands."

"That is all well, dear friend Seekabo," pondered Hopoithle Miko. "But we could not do such a thing alone, and the Lower towns would never join such a fight. What of the Choctaws and the Seminoles?"

"Our Choctaw and Seminole brothers are prepared to fight. They await your leadership."

"We must know more. If we are forced to fight we must know which tribes and villages to trust. We will destroy ourselves and forfeit all that you beg us to protect if we act in haste and by mistake."

"Then I urge you to seek the alliances of those that you trust, and swiftly before it is too late."

"I will make a pact with you, my friend, and with our brothers from Kailaidshi. Let us drink together from the sacred waters of the Tallapoosa in remembrance of Tecumseh, and as a pledge to do whatever is necessary to protect this mighty river and all the land that embraces it, and to preserve it for the Muskogi people forever. We may exercise different cautions, but we share common goals and concerns."

"Agreed!" spoke Seekabo, feeling that he had finally opened a crack in Hopoithle Miko's resistance. He waded into the river and scooped water into cupped hands, following the gesture of the old, wise chief. He drank, "In remembrance of the magnificent warrior Tecumseh. And we pledge death to all that dishonor his memory or defile the lands that he walked!"

7

Saul had worked the garden plots until noon, pulling up the last of the onions, then digging and storing several baskets of potatoes. There remained to be harvested an abundance of potatoes, the only major crop still in the fields.

After dinner he turned his attention to the new cabin. Additional furniture had to be built and the fireplace was not yet fully cured. Otherwise, it awaited its tenants.

Soosquana had already moved many items from the old structure. She worked daily getting the new cabin clean, airtight, and familiar. She also wanted to leave the other in as good shape as possible for Cal. When time became available, she spent it lovingly crafting a cradle from bent saplings for the coming little one.

Saul labored through the afternoon on the log bridge between the cabins. It was strong and wide enough for a horse and a loaded wagon to cross safely, but it needed rails and additional gravel from the river for the approaches. Fashioning the rails had his attention this day.

A spring-fed brook ran between the cabins. It flowed briskly over a stone bed toward the river. Saul and Cal had diverted part of the stream to form a pool at the animal pen. The excess and waste water drained south through the woods behind the new cabin to the river. The natural branch slid beneath a small foot bridge and continued on past the cabins to pour freely off a boulder. Water for drinking and cooking was collected there. The rapid flow next passed under the sturdy rail bridge and on to another rocky drop into a small reservoir, convenient for washing clothes, tools, equipment, and people. Another twenty yards and the branch plunged off the bluff to the river below as a thin but pretty waterfall.

Saul pondered the concerns for their safety he and Pokkataw had discussed. Saul and Cal had little cause to fear the Red Sticks; Pokkataw himself was a Red Stick. But things could explode any day and could threaten the Murphs. White settlers were the root grievance among the Creeks, and he and Cal were the only whites in the region. There was no doubt some of the more excitable militants would welcome an excuse to tear into the Murphs.

Perhaps we should be more worried, Saul mused as he buttressed an upright against a side of the bridge. Maybe Pokkataw knows much more than we do. Maybe he isn't telling all he does know.

Shadows had just begun to stretch and flatten when a rustling sound filtered from the woods in the direction of the road. Saul made a quick move for his musket, but after a single step relaxed at a second noise. It was the happy bray of George as the mule sensed the familiarity of home.

Saul walked around the corner of the cabin to peer toward the woods as the first horse cleared the trees. Soosquana came and stood beside him. They marveled at the sight. Cal and a stranger rode side-by-side mounts ahead of the mule pulling a heavily laden cart. A woman. As they drew nearer, Saul recognized her as the farmer's redheaded daughter from along the trail to Turkeytown.

"Holy hell!" Saul exclaimed.

Soosquana looked at Saul. "Who is she?"

Cal halted his party in front of the cabin. "Hi there, big brother," he greeted with a wide smile. "Hi, Soos. Miss me?"

"Is this the young lady I think it is?" asked Saul, as he caressed the mule's cheek and patted his neck. He laughed. "Did you kidnap her, Cal, you fool?"

Cal's smile changed to a happy blush. "This here's my, my wife. This is Adelin. We got married back at her folks' place. Adelin, I think you remember my ugly brother Saul, don't you? And this is his wife, Soosquana. Call her Soos. You'll like her. You're probably gonna hate Saul."

Cal and Adelin dismounted. Adelin took the hand offered by Soosquana, then by Saul.

"Welcome, Adelin," smiled Soosquana.

"Me, too," offered Saul. "I can't imagine how you got talked into this."

Light conversation continued as the men unhitched George. They would leave the cart in front of the cabin for easier unloading. Soos and Adelin rummaged through the cart's contents. Saul and Cal left the women to get acquainted as they led the four animals, one with its cargo of chickens, up the path to the animal pen and shelter.

"You finally snagged that little girl you've been sweet on, huh? You surprised me but, hell, congratulations."

"Thanks, brother."

The brothers walked side by side, smiling. Saul's brown hair and mature carriage contrasted with Cal's dark blond, unruly locks and smug grin. Scattered freckles accented Cal's forever boyish face that conveyed perpetual enthusiasm. He stood two inches shorter than Saul's almost six foot height. Both were lean and muscular, essential characteristics for thriving in the wilderness, but Saul carried his heft on a slightly larger frame.

"How did you find Turkeytown? Any news from Virginia? Did you hear anything of our old friends in Big Spring?"

Saul asked his questions rapidly, not allowing Cal a chance to answer. He paused with the Big Spring question. The Murphs had wintered there in 1810 before moving on down into the Territory that spring.

"Only that it ain't Big Spring no more. Word in Turkeytown is that they wanted to name it Huntsville. Already did, 'bout two years ago, I guess. After Old Man Hunt that used to claim all the land up there. Why they wanted to change the name nobody can understand."

"I don't like that. Big Spring sounds right to me. Humph! Huntsville?"

"'Least that's better than what loony Leroy Pope tried to name it while we were there, after he bought up all the best claims. What was it, Twickersham, Trillerhan, something like that 'cause he liked the British? But no matter, how have things been here while I was gone?"

"Fairly quiet, except for the other day when some of those young troublemakers running down the river trail raised a ruckus. Just blowing off steam, though. Nothing to it. Pokkataw came by a little later to check on us."

"Well, about that. That's the other news from Turkeytown. You ain't gonna like this."

The brothers went about feeding and cleaning the animals while Cal retold the stories of Burnt Corn Creek and Fort Mims and rumors of a military campaign. As the Holmans had been, Saul was horrified.

"Damn! All this country needs is for soldiers to come nosing around down here and fighting to break out. Don't they realize how riled up the Creeks are already?"

They finished the chores and walked back toward the cabins. The setting sun painted the hazy sky in orange and golden splendor.

"I guess me and Soos better move into the new cabin tonight, huh? You and Adelin need your space."

"Yeah. We'll help you move after supper."

"Hey!" Saul pulled up short, suddenly realizing an absurdity. "Cal, since you knew about all the trouble, and that we very well could catch hell, how come you brought that gal down here? Are you daft?"

Cal half smiled. "Brother, you just don't know. Seems that once I stepped in it, I had really stepped in it! She wasn't gonna let me step out of it, either, and she wouldn't take no stuff from me or her daddy on the matter."

Saul snorted. "You really tried to talk her out of coming?"

"Yeah, we did, honest, but wasn't no stopping her. Can't say I was disappointed, though."

"Did you tell her how things might get here?"

"She knows the situation, but she was coming anyhow. She's one tough filly, brother."

"Not a good idea to rile her, huh?"

"Yeah." Cal smiled. "She just might chew both of us up."

Saul laughed out loud. "Couldn't stop her, you say?" Cal appeared puzzled at his big brother's sudden amusement. "Doesn't that remind you of someone else about four years ago?"

A broad grin slowly creased Cal's face as he remembered . . . .

8

Henry Murph gazed across the bean field where his oldest son weeded the crop. Another two weeks and the beans would be ready for first picking.

Henry knew Saul had become restless. He was twenty-three years old and more than ready for a place of his own. Saul had developed into a master farmer, equal to Henry himself, and capable of operating alone a farm the size of the Murph place. Henry had more than half of his thirty acres planted in apples and grapes, with just enough acreage devoted to vegetables and lifestock to support the family. His other four children would be more than sufficient help, so he could afford to let Saul go. It would be unfair not to give his blessing.

"Thank you, Father," said Saul after Henry brought up the subject and revealed his feelings. "I've wanted to tell you for a while but I didn't know if you would agree to the idea."

"Son, you've done your share for your mother and me and your brothers and sisters. You have your own life to live and it's time you got on with it."

"Well, Father, there is something else." Saul hesitated. His father might not be so agreeable to the remainder of his idea. "I don't think I want to stay around here, in the Roanoke area. These mountains are my home; I've never known anywhere else. But . . . "

It was true; Saul had lived his entire young life thus far on the Murph farm. He had been born a year after Henry and his bride Mary, a beautiful young lass from outside Petersburg, had broken the land. Henry had claimed the stake as his promised payment for honorable service with George Washington against the British on Yorktown Peninsula. Saul had remained an only child for six years until brother Callister was born, then sister Pauline two years later. Brother Nathan followed the next year, and finally sister Mary in another three years. Five children in all and they were growing fast, too fast to be confined for long on thirty acres.

" . . . but I just feel real strong that I don't want to settle around here. I think I need to go where there's lots of land."

Henry paused in currying one of the horses he and Saul were feeding and cleaning after another long day in the fields and orchards. "There's plenty of land here, son. No need to go very far adrift."

"No, Father, there ain't land here. Not for long, for certain. There are people coming down the Shenandoah Valley and over the Blue Ridge Mountains every day. It's getting crowded here."

"What do you have in mind then?"

"I think I want to go west."

"Eh?"

Saul wiped sweat and mud from leather harness. "I'm smart enough to know that most of the tales of easy riches in the west are not true. I don't think stories of bloodthirsty, vicious Indians and monstrous animals are either. But the land is there and I hear it's good dirt, the kind a hard-working farmer can make a fine living from. Too, I've heard they are begging for settlers in Tennessee."

"Yes, son, I'm aware of that. Your mother and I will hate to see you go so far away, but if you must, you must. We understand and we'll give our support. Or you might consider heading down

Georgia way. I hear there is new land opening up down there. And if that didn't work out you could keep on going to the south of the Mississippi Territory. I understand there is a new road being cut through from Milledgeville in Georgia to Mobile and New Orleans."

"Ah, I don't know about that. That don't sound like our kind of farming. I'm a mountain farmer. I think I might just continue down the Blue Ridge range and see what I can find."

So the Murphs agreed, though reluctantly, to cut big brother Saul loose to explore the west and settle a piece of it. He would leave when the harvest was far enough along for the rest of the family to easily complete it, but early enough to travel ahead of mountain snows. Saul figured he could make it to somewhere in Tennessee by winter and be ready to stake a claim in early spring, perfect timing to clear and plant. Henry would award him the younger mule, George, a small cart, and a modest supply of basic farm tools and seeds to go with Saul's own saddle horse, James. That would be a fine start to developing a nice little farm.

As late September approached, one member of the Murph family began to see a flaw in Saul's plan. Seventeen-year-old Cal thought it should include him as well.

"But, Saul, you could use some help," he reasoned. "You know that. Admit it, you'd like me to go with you, wouldn't you?"

"Even if I did, Mother and Father would never allow it."

"Of course they would if you asked them yourself."

"Well, I'm not asking. Mother would slap my nose off my face for asking such a thing."

"So what if I asked and told them it was all right with you? That you would like for me to go with you?"

"Maybe. No promise. But they ain't gonna let you go; might as well forget it."

Cal didn't forget it. That same night around the supper table he shocked his parents with his request. "And Saul says he would welcome me along," he finished.

Every eye turned to stare at Saul. His mother, deliberately and scoldingly, inquired, "You said that, Saul?"

"Well, no, ma'am, not exactly."

"What, exactly? Your brother is only seventeen."

"I know, Mother. I told him I wouldn't stop him if he could convince you and Father." Everyone's eyes rotated back to Cal, but Saul had something to add. "But if he truly wants to go, I would indeed welcome him along. Father, you know Cal is already as good a woodsman as either of us, and a better hunter than we are."

"Yes, he is that," Henry Murph acknowledged, sounding as if he argued with himself.

Saul continued as Cal smiled proudly and hopefully. "Cal may never be a natural farmer, but he'll make his way. If you let him, I would like for him to go west with me."

"Harrumph!" snorted Henry. "Well, we still have plenty of time. We'll talk more about it later."

They did. Every day. But Cal could not be shaken. Mary and Henry Murph tried every argument while Saul stayed neutral. He said nothing else in Cal's behalf, leaving little brother to fight the battle for himself. If Cal could win over his parents to agree to such a huge turnover in their lives, and in Cal's, then Saul figured his brother could surely make it in the wilderness with him.

When it was time for Saul to leave, Cal stood firm and his parents reluctantly gave their blessing. They could work the farm with the help of the remaining siblings, and they knew that soon they would have to cut Cal loose anyway. They trusted their sons and since the two had always been close, they concluded that traveling and living together had to be best for both. Thus, Saul and Cal Murph left their native Virginia behind to find the rest of the world.

After only one day the two adventurers crossed the New River and began the climb of the Blue Ridges to the mountain divide and down the other side. In less than a week they stood on a high ridge overlooking the Holston River.

"If we follow this valley," announced Saul, "we should make it to Knoxville in a few days. Least ways, that's what I've been told."

"Let's get going then," prodded Cal, still enthusiastic, as he urged his horse, Tom, down the slope. He tugged on the lead rope to George, who faithfully pulled the cart. The mule occasionally voiced, with a happy bray, his pleasure to be traveling.

Less than a week later, the Murph brothers pulled into Knoxville, a growing town high on the bluffs above a bend in the Tennessee River, and the capital of Tennessee, a state for only thirteen years. They decided to stay a few days to rest the animals and to gather as much information as possible about prospects west.

"Where you young fellas aiming to end up at?" asked old Ev Stang, who seemed to be a permanent fixture on the bench in front of the feed store in town. Ev had taken a liking to Saul and Cal after just two days. "You not gonna settle around here, are you?"

"No, Ev, no, we're not," chuckled Saul. Ev was an amusing character but he also seemed to know a lot about the comings and goings through Knoxville. "Too crowded. We're headed toward Nashville and figure to go past there till we find the good farm land we need."

Ev screwed up his whiskered face and spat a charge of tobacco juice. "Well, I tell you, fellas, if you want good land and open spaces, you're going in the wrong direction. Oh, the land out there is fine soil all right, but all these other folks moving west are after it, too."

"You're saying there ain't much more room out there than there is here?" asked Cal.

"'Tis now all right, or so I'm told. But won't be long. Gov'nor Sevier been begging for people to settle west of Nashville down the Natchez Road, and they been going. Listen to old Ev, won't be long 'fore he's begging for some place to put all those folks."

"Hmmm. So you don't think we should go to Nashville, huh, Ev?" surmised Saul.

"Naw. Not you young fellas. I got a better idea. If it was me a heading out with what y'all want, I'd head down to Big Spring."

"Big Spring? Where's that?"

"Down south of Nashville, over into Mississippi Territory. I'm told the gov'ment is a'selling land down there and there's lots more on past, 'specially below the river."

"The river?"

"Tennessee River. That'n out there." Ev gestured toward the river below the bluffs. "Runs south, then turns west. Some say it turns back north somewhere, but I never been out that far to see for myself."

"But ain't people settling down there, too? Down there at that Big Spring?" Saul was interested but a little confused.

"Naw, not many. Not hardly any south of the river where the best land is. Least that's what I hear all the time. Pretty reliable tellings, too."

"Why not?" asked Cal.

"Hell, that's the bad part." Ev spat again. "Too many Indians. Mean fellas, too, so they say. But if you can tolerate mean Indians, you two oughta do good for yourselves."

"Ev, you got me interested, Indians or not. We always got along just fine with the Cherokees back home. We'll check around and see what some others think about it. We're obliged to you for the information, friend."

By the next day, Saul and Cal had heard all the tales they cared to, including one trapper who told of " . . . Indians at least ten foot tall that were eating human flesh. I seen 'em with my own eyes and I ain't lying!"

Ev cackled when the brothers returned to his bench and told him the story. "Warn't no ten foot tall Indians the one time I was to down there. Didn't see none much over nine foot tall myself." He doubled over laughing. "Didn't see 'em roast no people parts, either."

"Anyhow, Ev," Saul announced, "Cal and me 'bout decided to do what you think we oughta, go down to Big Spring. Figure we can spend the winter there and by spring we'll know what we want to do. If things don't work out we can always head on back up to Nashville."

"I knew you would. You boys are too smart not to listen to old Ev."

"We reckon we'll leave tomorrow. Do you know the best route?"

"Shore I do, and it ain't how most folks go. They take off down the Tennessee and stay with it. If you ain't going by boat, that's the wrong thing. Too many creeks and other rivers running in that you have to work across. Naw, if you listen to me you'll follow the river south till it meets up with the Clinch River coming from the right. 'Bout thirty, forty miles, I reckon. There's a little army outpost thereabouts somewhere. After there, find the first gap in the mountain to the west. Cross over that and you'll be in the Sequatchie Valley. Follow that little river until you clear the mountains and run into the Tennessee again, then work your way west hugging the north edge of the river valley. You'll run right into Big Spring 'bout sixty miles after you leave the Sequatchie."

A week later, the Murph brothers pulled into Big Spring, a small but busy community centered around a large natural spring near the foot of a dominating mountain.

"You'll be mighty welcome to use old Josh's cabin for the winter," offered the first resident they asked concerning temporary living quarters. "He ain't been back here in a couple years now. Somebody needs to use the place."

"Well, that's very neighborly of you," Saul responded, "Much obliged. I think we're gonna like it here."

"Y'all look like nice folks, so we're glad to have you. The cabin is about a half mile south of the spring, toward the river. You can't miss it. Make yourselves at home."

Saul and Cal soon realized that everything around Big Spring was not so nice and friendly. They had arrived in the midst of a bitter controversy.

The previous year the legislature of the Mississippi Territory had created Madison County and the governor had put up the land at auction. Leroy Pope, a wealthy newcomer, and a British sympathizer at that, bought most of the prime parcels surrounding the spring and the nearby mountain for twenty-three dollars and fifty cents an acre. No one else could afford such an outlandish price, not even John Hunt himself.

John Hunt had built the first cabin at Big Spring in 1805, had opened the settlement, and invited any and all to join him in developing a thriving, congenial community. Now he couldn't afford to bid for his own property, and neither he nor anyone else in Big Spring could pay Pope's asking price.

Leroy Pope had petitioned the Territorial legislature to name the settlement, which had been selected as the county seat, after the home of his favorite English poet, Alexander Pope. Thus the new official name for Big Spring was Twickenham, which the majority of the residents despised. They had immediately clamored for the legislature to reconsider, but since Leroy owned most of the land, they had not been successful.

The argument raged, not only about the name but also about Leroy's greed. Residents accused him of wanting to make Big Spring and Madison County a sanctuary for the British. They were convinced that Leroy was related to this Alexander Pope, but Leroy insisted that the name was a coincidence. New stories and rumors circulated every day, none favorable to Leroy Pope.

Saul and Cal Murph dared not concern themselves with local politics and so passed a pleasant winter of 1810. They talked to many people about the surrounding region and collected much information and advice. Sorting it all out by the first of March, they had decided to go south in search of their dream locale.

The best place to settle, some told them, would be somewhere east of the Coosa River. "But don't you go too far south," they warned, "and certainly don't wander nowhere near the Tallapoosa River. That's Creek Indian lands and them savages don't welcome whites. They'll have your scalps quicker'n lightning."

Three days into March found Saul and Cal following a faint trace through the wilderness. They read it as old wagon tracks but didn't understand why they were there. Then, peering past a clearing ahead, Saul stopped short.

"Hell, Cal, look at that. I can't believe it."

They had stumbled on a large, thriving farm located dozens of miles from the last sign of white settlement. The farmer's name was Daniel Holman. He, his wife, and three children—two grown but young daughters and a younger son—welcomed them.

"Why don't you boys stay with us for a few days?" urged Daniel Holman. "We would be mighty pleased with your company."

Mrs. Holman and the siblings echoed the invitation and left them no choice but to accept. The kids lavished loving, skilled care on James, Tom, and George and fed them daily with double rations of oats. Daniel inspected and strengthened the cart and greased the wheels. Mrs. Holman fed them the finest food they had tasted since leaving Virginia, which coincidentally was also the homeland of the Holmans.

"Clinch River Valley," confirmed Mr. Holman. "We were practically neighbors of your folks before we left six years ago. We hated to leave Virginia, but we sure are glad we came here. This has to be the richest dirt on the planet." Daniel walked Saul around his fields and mesmerized him with tales and tips of successful planting.

The boy, Zack, marveled at the Murphs' tales of adventure on the trail. But the girls, Adelin, the oldest, and Bess Marie, were more interested in the towns the men had visited and the people in them.

"Mr. Murph," asked Bess Marie, directing the question to either of them, "how big has White's Fort become by now?"

"Oh, you mean Knoxville," remembered Saul. "It ain't been White's Fort for quite a while now."

"Oh yes, I forgot. Well?"

"How big? Well, I suppose there's three or four hundred folks there. Maybe more."

"Whew, that's huge! How about Big Spring?"

"Big Spring has at least a hundred people. We just came from there. We spent the winter with those good folks."

"Mr. Murph," began Adelin, looking directly at Cal, "why did you want to leave Virginia and come south?"

"Oh, oh, I," stammered Cal, "I don't rightly know how to say it. I just wanted to see the country and I decided it would be a good idea to follow my brother."

"Are you glad you did?"

"Yeah, I, I believe I am. I think we're gonna like it wherever we finish up."

"I think you will, too," Adelin encouraged him. "Maybe it'll be close around here."

With the weather brightening each day, Saul decided it wouldn't be wise to extend their stay any longer.

"How much farther you plan to go?" asked Daniel Holman.

"Till we find land to our liking, I reckon," said Saul. "It seems that this land is wide open and we can choose where we please."

"Pretty much," agreed Daniel. "But make sure you get along with the Indians."

"What's your reckoning on the Indians, Mr. Holman? We never had any crossings with the Cherokees back home, but we've heard all kinds of stories and warnings about the Indians down here."

"Well, son, these Indians ain't Cherokees. They're Creeks. Most of 'em ain't too neighborly toward whites, but we've got on with 'em just fine. I've found that if you treat 'em fair and treat 'em as equals, they'll regard you the same."

"Are any of the stories about Indian attacks true?"

"Naw. Leastways not like those trappers and hunters we see once in a while make it sound. Oh, the Creeks have their hotheads, so be sure to stay away from them if you can. Most of the Creeks are all right, though, if you respect the land and respect their ways."

For three days after leaving the Holman farm, Saul and Cal skipped from ridge to ridge not knowing where they were and having nothing to illuminate the trail but their woods skills and sharp instincts. They didn't know they were near a river until one afternoon they stood atop a hill and through the trees saw the water several hundred yards away.

"Where you reckon we are?" asked Cal. "What river is this?"

"Can't be the Coosa," Saul reasoned. "We're too far east. It can only be the Tallapoosa. There ain't no other around here."

"Sure is pretty," said Cal. "Maybe we should settle here."

"Maybe so," Saul agreed. "We'll camp here for now and search for possible sites in the morning."

The brothers explored the river for three more days and found their home on a bluff overlooking a shoal from the west bank. The bluff stretched away from the river across level ground for many hundred yards, enough for a large field for crops and ample room for a compound of a cabin, an animal shed and corral, smokehouses, and other out buildings.

"All right, we agree," announced Saul. "This is the place. First thing to do is clear a small patch of land and get a crop going. Then we build a cabin. Little brother, we have a summer of hard work ahead of us."

In the following days the two felled a couple dozen trees, burned the stumps, turned the soil, and planted corn, beans, and potatoes from their supply of seed stock. They stripped the logs and dressed them for use on the cabin. They collected large stones to build pillars, for which they dug footings at a prime location about forty yards from the lip of the bluff.

A small brook rushed past the cabin site to drop off the bluff to the river below. Saul and Cal diverted part of it into a reservoir for the animals near a spot they selected for the livestock shed. From there a small drainage ditch directed waste water to the river downstream from the compound. Drinking water was taken from the main channel of the little stream near the cabin.

Weeks passed. Not an hour of daylight was wasted. The river yielded a bountiful harvest of fish. Cal shot a deer for a supply of venison. Plants poked through rich garden soil and appeared green and strong. The cabin's solid stone foundation, held together with a hard compound of dried mud, supported a frame, a floor, and part of a roof.

Saul, working on a corner support of the cabin, and Cal, on the roof, were both too busy to notice the man standing thirty yards away at the edge of their clearing.

Since their arrival, Saul and Cal had not seen a single Indian. That worried them somewhat for they thought that surely the natives knew of their presence and probably watched them constantly. Thus, when Cal looked up and saw a man standing erect and motionless with his arm raised in a sign of peace, he yelped in surprise.

"Saul!" Cal reached for his musket but didn't cock it or raise it.

"Hold on, Cal," cautioned Saul. "Let's see what he wants."

Both men cradled their weapons across their arms and stepped cautiously toward the Indian, their own arms held similarly to the visitor's. They stopped five yards before him.

The man wore leather moccasins, deerskin leggings from the waist to a tight gather at the ankles, and a long deerskin shirt, cinched tightly at the waist with a crude belt. On the belt hung a long bone-handled knife and a pouch which probably carried ball and powder for the long-barrel musket at his side. A wrap of a coarse cloth tightly encircled his head above the brow. Colorfully dyed beads and tiny shells decorated his garments.

"Hello," greeted Saul. "Welcome." The man lowered his arm and nodded behind a quizzical look, obviously understanding no English. Saul pointed to himself and then to Cal. "I'm Saul Murph. This is my brother Cal."

The Indian pointed to Saul. "Saw?" Then to Cal. "Cow?"

Saul smiled and using his finger again as a pointer, enunciated carefully. "Saul. Cal."

"Saul. Cal." The man smiled in self-congratulation when Saul nodded approval. He then pointed to himself. "Pokkataw. Pokkataw," he repeated slowly.

"Poke Atall," guessed Saul.

"Pokletaw?" was Cal's version.

Pokkataw patiently repeated the name several times until the brothers got it right, upon which event the three dissolved into laughter.

Through sign language and physical props, each learned a few words of the other's language that day and more in the following weeks. Pokkataw learned faster and better and so halting English became the official tongue of the friendship.

Over the remainder of the spring and the length of the summer, Saul and Cal developed a cordial and beneficial relationship with the Creeks. They offered food, farming and hunting tips, and a few tools to Pokkataw and his compatriots. In return, the Creeks shared native pottery, advice on fishing techniques, and Indian seeds for the field. Several times the Murphs invited Creeks for supper, Pokkataw always serving as the emissary. Saul and Cal found it especially interesting that the Indians enjoyed American coffee, the stronger the better.

Pokkataw and his friends pitched in to help complete the cabin, learning something of the white man's construction methods. From them, Saul and Cal learned to better seat and seal the split-pine shingles on the roof, and to make tables, chairs, other furniture items, and frames for stretching and curing animal skins. Soon the cabin was finished and attention shifted to the livestock shelter. Timber for the structures was cut from the area Saul wished to till for his crops, and thus he was able to put in a late planting for a good fall harvest.

When leaves began to turn and the wind gained a bite in late October, Saul and Cal Murph had happily established their dream settlement. As a bonus, they had become good friends with some of the best neighbors they had ever known.

9

The Murph settlement, early November, 1813

Adelin, the newest Murph, adjusted well to her new surroundings as the remainder of October passed easily into November. Periodic heavy rains meant there would be moderate flooding downriver.

"Will raise the water level," reasoned Saul. "Oughta wake the fish up. Bring some of them big mudcats up off the bottom."

Both Murph cabins underwent changes, became homes. The new mistress of each fussed to transform her respective abode to her own tastes. Soosquana decorated her walls and shelves with utensils and clay pots marked with Muskogi tribal designs in bright earth colors. Adelin captured some of the flavor of her Holman farm home with personal and household articles she had brought with her. The husbands preferred to work outdoors, but rain often trapped them into doing the wives' bidding within the cabins.

The new goods from Turkeytown and the Holman farm were safely stored. Tom, George, Okra, and the nanny goat relished a long, leisurely recovery from the trip north. They worked at getting fat off newly harvested feed corn and sweet hay cut from the fields.

Soosquana was overwhelmed at Mrs. Holman's gift of the goat. She had already made a personal pet of her and milked her daily.

Adelin enjoyed trying her cooking and housekeeping skills. Her mother had taught her well, she thought, but she had never had the chance to test herself without supervision. She certainly wasn't unacquainted with preparing and eating venison and a wide variety of other wild game, staples at the Murph compound. There was a small supply of dried beef, but not the ample cuttings of fresh beef and pork she had left at the farm. The river teemed with fish, easily taken with net or spear, large turtles for meat and soup, and eels.

Soosquana thrived in the company of another female. Adelin quickly became a special friend, and not just because of shared gender. They admired each other. Soosquana's inner strength and goodness was evident to Adelin, and Adelin's independence and courage to Soosquana. For the upcoming birth of her first child, Soosquana surely liked the idea of another woman around.

On November first, maybe it was the second — the Murphs tried hard to keep an accurate calendar but often weren't sure of the days — the rain had cleared, leaving a sunny but cool day. Cal and Adelin commandeered one of the canoes and paddled downstream. Cal wanted to show her his beautiful river.

They marveled at the majestic water fowl that flew ahead of them to the large tree at the tip of the next point. Another, a white crane, fluttered from his roost and crossed the river over their heads to a new lair.

Later, Cal and Adelin stopped paddling and drifted aimlessly as they watched another large bird high overhead glide from the glare of the sun. It lazily circled lower and lower, not flapping its wings at all and only infrequently wiggling a wing tip to steady its flight. The distinctive rust-colored tail and speckled brown and off-white of its underbelly showed clearly.

"It's a red-tailed hawk," pronounced Cal as he and Adelin stared in wonder.

"He's beautiful, Cal," said Adelin. "What a magnificent creature."

The hawk caught a thermal and began to climb again, content to soar on invisible currents in widening circles. Cal and Adelin followed his flight until he became a tiny dot near the sun's corona. The red-tailed hawk had not flapped his wings once during the time his admirers watched.

A doe and her fawn frolicked on a sandbar, oblivious for long minutes to the intrusion of humans. They finally noticed the canoe and the mother chased the fawn into the woods, though the thick forest on either side of the river appeared impenetrable.

Adelin laughed nervously as the canoe barely missed a boulder submerged inches below the surface, then slid smoothly between two large ones protruding above water. A half dozen big turtles sunning themselves on a dead log ahead rolled off to the safety of a mud bank. The rocky bottom of the shallow river could be seen for long stretches, but then it would fall away into deep holes. The canoe crossed several wide shallows which would evolve into minor shoals or sandbars in times of drought.

They drifted slowly, perhaps a mile below their bluff, watching the elegant flight of yet another heron.

"Cal." Adelin saw the dark object first, on the water far ahead. "Look. Who's that?"

"I don't know. I'm sure they mean us no harm." Cal nevertheless checked that his musket lay handy in the bottom of the canoe, though he didn't dare pick it up. That might be interpreted as ill intent.

As the other canoe approached, Cal saw it contained three Red Sticks, one he recognized as a friend of Pokkataw. The man had once accompanied Pokkataw to the compound and had eaten supper with them. Cal remembered him as a pleasant enough fellow. He didn't know the man's companions.

Cal held his hand above his head, palm forward, in peace. All three Indians did the same. They exchanged greetings with Cal in

Muskogean as they drifted alongside. Cal understood little beyond the salutations. He attempted to introduce Adelin, but the warriors understood nothing verbal. They stared, couldn't stop staring, at undoubtedly the first redhaired woman they had ever seen, probably the first white woman of any plumage.

The Red Sticks paddled on upriver. Cal watched them closely until they were safely away. He and Saul had discussed the need to be extra careful and suspicious around the Creeks, no matter how cordial they seemed, at least until the current troubles blew over.

"Those were my very first Tallapoosa River Red Sticks," Adelin said, a little excited. "Are they dangerous, Cal?"

"I hope not. Up to now they've been friends. We just hope we can keep them being friends."

"They seemed nice enough. Was it their kind that attacked those poor people in the south?"

"Those were Red Sticks down there for certain, according to the stories in Turkeytown, but not these Red Sticks."

"There's a difference?" asked Adelin.

"What binds them in common is that they don't favor opening Creek territory to white settlement. That's what all the fussing is about with other Creeks, those that want to cooperate with Mr. Hawkins and the government."

"Other Creeks?"

"Those farther south and east, especially along the Chattahoochee River. But the Creeks on this part of the Tallapoosa, as mighty suspicious and fearful as they are, haven't had any run-ins yet with any settlers, as far as I know. Since we are the only whites anywhere around, I don't see why that can't continue."

"Will they fight if the army does come?"

"Probably. I think they would. They're fierce people, and proud, mighty proud. But they don't want to fight." Cal paused, dug deep on the next two paddle strokes. "They aren't savages like they were calling them back at Turkeytown. They are as civilized as we are. They respect their laws and their chiefs and their shamans."

"Shamans?"

"That's their prophets, their mystics. Most Creeks believe in unnatural beings, unseen demons. They seem to fear only one thing, and that's the unknown. They can be spooky sometimes. Anyway, each village has its own council and governs its own warriors. They punish lawbreakers harshly just like we do. Then each village — a village never has more than a couple hundred people, mostly less than fifty or a hundred — each village answers to the Great Council of Chiefs down at Tukabatchi."

"Where's that?"

"'Bout twenty, twenty-five miles south, at the big bend of the river. That's like their Washington, I guess. The Red Sticks don't shine to Mr. Hawkins and his boys messing around down there, but they ain't apt to start something with him."

An hour later, as the enraptured couple returned, Saul stood at the water's edge to catch and lift the bow of the onrushing canoe. "How was your voyage? What do think of our river, Adelin?"

"It's beautiful, Saul. I keep seeing new reasons why y'all like it here."

Cal handed his paddle to Adelin and helped Saul hide the canoe in the brush. The three walked up the path.

"Time we went after some venison for our winter stores," said Saul. "Should be some fat bucks out there with the summer we had. Now's the time to get 'em before cold weather leans them down."

"Adelin and I can go." Cal knew Saul would rather not leave Soosquana, not even for a few hours. "Give her a chance to show me some of that shooting she's been bragging about with that big blunderbuss of hers."

"Get a bunch of big furry rabbits, too. We need to make us all some new winter garb. Them bunnies also make mighty tasty stew."

At daybreak the next morning, Cal and Adelin hiked up the road and veered into the deep virgin forest, leading George behind them to haul back their bounty. They returned to the compound with the sun only at mid-sky. George labored beneath the carcasses of two giant bucks, nine big rabbits, and a fat wild turkey.

"I gave Adelin first shot on both of them," Cal recounted, not able to disguise his pride. "I didn't get my second shot either time. She got 'em both right between the eyes."

"Didn't want to spoil the hides with ugly bullet holes," she beamed.

"I shot most of the rabbits, though . . . ."

"No, you didn't. I got just as many as you did."

" . . . and I dropped the gobbler at sixty yards."

"I gave him first shot on that one," Adelin conceded.

The banter and boasting continued as the brothers spent the afternoon dressing the quarry, quartering meat, and stretching hides over frames for scraping and curing. Adelin led George to the shelter for feeding and care; she welcomed the chance to spend a few private minutes with Okra while there. She felt guilty for neglecting the mare and not finding more opportunities to ride her since they had arrived. Okra had always been her favorite pet as well as an excellent saddle horse.

Adelin returned to find Soosquana already roasting the turkey on the spit over the outdoor fire for their supper. She decided to help and fetched a wooden bowl full of potatoes to prepare for boiling. The two talked and laughed together as they worked.

Well after dark, an hour or so after Saul and Soosquana had retired, they were awakened by shrieks and laughter from the yard.

"What the hell?" Saul blurted, snapping upright in bed. He went to the shutter facing the river and cracked it. "Soos, I'm looking at two daffy people. They are in the wash pond frolicking and snorting. Don't they know this is November? They'll be blocks of ice by morning."

"Come back to bed, Saul," smiled Soosquana, "and leave them alone."

In the pond, Cal reached for the top of Adelin's head to try to push her under. Adelin squealed.

"No, Cal, no! Don't get my hair wet. I'm freezing as is!"

"Ah, it's not so bad, is it, once you're in?" He gave up trying to dunk her.

"You, sir, are a lunatic, and you're making one of me." She giggled and swept water into his face with both hands. He grabbed her and squeezed her naked body to his. She squealed again, laughed aloud, and returned Cal's kiss.

They splashed each other for another ten minutes, laughing, shrieking, caressing, kissing, loving. Then they jumped from the reservoir and ran to their cabin, hand in hand, bare butts glistening in the moonlight, to warm themselves before a roaring fireplace. They hugged and caressed each other dry, climbed into bed, and cuddled together. No matter a cool November night, Cal and Adelin felt very warm one with the other.

10

"Looka them guys, Thaddie. Looka them smug looks on their faces. Sonsabitches been fighting damn Indians and here we are digging a damn latrine ditch. Hell!"

"Lookit ol' Coffee. That bastard just sitting there on that damn nag watching his guys parade by. Makes me sick. I come down here to get me some savages, teach 'em a lesson, and he goes an' hogs all the glory for his damn cavalry."

The two privates watched General Jack Coffee's cavalry regiment ride into the two-acre clearing. General Andrew Jackson's two infantry regiments of Tennessee state militia, plus several hundred other enlistees he had picked up on the march into the Alabama wilderness, busied themselves with the construction of a fort. Fresh-cut logs lay in stacks all around the grounds, punctuated by random piles of brush to be used for firewood. Stumps dotted the clearing, evidence of the forest that had been there only days before. General Coffee sat on his horse at the head of the road and congratulated each trooper as he trotted past. The last of the column now moved by.

"We oughta joined up with the cavalry, Oscar, instead of Jackson's damn infantry, when he come through Big Spring."

"Not me. I'm akeepin' my feet on the ground, thank you. Horses and me don't get along. Ever' time I useta try to get on one of the mean ugly sonabitches I got bucked some'ing awful and throwed off. Ever' time! I give up and decided if I needed to go somewhere I could walk myself there."

"Well, it woulda been lots easier and we'd be fighting Indians by now."

A group of cavalrymen dismounted and walked toward them. "This thing ready to use?" asked one.

"It ain't finished but who the hell cares," replied Oscar. "Do your business."

"Hey, we saw you fellows ride in." Thad couldn't hide his curiosity. "How was it? We heard y'all killed 'bout five hunnerd savages. Where'd you go? Tellsatch, was it?"

"Tallashatchi. Least that's what the Indians call it. Company captain said General told him we got maybe two hunnerd. War'n't no five hunnerd, I know that. Did get some prisoners, though, and far as I could tell none others got away."

"How many did you get?" asked Oscar. "I mean, you yourself. How many did you shoot?"

"I don't know. Some, I guess." The cavalryman's buddies, scattered along the ditch in various stages of undress, smiled at the two young militiamen's interest. The horsemen's pride and their perceived superiority showed clearly. "I musta shot my musket twenty times or more. That's all we all did, just shoot. They were like fat ducks sitting on a cold lake."

"Did they shoot back? Any of our fellows get hit?"

"Yeah, hell, they shot back. But they couldn't seem to hit nothin' with them British pieces of theirs. Most couldn't hit the roof of a church if they were sitting on the steeple."

Another soldier sought to answer the question about casualties. "I think we lost four or five, or so somebody said. A couple of those by getting stuck with arrows. I didn't see anybody fall myself, did you, Matt?"

"Naw," replied the first man. "A coupla dozen got nicked. I saw some of them, but I didn't see nobody get killed."

Several dozen cavalrymen had made their way over to use the sanitation ditch Oscar and Thad had spent several hours digging. The two leaned on their tools and listened to excited tales of military glory while the men tended to business. To hear the stories and receive firsthand information made worthwhile the extra time it would take the two novice militiamen to finish the latrine. This was the first major battle of General Jackson's campaign against the rotten bloody Creeks that massacred those poor souls at Fort Mims and they had to know what to expect when it was their turn to go after Red Sticks.

"Where you young fellows come from?" asked a cavalryman.

"We from Big Spring. We joined onto General Jackson's outfit when he come through last month. And we ain't no young fellows, neither. We're plenty old enough and we're good Indian fighters."

The soldier exchanged amused looks with his compatriots and decided not to pursue the conversation. The ditch had nearly cleared of cavalrymen. Oscar and Thad reluctantly resumed work.

"Damn, Thaddie, when you gon' learn. It ain't Big Spring no more. It's Huntsville."

"I know, but ever'body still calls it that 'cause ever'body still did all the time they said its name was Twickenham. Ain't nobody liked that. And you quit calling me Thaddie. I keep telling you not to."

"Hell, that's what your Ma calls you."

"You ain't my Ma. And I ain't no kid no more. I'm grown and I don't like no baby name. I told you over and over to call me Thad or Thadeus. That's my name."

"I always called you Thaddie. Been doing it since we were four years old and I ain't about to change now. Thaddie!"

"You piss pot!"

Four days later General Jackson's fort was almost finished. The rugged, energetic general stalked around like a mad bull, impatient, grouching. He grimaced each time the pain in his arm stabbed again. He tried hard to disguise the discomfort, inflicted by a pistol ball he had received above the elbow in a dispute back in Nashville. He occasionally carried the arm in a sling but mostly just held it tight against his ribs, grinding his teeth and cursing to himself that coward Jesse Benton for each throb and ache.

Jesse was the brother of Thomas Hart Benton, formerly Jackson's emissary to Washington. Thomas Benton accused the general of encouraging a duel between incompetent Jesse and Colonel Billy Carroll. When Carroll received a shot to his thumb and sent in return a pistol ball that seared both of Jesse's buttocks, Thomas took offense for the humiliation. He and Jesse confronted Jackson at a hotel in Nashville. When Jackson angrily chased Thomas Benton through the hotel, Jesse stepped up at close range and sent a shot into Jackson's arm. The wound had barely begun to heal when the alarm from Fort Mims swept Nashville.

Three wagonloads of provisions arrived at the new fort and were cached inside the stockade along with stores of weapons, ammunition, and surgical supplies. For over two thousand men, the food would have to be thinly rationed. Wild game that could be harvested from the forest could not feed that many soldiers and would soon be depleted.

General Coffee's cavalry camped by the river, the infantry in tents around the edges of the clearing. A six-pound cannon, one of only two artillery pieces possessed by Jackson's forces, guarded the front gate. The three-pound piece was positioned at the rear portal.

On the cool, clear morning of November eighth, assembly

sounded. Within minutes two regiments of infantry and one of cavalry and mounted sharpshooters stood at attention on the grounds before the fort. General Jackson faced them, tightly reining a horse as impatient as its rider. Moderately tall at five feet, eleven inches, the general sat much taller in the saddle.

"Gentlemen," he began, "we have learned of hostile Creeks about thirty miles south. They are besieging a town of friendly Creeks that wish to ally with us and who beg our help against the godless barbarians."

"Could that be close to Fort Mims, reckon?" Oscar whispered to Thad standing next to him deep in the ranks.

"What's a barbarian?" countered Thad.

Jackson continued. "You have one hour to prepare for the march. We will camp near the site of engagement and at first light move against the enemy. We intend to send those murdering savages on a short trip to hell. Captains, issue full lots of shot and powder and campaign rations. Column up your companies on the hour. Good shooting, men! Sergeant, dismiss the battalion."

"Hot damn, we're finally gonna get us some Indians," whooped Oscar, running with Thad to their tent.

"Yahoo! Hell, yes, this is gonna be fun!" Thad leaped as he ran and waved his hat in the air. "Look out, you damn savages! I'm coming after yore hides!"

Jackson's army bivouacked that night a few miles from the Creek town of Talatigi, located on a stream of the same name flowing into the Coosa River from the east. The next morning they surrounded and attacked a thousand Red Sticks harassing the passive villagers. Oscar and Thad kneeled in a rank of militiamen providing cover fire for a cavalry probe.

"I got one!" yelped Thad.

"No, you didn't."

"Did so. I saw him jump."

"Hell, Thaddie," scoffed Oscar, awkwardly reloading his musket, "you can't see nothing for all the smoke. You ain't shot no Indian."

Thad's musket ball rolled out of the barrel before he could push it snug with his ramrod. He picked it up, blew dust from it, and stuffed it back in the muzzle. "Shot more'n you, I bet."

A voice boomed behind them. "Fix bayonets! Prepare to march forward in skirmish ranks! Be ready to charge on the order!"

"Oh, boy!" squealed Oscar, fumbling at his side scabbard for his bayonet. "Here we go!"

"Watch 'em run from us now!" yelled Thad.

After the battle, decisively won, militia officers counted over three hundred enemy dead. Another seven hundred had escaped.

"What the hell you mean they escaped?" raged General Jackson. "Exactly how did they do that, Captain?"

"Seems that Lieutenant Jarvis's platoon failed to close off the gap left by E Company's flanking move, sir."

"Get that son of a bitch — what's his name, Jarvis? — get that son of a bitch Jarvis over here! His company commander, too. I won't have the enemy escaping through my ranks. Not one, you hear?"

Jackson continued to yell, unhappy with imperfection. Nevertheless, he convinced himself he had struck a fatal blow to the warring Creeks and had avenged the massacre at Fort Mims. He immediately dispatched a message boasting such to Governor Willie Blount in Nashville.

The Battle of Talatigi was a glorious victory for General Andrew Jackson and his Tennessee militiamen. He lost just fifteen of his soldiers killed and eighty-five wounded.

Thaddie from Big Spring lay among the dead with a musket ball through his forehead. Oscar, Thad's lifelong pal, screamed with the pain of his splintered right knee until he passed out just as the surgeon began to amputate the leg.

Both boys were seventeen years old.

11

The Murphs learned of the incidents at Tallashatchi and Talatigi during the second week of November. Travelers along the river displayed increased excitement and anger, raising concerns at the compound. When a group of trusted warriors happened by, Saul hailed them and Soosquana questioned them, interpreting to the others.

"What the hell are troops doing in this part of the Territory?" fumed Saul after the Creek neighbors had continued on their way. "Nothing has happened here yet."

Neither Saul nor Cal knew anything at all about the two villages the army had attacked, or even where they were, and Soosquana knew little more, but there was small doubt that trouble had come to the region.

"I thought it was Fort Mims they were upset about," said Cal, "and Fort Mims must be two hundred miles away 'cording to what they said at Turkeytown. Seems to me the Creeks fighting each other is none of the government's business. And that's all that's going on around here."

"That part of the Coosa, if I know about where they are saying," offered Adelin, "isn't far from our farm. It must still be sixty or seventy miles from here."

"So maybe we ain't got nothing to worry about." Saul looked relieved. "Not yet anyway. Just hope those fool soldiers don't come on down here."

"Hope everything is okay with my folks," fretted Adelin.

"Think we should take a run up there and see?" asked Cal. "We can if you'd like."

Adelin thought it over slowly. "No," she finally said, "They wouldn't bother the farm, neither the Indians nor the soldiers. Not if they are over on the Coosa fighting each other. They'd have no call to be that far east. Besides, we couldn't do any good, and we're needed here with Saul and Soos."

It seemed a good idea for someone to keep vigilance over the river from the edge of the bluff whenever possible. The task fell mostly to Soosquana, not only for her sharper perceptions concerning her native people, but also because she was slowing considerably and needed more rest for her bulky body, now in its seventh month of pregnancy. But over the next several days nothing else appreciable happened and there was no further news of the American military.

On November fifteenth, Pokkataw and a small band of Hillabi Red Sticks stopped by on their way south to Tukabatchi. He had not been to the compound in several weeks, not since Adelin arrived. The presence of such a respected warrior impressed Adelin and she instantly liked him.

"Good wife!" Pokkataw congratulated Cal. "Smart. Pretty. Strong."

Pokkataw had been delegated by the Hillabi villages and the large town of Oakfuski to report to the Council at Tukabatchi about peace negotiations that had occurred over the last several days with militia officers. The commander of the government force, a general by the name of Jackson, was apparently convinced that he either had broken the power of the Creeks at Talatigi or that he had penetrated far enough into the Creek Nation to secure the safety of American settlements. An accord, Pokkataw said, had been reached with Jackson's emissaries that promised no further hostilities.

The Hillabi leaders thought such an agreement struck by the important Red Stick villages scattered the length of Hillabi Creek might reunite the Upper Creek warring factions. Peace with the whites was exactly what the villages that advocated coexistence with settlers wanted. Pokkataw was excited about his mission and the Murphs were relieved.

Two days later, on the seventeenth, Pokkataw stopped by again on his return trip from Tukabatchi. The chiefs had welcomed the news and urged the Hillabis to keep bargaining in good faith with General Jackson's representatives. Each town along the river was likewise encouraged, although some Red Stick zealots expressed suspicions and distrust.

Perhaps the threat of war had ended.

The next morning Cal and Adelin went after more rabbits, happy in the hope that the woods were once again free of conflict. George stayed at the compound; they figured they could lug the day's takings themselves. They explored and played and enjoyed the outing, and they shot eight more rabbits for fur and stew. They took their time, stretched the day, loving the woods and each other's company. The sun slid deep on its downward arc when they returned home.

Saul and Cal skinned and dressed the rabbit meat before dark but decided to wait until morning to stretch and scrape the hides. With this task they were engaged two hours after sunup on the nineteenth. Soosquana and Adelin busied themselves stitching together some of the skins from the previous hunt with fishbone needles and thin deerskin thongs. They talked excitedly and happily about the baby.

A clatter arose from the woods in the direction of the road. Horses. All four Murphs looked first for their muskets, then toward the source of the disturbance. Riders appeared.

Eight cavalrymen in tattered, mismatched military uniforms and two Indians, apparently Cherokees, approached cautiously, muskets cocked, bayonets fixed.

"What the damn hell are you people doing in these damn awful woods?" bellowed the leader, a sergeant.

"We live here," replied Saul evenly. "We're Saul and Cal Murph and these are our wives. Who are you and what is your mission?"

"Goddamn! We heard rumors that a white family lived somewhere on this part of the Tallapoosa, but nobody believed it." He relaxed his musket and signaled his men at ease. Tobacco juice leaked from the left corner of his mouth to run in rivulets through the thick stubble of his chin to join brown splotches already dried. "How long you folks been squatting here?"

"Over three years now. We don't see ourselves as squatters. We are mostly welcomed. Why are you here? Are you from that General Jackson's army?"

"Hell no! We got no truck with that yellow belly Jackson. No sir. I'm Platoon Sergeant Mordecai Barnes. We're attached to General James White's East Tennessee Militia, answering to Major General John Cocke. Real Indian fighters."

"I ask you again, sir, what business do you have?"

"We been chasing Indians all night and we run across your track a few miles back and followed it to here."

A chill of terror ran through the Murphs. They swapped concerned looks.

"What the hell you mean you been chasing Indians?" Saul demanded. "Chasing them from where? And for what?"

"From up on Hillabi Creek, that's where. We wiped out four

towns full of the murdering savages yesterday," boasted the sergeant with a proud smirk. "Burned 'em to the ground, too."

"You what? Sir, what have you done? Those people are not your enemy."

"Hell they ain't! Our boys are out after more of them pagan Indian villages this morning, and we're chasing stragglers. Lost 'em in the night, but we got the dirty bastards on the run all right."

"You son of a bitch!" Saul was furious. He tightened his grip on the musket. "The Hillabis don't want to fight nobody. Just two days ago we got word that they had struck peace with Jackson's army."

"Told you we don't cotton to General Jackson. He's been hogging all the glory and General Cocke says he's having none of that." Barnes spat a stream of tobacco juice off to one side. He wiped his mouth with the back of his hand. "Our boys are just as good — better! — as them weasels from over Nashville way."

"You son of a bitch!" repeated Saul.

Sergeant Barnes laughed. "We done got us a couple more towns, too, General White did. On the way over here, up close to where the Little Tallapoosa runs in."

"Hell, Sergeant! You probably done gone and started an all-out war with the Creeks. That, sir, is stupid!"

"Careful who you calling stupid, boy. You some kind of Indian lover or some'ing?"

"As a truth, we are, I suppose. They are our neighbors and our friends and they wouldn't burn a village of yours without cause."

No one had spoken but Saul and the sergeant. The latter looked intently around the compound from where he sat on his mount, then stared at the other Murphs, studying each in turn.

"You got any Indians hid out 'round here? Besides that pregnant squaw there, I mean? You buy her as a slave?"

"That's my wife, sir." Saul struggled to keep his voice even. "I'll ask you to leave now. I regret that you are no longer welcome on these premises."

"That little redhead filly there. You buy her, too?"

"Sir, you . . . !" Cal exploded, but was interrupted.

"Listen, you slimy murdering bastard!" Adelin, angrier even than Cal, took a step toward Sergeant Barnes. "You are a disgrace to our country. Ride your asses out of these woods and leave these good men to try to repair your treasonous deeds." Cal, Saul, and Soosquana had not seen Adelin so angry, nor heard such language from her. They feared she might have shot the sergeant had not Saul put his hand on her musket barrel. She wasn't finished. "You will best serve by turning your horses back toward Tennessee. And tell your Generals White and Cocke and Jackson to go as well."

"Ain't you the fiery one!" mocked the sergeant. "You boys let this pretty little wildcat fight your fights for you?"

Adelin tried to raise her musket again. Saul tightened his hold.

"Sir," Cal's voice had calmed a little, "you had best heed her calling. We might just turn her loose and let her whip your sorry, cowardly ass. Now get off our place and honor us by not ever coming back."

Barnes glared at each of them one final turn, then slowly reined his horse around. He motioned his men to follow. "We just might be seeing you folks again. Look out for us."

The militiamen rode off at a brisk trot. The four Murphs went limp with relief, but still fumed. Cal sat against a tree. Adelin turned and stalked away toward the edge of the bluff. Saul stood fixed, unable to move or gauge his thoughts. Soosquana walked to her husband and put an arm around him.

"Holy hell!" spat Cal. "What now? So much for peace with the Hillabis, eh?"

"Yeah," agreed Saul sadly. "The Creeks, Red Stick or not, ain't gonna trust Americans anymore. Dammit, and we're Americans. We could be in for a helluva lot of trouble ourselves 'cause of this. Them damn stupid generals! They can't find a real enemy, like down to Fort Mims or somewhere, so they just make up one. Anything to pick a fight. Damn, damn!"

An hour after Sergeant Barnes's squad departed, Pokkataw and several fellow Red Sticks stepped from the forest.

"Good to see you," the Murphs all said at once. "Is it true? Are your towns destroyed? You and your family okay? Was it you the cavalrymen were chasing?"

Soosquana took control. She got the story from Pokkataw and his friends in Muskogean and relayed in English. Cal, Adelin, and Saul listened anxiously. The soldiers had attacked at dawn the previous morning. At least four and probably seven or eight Hillabi villages had been burned. Many Hillabi warriors and some women and children had been killed, no way to tell exactly how many. The aggressors had been different soldiers from those they had been talking with the past week or so. Hillabi warriors had scattered all over as the battles were lost, but would soon regroup, this time for war with the whites. And no, the horsemen had not chased Pokkataw's band. Quite the opposite. Pokkataw had stalked the soldiers all night, never losing sight of them, making certain they didn't move to attack another village.

"We're grievously sorry, Pokkataw," offered Saul. "This should not have happened. We are still your friends. We hope you remain ours."

"You friends. Peace. Not soldiers. No treaty. No peace. Kill soldiers. Or die. Never surrender. Never! Never!"

Pokkataw and his party disappeared into the woods, merging with the trees and shadows as stealthily as they had come. The Murphs would not see him again for three months.

12

The Executive Mansion, Washington, D.C., late November, 1813

President Madison again riffled the stack of papers with his thumb. He continued to scowl, more at the papers than at the visitors to his Blue Room office.

"Congressman, what is going on in Tennessee? Has your governor lost his senses?"

"Sir?" Congressman John Sevier furrowed his eyebrows, puzzled.

"These dispatches, Mr. Sevier." Madison pounded two fingers onto the papers on his desk. He glanced at Secretary of War John Armstrong seated to the side. "They are reports from Governor Blount and from General Jackson, directed to myself and to Mr. Armstrong, regarding their military campaign into the Alabama country against the Creeks."

"Sir, they are there to guard our border against unfriendly Indians."

"Poppy seeds! The Creeks may be unfriendly, but I can't see that they are threatening your border. Why, Jackson is half way to Florida fighting Indians. Or," the President held up the papers, "according to his own report, slaughtering Indians." He angrily threw the document back on the desk.

A soft knock at the door interrupted the men. A maid stepped inside. "Beg pardon, Mr. President," she said in a quiet tone, "would you and your guests like some tea?"

"I would, Ora. Congressman?"

"I'll take a cup of strong coffee, if I may."

"May I suggest a dollop of rum stirred in?" said Madison with a twinkle. "Does something for it."

"Sounds interesting," smiled Sevier.

"You, John?"

"Tea, Mr. President," replied Armstrong. "And a dollop for me, too, Ora, if you would."

"You know how I like mine, Ora. Thank you." The President dismissed the maid with a wave. She curtsied and backed out the door, closing it behind her.

"If you please, sir," asked Sevier, "may I see those dispatches?"

"Certainly." Madison slid the reports across the table. He didn't wait for Sevier to read them. "Jackson says he has attacked and defeated two Creek villages. He boasts that he has broken the backs of the Creeks and, his words, avenged the attack on Fort Mims."

"Yes." Sevier looked up. "Sir, General Jackson is a capable military leader. I've had my differences with him and we don't get along at all. But I'm sure he has done what he set out to do."

"I'm sure he has!" The President aimed the contemptuous retort directly at the congressman. "I . . . ."

Another knock stopped Madison short. Ora entered with a tray of steaming cups as another maid held the door for her. The two women distributed the refreshments, set out a plate of buttered crumpets, and hastened to retire.

"Thank you, Ora," acknowledged Madison. "You, too, Carrie." The two maids curtsied again, backed out, and closed the door.

Sevier finished reading the reports and took up his cup. The first sip caused an involuntary grimace. "Bracing."

"Congressman," Madison resumed, "I've some knowledge of your history with General Jackson. And I'm well aware and very appreciative of your own military adventures. Yours is a heroic record."

"Thank you, Mr. President. You're very kind."

"That is why I'm seeking your counsel. You, without a doubt, know more about General Jackson, and Governor Blount, too, than anyone in Washington."

General John Sevier, a Revolutionary War hero, had led a company of two hundred forty Tennessee militiamen across the Smoky Mountains to fight the British at Kings Mountain, and another two hundred the next year to the service of Francis Marion. In 1780, between those two incursions, he began a campaign against the Cherokees, the first in a long, continual series of Indian harassments.

He had been the first governor of the State of Tennessee, serving six two-year terms. After the first three terms, not permitted a fourth consecutive by the state constitution, he ran for the major-generalship of the Tennessee militia, a commission he coveted and for which he was easily the best qualified and most experienced candidate. When the vote of the legislature resulted in a tie, the new governor, Archibald Roane, cast his deciding vote for his political ally, Andrew Jackson. Sevier, the head of the east Tennessee faction, and Jackson, the principal supporter of the Willie Blount clique in the west, had already feuded as bitter political opponents. The animosity stemmed from an argument in 1796 and quickly blew to more than a rivalry; they became enemies. The generalship controversy and subsequent charges of corruption and fraud by Roane and Jackson against Sevier intensified their dislike for each other.

Roane's single term ended in defeat when Sevier ran against him and won. Sevier served his second set of three consecutive terms as governor, followed by a stint in the state Senate. He was then elected to the United States House of Representatives in 1811.

"I believe you have served in Washington before, have you not, Mr. Sevier? Even before General Jackson was here?" Madison had taken his tea to one of the tall windows fronting the Blue Room. He sipped the last swallow as he watched a carriage in a swirl of dust clatter along the far boulevard. Two dueling crows flitted across the expansive field that was the rear grounds of the magnificent new presidential mansion. He pondered the complexities and contradictions of John Sevier, and of Andrew Jackson by extension, trying to understand.

"Yes, sir, but that was long ago."

Sevier had previously been elected to the House in 1789 as the representative of the Wautauga-Holston region of Tennessee, a North Carolina district before its cession of the territory to Congress in 1791. He saw his return to Washington in 1811 as a fulfillment of duty to his constituents. However, his associates and friends knew that he would much prefer to be back home in east Tennessee.

Madison returned to his desk and put down the cup.

"General Sevier," asked Armstrong, "am I to understand that you stand in support of General Jackson's current campaign?"

"I don't think General Jackson is necessarily the man to lead our forces, but, yes, I wholeheartedly believe that Tennessee has the right and the duty to defend ourselves and neutralize the Creeks."

"Neutralize them, Mr. Sevier?" reacted Armstrong.

President Madison wiggled a hand at Armstrong. "But if Jackson has already defeated the Creeks, as he claims in his report, why does he continue to ask for regulars?"

"Oh, Mr. President, there are a lot of Indians in the Mississippi Territory. I'm sure that General Jackson isn't through yet and can use all the forces we can muster for him."

"I see. Now, Congressman, tell me about your General Cocke."

"General John Cocke, sir?"

"The same. He has joined up with Jackson in the Alabama wilderness."

"I was not aware of that. Cocke is actually a Virginian, young for a general, only thirty-three, I believe. He has risen rapidly in rank on a sterling record and has agreed to command a brigade of east Tennessee militia, but I did not know that he had been deployed to Alabama country. I know little about him personally beyond what I've stated, but I'm sure he is a big asset to Jackson."

"Not according to Jackson himself." President Madison fanned the pages of the reports, back on his desk. "He claims Cocke sabotaged an agreement he had from a major faction of the Creeks for their surrender."

"Sir?"

Madison looked at Armstrong. "Relate the details, John."

"Yes, sir. According to the report, Cocke, unknown to Jackson, ordered one of his regiments to attack a group of Creek villages. A regiment commanded by General James White. I believe you know him, Mr. Sevier."

"Yes, I do. Very well. A fine man."

"The Indians he annihilated were on the verge of accepting Jackson's terms. Wiped 'em out, killed hundreds. Burned several villages. Now none of the Creeks will talk with Jackson's negotiators. Can't blame the devils, can we? Jackson claims to be furious and is complaining about Cocke acting independently and against his orders."

President Madison was certain that he detected a subtle, satisfied smile from Sevier, a smile that betrayed a hatred for Indians possibly more acute than his contempt for Andrew Jackson. "So, Congressman, what is your advice? How should we regard these developments?"

"Mr. President, you honor me by asking. I must offer my full support for our brave Tennessee lads. If you would respect my recommendation, I urge you and Mr. Armstrong to send General Jackson the supplies and ordnance he needs. Also, Mr. President, I believe regulars should be attached to Jackson; two, perhaps three regiments."

"I wish we could spare two or three regiments. But I thank you, Mr. Sevier. Be assured, your counsel is valued."

Armstrong lingered after Congressman Sevier left. "Mr. President, perhaps we can search the Quartermaster Corps for additional supplies, and even some ordnance, but we can spare not one soldier for Jackson."

"I know, John. We have much greater needs on more pressing fronts. But what concerns me in the Alabama country is whether Jackson's antics are serving to hold the British in place along the Gulf, or if the Creeks are being pushed closer than ever to joining the British cause."

13

The Murph settlement, late November, 1813

Saul and Cal speculated that General White or General Cocke, whichever was responsible, had sanctioned the massacre because of several factors. Their line of march carried them over the upper reaches of Hillabi Creek. The Hillabi towns, clustered close along the shallow, accessible stream, presented convenient targets. These generals must not have known of Jackson's peace negotiations. Maybe more importantly, they were anxious to fight, jealous that Jackson had already skirmished with the Red Sticks and was probably being saluted as a hero back in Tennessee.

The incident surely would end the threat of civil war among the Upper Creeks and unite them against the white man. The militant Red Sticks would have their way, and would now be joined by most warriors who had until now condoned white settlements. There certainly would be no more peace talks. Pokkataw had vowed as much himself, and surely that sentiment would prevail among the Creeks. Muskogis were proud people and they were not afraid to defend their land and their honor. Pushed, betrayed, invaded, even if overwhelmed in men and arms, they would fight to their deaths.

The Murphs had to again discuss the possibility of leaving, of fleeing north out of danger, at least for a while. None of the four wanted to, though all agreed it might be the wise thing. The compound was vulnerable to any serious attack, but a party on the open trail would be even easier prey. The Creeks knew the Murphs and knew they meant the Indians no harm; on the road they would have no identity and no protection. The clincher was that Soosquana couldn't very well travel. They would stay.

Monitoring movement along the river began anew. There was little. The Red Sticks had apparently gone into hiding and their women and children dared not stray from the safety of the villages. The river ran in solitude, silent except for the continuous rush of the shoals and the night sounds of forest creatures.

No further word came of American soldiers. Three days of steady rain and cold wind depicted the first serious signs of oncoming winter. The Murphs welcomed the bad weather, hoping that it would dampen the passions of American militiamen.

"Maybe they'll rot cowering in their tents," mused Cal.

The weather cleared. A week had passed since the Hillabi attack. Still no river traffic except for an occasional small hunting party.

Soosquana watched from the bluff one morning. "Saul!" she called in a low voice, alarmed.

Saul ran to her and peered over the bluff. Six Red Sticks, all apparently in their teens, stood on the rocks at the head of the shoals, glaring up toward the compound.

Saul pushed Soosquana back. "Get to the cabin," he ordered, taking her musket as he had not bothered to fetch his. Cal slid beside him, his musket ready.

"What do they want?" Cal asked.

"Don't know." Saul recognized the leader as the angry showoff who had mocked him from that very spot a month and a half earlier. Some of his present companions had also been along for that incident, Saul was certain. "I hope they are just beating their chests again."

"They got more to beat 'em about now, I reckon," offered Cal.

One of the young Creeks yelled a threat. The others joined with taunts and curses. The leader raised his arm to quiet them. He looked to his musket held at his waist and pulled back the lock to full cock. He slowly raised the weapon to aim at the compound as he had done before with an uncharged musket.

This time it wasn't empty. The pan flashed and smoke spurted from the muzzle. A musket ball whistled inches above the heads of Saul and Cal and slammed into the trunk of the big oak behind them.

Cal raised his musket.

"Hold it!" cautioned Saul. "Don't show nothing unless they start up the bluff."

Long moments passed. Nothing moved. The other Red Sticks made no threat with their weapons. They stared, chests ballooned and squared toward the Murphs, unseen but surely present, daring retaliation. Finally, the shooter laughed, shrieked defiantly, taunted the bluff with wild swings of his red war club. His companions pumped their clubs, yelling curses anew and screaming challenges. But none of the warriors moved closer.

After long minutes that seemed hours, the young troublemakers gave up. They retreated from the rocks to the opposite bank and headed downriver, triumphant, boisterous, obviously pleased with themselves.

Saul and Cal relaxed.

"Let 'em have their fun," counseled Saul. "Let's make sure we don't react no more than is called for."

They turned to see to the women. Two muskets pointed toward them from narrow openings in the shutters of Cal's cabin. One shutter opened wide as its musket was withdrawn.

"Did we win the skirmish?" joked Adelin to her returning heroes. "Or do we need to hail General Jackson to protect us?"

14

CALABI CREEK, SOUTH OF THE
TALLAPOOSA RIVER, NOVEMBER 29, 1813

Lieutenant Titus Alderman trotted his mount across the gravel bed
of shallow Calibi Creek to where his commanding officer waited.
He served as aide to General John Floyd, commander of the
Georgia militia out of Fort Mitchell on the Chattahoochee River.

Smoke billowed from the Upper Creek village of Atasi behind
him, black smoke, white smoke, pillars of it from dozens of Indian
houses. The stench of spent gunpowder almost overpowered that of
the burning town.

"Casualty report, Lieutenant?" inquired General Floyd. He sat
astride his mount, impatient for Alderman's information.

"Some, sir. Few killed, exact number not yet known. Several
dozen wounded. Overall, it looks like acceptable attrition, sir."

"Very well, Lieutenant. And the enemy?"

"Heavy casualties, sir. We certainly have won a handsome
victory."

"Good. Now we must press on. There are more villages upriver
that must not survive. Get a message to Infantry Companies Two
and Five to hold here, complete a final canvass, and establish a
secure rear line. Sound assembly and have all other forces gather on
this side of the creek."

"Yes, sir!"

Alderman pulled his horse sharply around and galloped back through the water. Sporadic gunfire still sounded in parts of the village, scattered for hundreds of yards along both sides of the creek and on the banks of the Tallapoosa, wide and swift and deep at this point. Calibi Creek merged with the river about ten miles below the great falls and four miles west of the right angle bend that changed the flow of the river from south to straight west.

General Floyd turned in the saddle to face his staff officers mounted behind him. "Major!"

"Yes, General," answered the youthful major. He spurred his mount to a position adjacent to the general.

"Major, prepare the cavalry and the Cherokees to march at quick time along the river to our other objectives."

The other objectives were the small village of Nafoli, spread near the river bend, and the large and powerful warrior town of Talisi above the mouth of Yufabi Creek. Before Floyd's army left Fort Mitchell, their base on the Chattahoochee River, Indian Agent Benjamin Hawkins had speculated that little resistance could be expected at Nafoli. However, Talisi would be much more difficult, though Floyd's nine hundred fifty Georgia state militiamen, half of them cavalry, and four hundred Cherokee and Lower Creek mercenaries should be an overwhelming force versus Talisi's projected maximum of two hundred warriors.

Floyd continued to bark orders. "Have the other infantry companies follow at double time. We may need them in reserve."

The major trotted his mount to the point of assembly to await the arrival of company and regimental officers. Shooting had all but ceased. Soldiers streamed from doomed Atasi town toward the creek, hungry for more action. Opposition from Atasi had been sharp but brief. The attack had caught its defenders unaware and unprepared, with no chance to gather reinforcements from nearby villages. There was no hope to surprise the Creeks at Talisi, though. Most of the warriors that escaped from Atasi would no doubt go there to help with its defense. They would be ready and they would be angry. And they would fight to their deaths.

Fifteen minutes after General Floyd's order, fresh shot and powder had been drawn by each soldier and the troops began their trek toward Talisi. They would not follow the sandy river bank, but instead find more solid ground a few hundred yards parallel to it. Still, riding was difficult through marsh grass, thickets, and mud bogs. The horses could not make the distance at full gallop, so Floyd's cavalry set off at an easy canter with the general at the fore.

After approximately four miles, the column veered hard by the sharp bend of the river that turned its route north. The adjacent land was flat, as the fall line at the great falls marked the transformation of the last of the Appalachian foothills into coastal plain. The river banks were steep and deep so as to contain the river in times of flood, and they were alternately muddy and sandy. Access to the water was limited and traverses down from the bank were difficult to locate.

Around the bend, occasional Indian houses began to appear, then clusters. No warriors guarded them, not even women and children. Nafoli had been abandoned.

"Torch them," ordered General Floyd. "Major, leave a detachment to see to it."

"Yes, sir."

"Move on!" The general spurred his horse forward at a faster pace than before.

Canoes dotted the surface of the river, their occupants paddling for the opposite bank. Probably most of the women and children of Nafoli were aboard to seek refuge at Tukabatchi.

The cavalrymen again left the river bank, angling northeast

where two miles away Yufabi Creek spilled into the Tallapoosa at the toe of a sharp horseshoe peninsula jutting from the west bank. Fortunately for the attackers, this natural fortress lay under the control of the Tukabatchi council chiefs and not the Red Stick warriors of the east bank. To dislodge a defending force from the interior of such a bend, or even to reach them from the opposite bank of the river, would have been virtually impossible.

Agent Hawkins had forecast no difficulty in traversing Yufabi Creek, but as Floyd approached and ordered his companies to fan out for an assault across the stream, an obstacle appeared. The wide creek — thirty yards in places — was extremely shallow, never deeper than a few feet and mostly less than a foot, often not enough draft to float a canoe. But its banks were high and steep, almost matching those of the river. Horses could not safely slide down one bank, and certainly would not be able to climb the opposite slope.

"Major, pass the order," decided the general. "Dismount and prepare to assault across the creek on foot."

The first volley of musket fire exploded from the trees north of the creek. Horses were led out of danger away from the bank as soldiers scampered for cover and primed their weapons.

"Prepare to return fire, Major," ordered General Floyd. "When ready, fire at will. We will continue the barrage until we gain a reasonable run at the creek."

Staccato explosions from hundreds of muskets shattered the woods. Billows of smoke veiled both sides of the divide. Burning gunpowder strangled the air with a stifling odor. A few soldiers fell, but under the superior weaponry and marksmanship of the Georgians, the Red Sticks suffered considerably more casualties. Finally, Floyd saw an opening.

"Send half the Cherokee contingent east along the creek," he ordered. "Have them cross it and outflank the enemy. Have two companies set up along this side to provide covering fire. All other units prepare for a frontal charge as soon as the Cherokees have drawn attention away from us."

Twenty minutes later, gunfire from across the stream dwindled sharply. Simultaneously, a clamor arose in the forest to the east. The nearly two hundred Cherokees had apparently found a way through and were attacking.

"Major, pass the order." General Floyd panted with excitement. "With bayonets affixed and weapons primed, on my signal, charge."

"Yes, General."

The commands reverberated down the line. Allowing only a minute to make ready, General Floyd decided he could wait no longer.

"Charge! Overrun the scurvied bastards, men! Charge! Charge!"

All but his first command was drowned by the renewed barrage of protective musket fire of the covering marksmen, and the yells of hundreds of men sliding down the bank and dashing through the sand and gravel and shallows of the creek bottom. A soldier pitched forward and splashed face first into the muddied water, mortally wounded. Another screamed and twisted as he fell into the creek, his musket flying away as he clutched for the arrow in his thigh.

Dozens of soldiers with bayonets pointed skyward tried to sprint up the creek bank, only to slip backward and struggle for footing. Thirty or more Red Sticks ran to the lip to repel them with muskets and knives and red war clubs. Many of the warriors immediately fell to musket fire from across the way. Others were jerked down the bank and bayoneted, but not before inflicting bloody mayhem on the attackers.

The first soldiers to gain the bank sought shelter behind the nearest line of trees. They hastily reloaded and fired into the woods as others joined them behind a choking curtain of gun smoke. Soon the north bank was won and troopers began to penetrate cautiously into the forest, still meeting strong resistance from Creeks fighting from behind almost every other tree.

Lieutenant Alderman pounded up and reined his horse hard next to General Floyd at the command post a hundred yards south of the creek.

"General, sir, the cavalry company we dropped at Nafoli has arrived. They were relieved by a company of infantry. Captain Noble sends his compliments and congratulations and reports that the infantry column is now less than a mile away. He begs your orders, sir."

"Very good, Lieutenant. Have the cavalry follow the creek west to the junction of the river. If they meet little enough resistance, cross the creek and secure the river bank as far north as they can push. If they are unable to cross, direct Captain Noble to secure positions and have his sharpshooters fire on anything trying to cross the river. In either direction, Lieutenant."

"Yes, General. Immediately. And the infantry?"

"Have Colonel Coxwell report to me the moment he arrives."

"Yes, sir!" Lieutenant Alderman spurred his horse to a gallop.

Black smoke rose from beyond the trees. The Cherokees on the flanking maneuver had apparently reached Indian houses and torched them. Fighting still raged through the hundred yards of woods, but resistance had weakened. Soldiers broke into the clearing where stood at least a hundred widely spaced sturdy log houses and an equal number of dome-shaped huts, constructed of pole frames with pine bough roofs and walls, several afire. Militiamen scattered toward the houses, where they met renewed resolve from the defenders.

The infantry arrived and stormed across Yufabi Creek. The contingent of cavalry that had so effectively provided the cover that assured a foothold on the north bank, that job now done, began gathering dead and wounded.

In Talisi town, the battle had dissolved into house-to-house fighting as soldiers steadily gained ground. Casualties mounted for both antagonists, but much heavier on the side of the Creeks. The attackers' superior numbers had gained nearly three-quarters of the town's perimeter.

Warriors held their ground at each village structure until overrun. A woman stood defiantly in a blazing doorway, refusing to move. Her toddler children ran away screaming to the next house. She tightly gripped both sides of the portal but didn't make a sound or move an inch as fire engulfed her body. She died standing; her charred, still flaming corpse finally collapsed to mix with the ashes of her home.

A squad of soldiers turned a corner around a large, prominent house to find themselves facing a fierce, middle-aged warrior and three stout youthful ones. Both groups stood for a long moment, glaring at the other. No man on either side held a charged musket. Three soldiers to the rear frantically attempted to reload while their companions squared off with the Red Sticks before them.

"I am Naupti, brother of our chief," spoke the older warrior defiantly, struggling to mix as much English as possible with his native Muskogean. "I and my sons fight with the protection of the Spirits. May you and your evil die in dishonor and damnation!"

Naupti raised his war club and charged. He ducked a thrust of a bayonet and smashed the unlucky fellow behind it into eternity. Another soldier swung a musket stock into Naupti's face, smashing him to the side. Naupti turned back, prepared to swing the blood-dripped club again. A bayonet went through his throat with the club still on the backswing.

One of the young warriors dispatched two militiamen with the butt of his musket before it was wrenched from his grasp. He pulled a bone-handled knife from his waistband and leaped onto the nearest soldier and cut his throat. A bayonet pierced him through the rib cage. After slashing at another of the enemy without knowing whether he connected, the warrior passed into unconsciousness. His two brothers, fighting valiantly with gory war clubs, continued to take a deadly toll.

A soldier at the rear finally primed his weapon, cocked the flint and positioned the strike in one motion, leveled and fired without aiming. The point blank charge ripped through the heart of one of the warriors. The remaining one, enraged anew, attacked again, only to be felled by a musket stock across his forehead. He crashed to the side, motionless and bleeding heavily, as the soldiers stepped past, their new goal the tribal council lodge in the town's central square.

Skirmishes continued for another hour, until surviving warriors had been pushed into the forest or the river. Soldiers rounded up some wounded warriors as captives and killed others. They gathered women and children that did not flee, huddled them near the river bank, and awaited orders for their disposition.

Finally, recall sounded. Companies assembled slowly in the wide square. Details of soldiers gathered the dead and treated the American wounded. Trails for horses had been cut into the creek banks so casualties could be conveyed out on litters. Most of the houses of Talisi smoldered as ashes, but some still crackled with live flames.

General Floyd rode slowly into the clearing and continued in a wide circle to survey the spectacle. He walked his horse in silence, hardly believing. Not even two decades of military life on unforgiving frontiers had prepared him for such a grim scene.

"Lieutenant," Floyd turned quietly to Alderman. "Assemble my staff officers. Five minutes."

"Gentlemen," the general began when the officers had gathered, "we have won a significant, glorious victory. My thanks and my congratulations. Now it is vital that we make the correct next step. We have no means to cross the river in force to take Tukabatchi. Agreed?"

With little discussion, the staff affirmed unanimously Floyd's negative assessment of a potential attack on Tukabatchi. Several officers then urged the general to push on to towns farther up the river while they had the Red Sticks running and disorganized. The town of Saugahatchi would be an attractive objective, Ipisoga another. Others thought it better to backtrack to Atasi and campaign westward along the river to the confluence of the Tallapoosa and the Coosa; and perhaps then on to an assault on Holy Ground where Chief Red Eagle was rumored to be hiding since the Fort Mims massacre. Still others suggested that the army return to Fort Mitchell to resupply, not willing to trust unreliable supply lines to replenish provisions and ammunition.

"I believe that may be the wisest course," General Floyd said of the latter argument. "Our directive from Milledgeville only included Atasi and Talisi, and Tukabatchi if possible. We have no authority to campaign farther. I certainly have little desire to push northward above the falls. Marching a battalion of cavalry over unfamiliar hilly terrain in the face of hostiles is not a sound military tactic. As for Holy Ground, we have no reliable intelligence as to what would await us. And I, too, do not wish to stake my command's lifeblood on supply trains."

The general gazed wearily at each of his staff officers. "Gentlemen, I thank you again for your valor and your valuable counsel. But, no, I fear that our campaign must end for now. We shall go home to Fort Mitchell and I will make my report to Milledgeville."

Before dusk, General John Floyd's Georgia militia had begun its slow trek away from Talisi town on the first leg back to its Chattahoochee River base. They left behind hundreds of incinerated Creek houses, scores of dead and wounded Creek warriors, and deeply buried aspirations for Agent Benjamin Hawkins's Civilization Program for the Muskogi Nation.

15

THE MURPH SETTLEMENT, DECEMBER 1, 1813

Soosquana stood on the porch of her cabin in the early morning and watched November blend into December at the Murph compound. It was to be another gorgeous day. The weather remained moderate, comfortable, no sign of real winter yet.

Movement of Creeks along the river had not increased and no further threats from militant Red Sticks had been made. Everybody agreed, however, that they must remain watchful.

Soosquana saw across the compound that Adelin already worked at sorting a large pile of deerskins and rabbit pelts at one of the outdoor tables. She and Adelin were to work on them this morning, sewing some into winter clothing and dressing the remainder into prime condition for trading next summer. Saul and Cal appeared on the trail from the animal shelter leading all the livestock.

The animals needed exercise. They hadn't been out in weeks, not since the trouble began and their masters had become cautious about venturing afield. Occasionally, they were staked out to graze, but that seriously limited their range of movement.

Soosquana's milk goat and the horses and mules were each fitted with a halter and a rope to which Saul or Cal now tied a hefty rock. Dragging a weight would allow freedom to wander around the compound but would discourage roaming too far or too fast.

Soosquana loved her goat but had not as yet named her. Too, she appreciated the nourishment the milk provided her and her unborn child. Hopefully, by spring or summer the goat would still be producing enough milk to help keep the little one happy and healthy, the little one due only a month from now.

Later, Soosquana and Adelin busied themselves with the animal skins in front of Cal's and Adelin's cabin. Saul and Cal worked at shoring up the foundation of both cabins and repairing the mud plastering between logs. Extra insulation would be important for the coming winter.

"Uh oh," said Cal. "Look at old George." The mule had strayed nearly a hundred yards down the trail toward the river ford, almost out of sight among the trees.

"I'll get him," volunteered Adelin. She put down her skins, got up, and walked after the errant mule.

"George, you naughty boy," scolded Adelin affectionately as she reached the patch of late autumn grass where the mule feasted. She gripped his halter, reached under his neck, and stroked his opposite cheek while caressing her face against his. "You know better than to trail away. Come on, let's go bac . . . ."

George leaped sideways, startled, as a powerful arm wrapped across Adelin's chest from behind, clamping her arms tight, while another hand flashed the sharp edge of a knife to her throat.

Adelin shrieked in horror, then recovered and froze, afraid to move against the pressing blade. The man spewed orders in what she recognized as Muskogean, but she understood none of what he said. He tightened his hold as she glimpsed other men stepping forward on either side.

She decided she had little to lose. "Cal!" she screamed. "Cal! Saul! Help!"

The man made no attempt to squelch her. Instead, he pushed her toward the cabins, keeping his choking grip, while his companions fanned out to his flanks.

"Let her go!" yelled Saul, blocking the trail thirty yards away and aiming his musket at the Indian's head.

"You do her harm and I'll shoot you dead!" threatened Cal beside him, in a kneeling stance with his musket also aimed dead on. "Put away the knife!"

The band of warriors edged closer with their captive.

"Soos," urged Saul to his horrified wife as she hurried to him from behind, "get to the cabin. Quick!"

Soosquana reluctantly took a step away. She scanned the scene as she started for the cabin, then stopped. She yelped.

Screaming at the Indians in Muskogean, Soosquana ran toward them, excited and angry. Saul held out an arm to stop her. She fought to get through.

"It is Tolokika and Ettepti-lopa! Saul, those are my brothers! From Talisi!" She reverted to Muskogean and resumed screaming at the Indians. She pulled away from Saul and continued to within inches of where her brother held on tight to Adelin.

Soosquana angrily argued with Tolokika, obviously ordering the release of Adelin. Her brother did not relent. His friends spread across the trail and behind adjacent trees, with ready muskets and bows and menacingly red war clubs. Soosquana turned to the other sibling with her argument. He, too, rebuked her, eyes flashing and hands gesturing, unyielding as his brother.

Saul and Cal maintained their positions, unsure what to do.

"They don't look like Soos's brothers we met at Talisi," blurted Cal. "Don't act like 'em, either."

"It's them, all right," said Saul. "I recognize them now."

Soosquana's brothers had welcomed them with friendship on their second trip to Talisi. They had approved the marriage of their sister to Saul and had enthusiastically celebrated the wedding.

Finally, both of Soosquana's brothers became less animated. Their tone softened as they began to listen to some of what Soosquana said. Soosquana quietened, was less insistent, and the debate calmed. She reached up and touched Tolokika's forehead which featured a deep, ugly slash from its center through the right eye socket. She turned to Ettepti-lopa and pulled back his shirt to examine his torso. She cringed at the bloody, festered wound to his rib cage. Her hands went to her face in fright as Tolokika continued to talk angrily to her. She now was not arguing back; just listening intently.

"Saul," said Soosquana, turning around to face her husband with tears streaming down both cheeks, "my father, Naupti, and my brother, Hakkali, are dead."

Saul and Cal looked at her increduously, not speaking but not relaxing their vigil with their muskets.

Soosquana continued. "Soldiers attacked our village, and attacked other villages. Killed many. Burned houses. My father and brother died fighting them. These two brothers wounded."

"Soos, I'm sorry," said Saul. "That's terrible. But what do they want here? Tell them to let go of Adelin."

Soosquana resumed negotiations with her brothers for Adelin. They remained belligerent and adamant.

"They say no. They are very angry. They say the white man must suffer."

"Suffer hell!" blurted Cal. "I'm gonna suffer a musket ball between his eyes if he doesn't let her go."

"Hold on, Cal," cautioned Saul. "Let's not cause any wrong move here. They're mad enough now. Let Soos handle them."

Soosquana didn't let up. She debated insistently, gesturing to Adelin, then to herself, then to Saul and Cal. She stroked her belly, obviously invoking the coming baby. Negotiations continued for long minutes more. No one on either side dared move except Soosquana and her angry brothers.

Finally, Soosquana turned to Saul and Cal. "They say they'll let Adelin go if you uncock your muskets. They don't trust you."

"It's hard to trust them, too," observed Saul. "That's all? What else do they want?"

"They want me to go with them."

"Hell, no . . . !"

"I told them no. I told them I would not leave here."

"Damn right you won't leave here!"

"Lower your muskets," insisted Soosquana.

"They'll do the same?" Saul had taken all negotiations on himself. "And let Adelin loose?"

"Yes." She turned to speak again to her brothers, then back to Saul and Cal. "Yes," she said again.

"All right. Let's try it."

Saul first, then Cal, slowly lifted their aim, raised the strikes and carefully lowered the flintlocks. They ported the muskets but maintained firm grips on them. Long, tense moments later, but only after Soosquana admonished them again, the Indians eased their own weapons.

Soosquana gingerly reached with one hand to pry loose Tolokika's arm that encircled Adelin, and pulled the knife blade from her neck with the other hand. Adelin carefully stepped away. Soosquana jerked her clear and embraced her. Adelin hugged back, emotional and still frightened, then bolted past Soosquana into Cal's arms.

At the further urging of Soosquana, the warriors, nine in all, moved to the oak tree at the edge of the bluff and sat in a wide semicircle, but still held their weapons close. With Soosquana as interpreter, the Murph men, yet as leery of the warriors as they were of the Murphs, sought details on the Talisi attack.

"Was it Jackson's men?" asked Saul. "Or Cocke's? The American general at Talatigi or the troops that attacked the Hillabis?" The Murphs had not forgotten the visit by the boisterous sergeant and his posse.

Soosquana relayed the questions. "No, they were none of those. They were soldiers from the east. Many horsemen. Many Cherokees also. Burned Talisi, Atasi, Nafoli."

"Must've been Georgia militia. Damn! Is everybody getting in on this? Those troops answer to Mister Hawkins, I think. He's supposed to be friends with the chiefs at Tukabatchi."

"When was the attack?" Cal wanted to know.

"Two days ago."

"Ask them where the soldiers went from there. Not upriver, I hope. We certainly don't want them coming up here."

Soosquana patiently extracted as many details as she could from the warriors. Hours after the battle, when the brothers had regained consciousness, both badly wounded, most of the soldiers had gone. The pair escaped into the forest and worked their way north over the next two days, joining with the others one and two at a time as they happened to find each other. They decided to visit the Murph compound out of concern for their sister and, for some of the warriors, with a bent toward possible revenge.

Soosquana learned that her mother and her sisters had fortunately been ferried across the Tallapoosa to Tukabatchi before the attack. There they supposedly remained safe with most of the other women and children of Talisi.

Tension continued to ease as Soosquana gradually convinced all parties that they should trust each other. She stood and walked to Tolokika. She tenderly fingered his head wound, examining it carefully.

"Saul," she said, "we should treat their injuries."

Not waiting for Saul to reply, Cal stood up in one quick, fluid motion. "I'll get the surgical pack."

Soosquana persuaded Tolokika and Ettepti-lopa to accept treatment. Three other warriors needed attention at least as much as her brothers, she was certain. Maybe after she successfully cared for Tolokika and Ettepti-lopa, they would not resist.

Cal returned with a bulky canvas bundle containing the Murphs' medical stores, consisting of cotton swabs and strip bandages, a strong poultice bartered from Turkeytown, and several herb and root extract potions boiled from native plants. The latter were concocted by Soosquana from the lore of her ancestors. She insisted that her people faithfully and successfully used these remedies. Indeed, they had seemed to work miracles on routine cuts and scrapes that Saul and Cal often suffered in their daily tasks.

Soosquana treated Tolokika's deep gash first. She took special pains with the part that intersected the eye socket, and she eventually fastened a neat bandage in place that should give the wound an excellent chance to heal. She informed Tolokika with a teasing smile that he could expect a prominent scar. He grinned as if that wasn't necessarily bad. Such a vicious trophy would present an imposing facade among his peers and, more importantly, to potential enemies.

Ettepti-lopa's stab wound to the ribs was next. It was worse than Tolokika's head slash. Infection already showed, but Soosquana set about cleaning the ugly hole as best she could. Though he tried mightily not to, Ettepti-lopa flinched several times from the pain.

"Aiiiee!"

His companions smiled as Ettepti-lopa let slip the slight yelp. His acute embarrassment only enhanced their amusement.

Having observed the touch of Soosquana with her brothers, the other injured men finally relented. One had a wound all the way across his stomach, caused by a musket ball that came from one side, penetrated the flesh hardly more than skin deep and continued out the other side.

A fortunate wound indeed; it could have been fatal had the shot penetrated at a deeper angle. The wound had already begun to heal, which made treating him fairly simple.

The next warrior's shattered shoulder was of more concern. The ball was still deep within and Soosquana knew not to try to extract it. She applied the root and herb concoctions, trying to work them as deeply as possible with a minimum amount of discomfort to the patient, and topped off the wound with a thick layer of poultice. Then she heavily bandaged the shoulder and reassured the warrior, but she knew she had not helped him very much.

Soosquana finally turned to the last patient's multiple wounds. His left bicep had suffered a bayonet slash, he had another deep cut on his left thigh, and there was an ugly bruise just forward of the right temple, probably from a musket butt. The head wound was the most serious, Soosquana recognized, though the absence of broken skin probably made it appear benign to the others. She dared not tell them differently, though she would confide in Saul, Cal, and Adelin later. Unfortunately, she could do less for the bruise than for the cuts.

When she had finally finished with the medical chores, Soosquana suddenly realized that the visitors probably had eaten little for three days.

"I will get food and drink," she volunteered.

"No," offered Adelin, stopping her, "you stay here with them, Soos. I'll get supper. We have enough roast venison to boil up a pot of stew."

An hour later the Indians eagerly devoured hot stew, cornbread, and strong coffee. Even then, most of the warriors kept one hand on a weapon while eating with the other.

After supper Soosquana took a slow, solemn walk along the bluff with Tolokika and Ettepti-lopa, mourning their father and brother and missing their mother and sisters. They talked quietly but emotionally and embraced each other several times. Saul, Cal, Adelin, and the warrior friends of Tolokika and Ettepti-lopa left them to their grief and solace.

By dusk they were gone, but most of the nine Creek warriors yet harbored a load of suspicion and distrust. The Murphs watched them make their way down the path to the shoals, cross the rocks to the trail on the opposite bank, and disappear among the trees upriver.

"They asked me again to go with them," revealed Soosquana. The others looked at her. "I told them I couldn't, I wouldn't leave. That I belonged here, that I belonged with you."

Saul squeezed his wife with the arm around her shoulders. "We certainly belong with you, Soos," he said.

"You were a hero today, Soos," said Adelin. "Thank you."

Soosquana still stared after her brothers. Another tear coursed down her cheek. After a long pause she lamented quietly and sadly, "I'll never see them again. They will join the Red Sticks upriver. They vowed that they would avenge our people's deaths, and would die doing it. They will, too, Saul."

Saul squeezed her tighter. "I know, Soos, I know."

16

"What the hell is the old fool gonna do?" asked Jeb Worthington as he stoked the fire again. "He ain't got much of nobody left if we all go home."

"Who gives a damn?" answered the man standing next to him, Lester Kevenhall. Kevenhall crowded the fire as closely as its heat would permit. "Damn, it's cold! I shore ain't chasing no more mangy Indians around this country for him no longer than I have to. 'Specially since him and his all-fired stupid officers don't seem to know what the hell they're doing."

"Now hold on," objected Silas Monck. "General Jackson has done what he said he'd do. He lit them savages out of Tallashatchi and Talatigi, didn't he? Hell, all of you were there. And all them Indians down along that Hillabi Creek ain't so tough and mighty no more."

"We didn't do the Hillabi Creek raids," corrected Worthington. "That's what I'm talking about. These stupid generals don't know what each other is doing. We were about to win over the Hillabis without firing a shot. Then come that blooming idiot Cocke and his thugs from up about Knoxville and killed a bunch and got 'em all fired up again. 'Cause of that we're still stuck down here in these woods in the middle of winter."

"I ain't staying, neither, past my time being up 'bout three weeks from now," said Kevenhall. "I don't know what made me join up when y'all came through Fayetteville in October. Stupid, I reckon."

"Well," insisted Monck, "I think them damn heathens still need to be taught a lesson. They can't go 'round murdering and scalping women and children like they done. We can't stand for it."

"Hell, Silas, if we was anywhere near that Fort Mims place where all that happened, I might say that myself. But I hear Fort Mims is way down 'bout Mobile or somewheres and I don't think we're anywhere near that. And General Jackson told us that was what this was all about when we signed on. Hell, the Indians we've killed ain't even had any white folks' scalps on 'em."

"Wouldn't be so bad, I guess, if they'd get the damn supply lines going like they promised," observed another dissident. "When's the last time we had a decent feed? Huh? Hard biscuit and fat back ain't my idea of a fighting man's rations."

"Well, I'm staying it through," boasted Monck. "I ain't running from no savages."

"Watch your tongue, Silas. Don't be saying nothing about nobody, you hear?"

"You can stay if you want," announced Worthington, "but me and my company are heading for Nashville in the morning. Our enlistment is up next week and we're getting an early start. And I'd like to see ol' Jackson stop us, too. He cowed down that bunch last week that wanted to leave, but we ain't gonna stay here and freeze and starve."

As if reacting to the word 'freeze', Silas Monck threw another hickory log on the already roaring fire. "Would you boys be staying if we was fighting Indians more than we are? And, of course, if they was feeding us better?"

"I don't know. Maybe. That's what we come for. But we ain't

fighting 'em and they ain't feeding us and we ain't staying. That's that."

In General Jackson's command lodge inside the stockade, Colonel Billy Carroll asked, "General, D Company from Nashville says they're heading out tomorrow; we gonna let 'em go?"

"Mutineers!" spat Jackson. "Damn 'em! They still have a week left on their militia enlistments. We'll hold them here till then if we have to shoot some of them, but after that I reckon we'll have to let them leave if they want."

"Yes, sir."

Jackson had initiated his campaign with a call to arms in Nashville on September nineteenth. He ordered his standing cavalry militia to active status and began the recruitment of additional horsemen and infantry. Hundreds of volunteers responded with three-month enlistments, reacting to news of Fort Mims and wild rumors of Creek atrocities in its wake. By September twenty-fourth Jackson had gathered his forces at Camp Good Exchange near Nashville and made ready to march.

Colonel John Coffee, Jackson's cavalry commander and the husband of his favorite niece, had assured his general that the campaign would be short and victorious and glorious. Jackson promoted Coffee to brigadier and directed him and his regiment to ride straight to Huntsville in the Mississippi Territory.

Jackson's infantry marched south through Columbia to Fayetteville, recruiting more men at every junction, reaching Camp Blount near Fayetteville on October seventh. He pushed on to Huntsville on the tenth upon hearing a false report of great numbers of Creeks attacking on all frontiers.

Another four day trek brought the full army to the southernmost extent of the Tennessee River. They crossed to the south bank and established Fort Deposit, which was to be Jackson's supply base for the campaign. Not a single hostile Indian had been encountered to that point.

From Fort Deposit Jackson had to cut a wilderness trail through virgin forests, finally arriving at Ten Islands on the Coosa River about November first. He had operated since from Fort Strother, which he had ordered built on the site. It was there that he lamented his plight on this cold December night.

"Can't really blame 'em, though, I guess," General Jackson conceded about the impending departure of most of his three-month recruits. "Goddamn food's lousy, it's cold as hell, and we're pinned down here with no battle provisions, thanks to those damn fools we left in charge back at Fort Deposit. Besides, we ain't seen a hostile Creek in a month."

"Yes, sir," countered Colonel Carroll, "but we have had some nice victories. The Creeks haven't attacked any settlers lately, not since we've been here."

"Hell, Billy, there ain't no settlers around here for them to attack! Not east of the Coosa anyhow. But don't tell that to the men."

"What about the family that one of General Cocke's sergeants says he ran across squatting down on the Tallapoosa?"

"Hell, that soldier is a drunk and a braggart. You saw what a damn fool he is, didn't you? He's lying. We've heard rumors about all kinds of things down here. There ain't no settlers on that part of the Tallapoosa. Ain't no white man that stupid, Billy. Or that brave."

"Yes, sir."

"All the business about Indians attacking settlers is going on farther south. All the big incidents, anyhow." Jackson's already hostile mood turned even darker. "Don't matter, though. The blood-thirsty vermin around here would lift your scalp in an eye blink if you turned your back. We can't trust 'em." He paused, scowled, changed the subject. "Goddammit! First light send a runner on the trail north to find out where that damn supply train's got to. They better get their asses here like Governor Blount keeps promising or we're gonna lose our whole garrison."

"Yes, sir, I'll see to it. Right away!"

"And have General Coffee get a cavalry detachment out and surround D Company. I don't want them leaving till next week, if at all."

17

The Murph settlement, December, 1813

"What are they doing in there?" asked Cal again. "They're up to something."

"Just have to be patient," laughed Saul. "They said it was a secret and we weren't supposed to know until they said we could know. Just leave 'em be. You can't figure out women."

Soosquana and Adelin had been holed up in the new cabin all morning working on what they called a secret project. Saul and Cal, in spite of the cold, sat in front of the old cabin trimming poles and saplings and shaping them to dry. They would fashion chairs and tables and other pieces of furniture from them later in the winter. One or the other of the women emerged occasionally and pranced by with a smug expression, but spoke not a word. Cal, especially, could hardly stand the teasing.

"Getting colder," observed Saul, looking up at dark clouds rolling in fast from the southwest. "Could be some snow."

"Naw, too early. Might rain, but no snow. Ain't snowed in December since we come here."

"Don't mean it can't."

They began thinking back and tallying. This was their fourth winter on the Tallapoosa and they had seen snow only a few times.

"Five," concluded Saul, "counting only the times it stuck."

"I only get four. And just one of those amounted to anything. Three inches or so two years ago, was it?"

"I think so," Saul laughed. "Sure different from in the mountains back in Virginia, huh? We had it up to our chins all the time back there out from Roanoke, remember?"

Adelin strutted by again and flashed another flirtatious smile. She said nothing. Cal gnashed his teeth.

Soosquana still mourned her father and brother and her home village, but the hurt had begun to heal. She made heroic efforts to attend to her chores and to involve herself with her husband and her in-laws. Despite the intense pain of her losses, her cheerful, busy, confident personality had reemerged, and she had taken charge again of preparing for the birth of her baby. She glowed with excitement more each day as the time drew closer.

Finally, late in the morning, Soosquana called out. "Come over. We're ready for you."

Saul and Cal dropped their work and walked to the cabin, stopping in the yard. The women were still inside.

"Ready?" Soosquana asked from behind the door. "I come out."

She stepped from the door in full ceremonial Muskogi dress, resplendent despite her enormous bulge. She had not looked quite so elegant or so native since her wedding, thought Saul. She stopped on the porch and smiled.

"Gorgeous!" said Cal.

"My! Soos, that's beautiful," declared Saul. "So that's what y'all been doing all morning."

"Only part of it. You not seen best thing yet. Adelin?"

Soosquana stepped aside as the door opened again. Out strode Adelin, and what a sight! She wore a dazzling Creek dress made of fine deerskin. Her moccasins were topped with colored bead tassels. The belt around the wrap-around skirt was tipped with more brilliant beads. A cloth and bone sash crossed her body from one shoulder; the small bones, uniform in size, were dyed red, blue, yellow, and white. More beads and tips of hawk feathers were woven generously through her auburn hair, combed long and flowing. Several tiers of beaded necklaces encircled her neck and looped to her breasts.

The Murph brothers stood speechless, mouths open. "Wow," Cal finally managed. "I mean, wow! Adelin!" He stammered. "Wow!" he repeated.

"You like it?" asked Adelin with a bat of her eyes at Cal.

"I must say you girls surprised us," said Saul. "You are both something. Absolutely beautiful!"

"Is Adelin not pretty?" asked Soosquana, gesturing proudly. "She very pretty. Adelin real Muskogi woman now. She is my sister."

When the women finished parading and the men overcame their amazement, the next surprise was a special feast of fried chicken for dinner, and the promise of venison steaks for supper.

"No special occasion," explained Adelin. "We just wanted to do it."

Worsening weather didn't dampen the festive mood, even though light rain began in the middle of the afternoon and the temperature continued to drop rapidly. The thick cloud cover brought darkness earlier than normal, and with it the drizzle turned to sleet.

By the time supper was finished and Adelin and Cal walked to their cabin, the precipitation had become equal parts of rain and sleet with a few flakes of snow showing. The wind had lessened somewhat but still blew from the southwest.

A half hour later, before preparing for bed, Cal opened a shutter to check again on the weather. "Uh oh. Look, Adelin. How about this?"

The rain had given over completely to snow. It fell steadily in medium flakes. The wind had died completely so that the only sound aside from the familiar rush of the shoals was the soft rustle of snow falling through the trees. White patches had already begun to stick around the yard.

"How beautiful!" declared Adelin. "Will it stay?"

"Looks like it. Maybe several inches by morning. I better get Saul and go check on the livestock. Probably take us an hour or so. All right?"

Adelin lay awake in bed when Cal returned. He undressed, blew out the last lamp, and climbed in. He pulled the blanket close, shivering slightly.

"Everything all right?" asked Adelin.

"Yeah, sure. We plugged a few more holes in the shed and put blankets and furs across their backs. Okra says to tell you hello and good night."

Adelin laughed and shuffled toward Cal. They turned, facing each other, naked body to naked body. He reached an arm around her and pulled her to him. Adelin snuggled her head under his chin. They lay quietly, drifting into haziness.

"Cal?"

"Mmmm?"

"Cal, I'm really happy. I am so glad you brought me here."

Cal squeezed her tighter. "Even with everything that's happening?"

"Yes, even with that."

"This is a hard land, Adelin. And dangerous."

"I know, and that's fine. It's also a beautiful land. And I do belong here. With you."

"I really love you, Adelin. You know that, don't you?"

"Yes. I love you, too, more than I ever thought I could." She shifted slightly and snuggled closer.

"This place is paradise, and you are the best thing in it."

Cal tilted Adelin's face to his and kissed her. The kiss lingered and she responded eagerly. They exchanged more kisses as they explored each other's bodies. Cal rolled Adelin to her back and she pulled him after her. He kissed her again. She moaned, and hugged his body tightly to hers.

18

If the Murphs had the date right, with their crude estimates of the progress of the calendar, Soosquana's labor began on New Year's Day. She and Adelin had finished preparing a special dinner to celebrate the occasion when she felt the first pain.

"Oh! I have to sit down, Adelin."

"You all right, Soos? Are you sick?" Then she realized. "Oh, oh! Soos! It's the baby, isn't it? Wow! I'll get Saul."

"No, wait. Not yet ready. Maybe it starting but baby not come yet."

"I'll get Saul anyway."

Saul and Cal were at Soosquana's side in less than a minute.

"We have to get you to bed," proclaimed Saul. "And then we have to, uh, we have to . . . . Soos, what do we do next? Adelin? Hell, I don't know."

Adelin laughed. Soosquana tried to laugh, too, but the next pain doubled her over.

"I see that you fellows are going to be a lot of help," reasoned Adelin. "She'll be all right; the baby will be a while yet." She reached for Soosquana. "Come on, help me put her to bed and I'll get your dinner for you. It's about ready."

Saul and Cal spent the afternoon walking in circles in the yard, with Saul having to look into the cabin at less than five minute intervals. It being a nice day for January, Adelin sat in a rocking chair on the porch and did finger work on a deerskin blouse. The men's worried antics entertained her. Soosquana mostly napped as the labor symptoms had subsided.

By supper, Soosquana had decided that the baby was yet days away, that the day's episode was just an early stirring. She finally convinced the others and prepared for bed.

Cal had said little all day, and had done even less to be helpful. As they walked to their cabin, Adelin hooked her arm in his and smiled. "You did good today, big boy," she teased.

"Huh? Whaddya mean?"

"Why, you didn't get in the way a single time. That's about as good as a man can do in these situations."

The quiet and the deep slumber of that same pleasant winter night was splintered by a panicked shout. "Adelin! Cal! Come over! We need you!"

Cal and Adelin jerked upright in bed in unison.

"It's Saul," said Cal.

"Soos's pains must be back. Let's get over there."

Contractions had returned stronger than ever, and this time it was unmistakably the real thing. However, the baby was in no hurry. After making all preparations for the birth and watching the men check everything over and over until it became annoying to both women, Adelin again banished them to the yard.

The time had to be a couple of hours past midnight. Cal decided he should check the animals and headed for the shed.

"You'll just wake 'em up," Saul called after him. "What the hell can you do in the middle of the night?"

Saul sat on the porch steps, got up and walked to the edge of the bluff, came back and sat down, got up and went to the door, opened it and spoke to Adelin who again reassured him. Saul closed the door and sat on the steps again. Perhaps three minutes had elapsed. A minute on the steps and he repeated the entire cycle. It would be retraced again with variations dozens of times before the moon set and a hazy gray softened the southeastern sky. Cal had returned to the porch sometime during the predawn and flopped down in the rocker. He hardly moved the rest of the night.

Through the night inside the cabin, Adelin's sympathetic conversation and excited giggles had mixed with Soosquana's occasional grunts, squeals, and tortured comments frequently cut short by sudden yips. As the sky lightened, the tone sharply changed. Soosquana's pain had become steady and acute. Saul ran to the door. Adelin let him in but soon had to again ask him to leave.

Cal laughed. "Big brother, you're just no good at this birthing business, are you?"

"I reckon you're doing a helluva lot of good yourself?"

Cal laughed at him again.

Saul offered his help a couple more times and was ejected from the cabin anew on each occasion. He walked across the porch, from one end to the other and back again, continuously. Cal grinned at him each time he paced by the rocking chair.

Suddenly, just as a big fiery sun poked through the treetops across the river, sounds of activity within the cabin stopped. Dead silence. Saul froze in the middle of the porch, facing the door, unable to move. Cal stopped rocking.

No sound. Nothing. Not even, it seemed, the murmur of the river washing over the shoals. Every movement had been suspended. Long minutes. Long, long minutes.

The door cracked. Then it swung full open. Adelin slowly walked out. She tenderly held in both arms a big bundled blanket.

"Daddy Saul," she smiled, fighting to control herself, "say hello to your beautiful, beautiful baby daughter."

Saul carefully peeked into the blanket as Adelin began crying, unable to hold her emotions longer. Sleeping in her arms was the most gorgeous baby Saul had ever seen. Everything about her, as far as he could tell, was perfect, right up to a full head of coal black hair.

"Is Soos all right?" he asked.

"She's just great," Adelin sniffed between tears. "She's dozing."

"Can I see her?"

"Of course. Go on in."

Saul looked past the doorway into the darkened room and nervously stepped inside. Soosquana appeared to be asleep. He quietly walked to her and leaned down and kissed her. She roused and opened her eyes and smiled.

"Did you see her?"

"I sure did," he said.

"Is she not beautiful?"

"She is beautiful. The most beautiful baby ever. She looks just like her mother."

Adelin still held the baby. "Do you want to hold her, Saul?"

"What? Hold her? Me? Yes. No! No, I might drop her. No. What, are you crazy? I can't hold her. I've never done that. I don't know how."

"Come on, don't be silly. You had little brothers and sisters back in Virginia, didn't you?"

"Yes, but I didn't touch them as babies."

"Sit down, you old softy, and I'll put her in your lap. Don't worry. I'll show you. You'll do fine."

Soosquana watched the drama from her bed, amused at her astonished husband. As Adelin arranged the baby in his lap, and he stared down at this amazing new creature, Soosquana's amusement turned to wonder and worship. Her Muskogi people believed in Spirits and depended on miracles, but what she saw in her husband

and child was more spiritual and more miraculous than anything she had experienced in life to this moment.

Later, Saul, Cal, and Adelin stood on the porch and noticed for the first time that a marvelous, bright day had dawned. Inside, Soosquana had fallen asleep with the baby at peace in the crook of her arm.

"I'll go to the cabin and cook some breakfast for everybody," volunteered Adelin. "You stay here and watch them, Saul. After we've all eaten, I'll stay with them. You boys need to get some sleep."

"Adelin," pronounced Saul, "you are not to be believed. What would we have done without you? You must be an angel." He looked at Cal. "And little brother, you were as useless as I was."

Cal and Adelin started toward their cabin. Adelin turned back.

"Saul," she asked, "what's the baby's name?"

Saul looked startled. "Name? Why, I don't know. I haven't even thought about it. We haven't talked about it." He stroked his chin. "Yeah, I suppose she needs a name. I'll have to ask Soos." He turned to reenter the cabin. "Yeah, I'll have to ask Soos."

19

FORT STROTHER ON THE COOSA RIVER, JANUARY, 1814

"How many men we got left, Billy?" General Andrew Jackson demanded the information more than requested it. He sourly chewed on a gnarled homemade cigar.

Colonel Billy Carroll didn't dare challenge the general's mood. He knew his commander was primed to explode, had been for the past month. "Less than fifty, sir, most of them cavalry of Coffee's troop. That's not counting your officers from the Nashville brigade."

"Friendlies?"

"About a hundred Cherokees and turncoat Creeks. The rest of the Cherokees left with General Cocke this morning."

"That son of a bitch!" Jackson repeated for at least the tenth time today. "What the hell did Cocke come down here for? He's here for less than two months and does nothing but jump on the Hillabis after we had 'em practically surrendered. Makes 'em madder'n ever and then goes home. Hell, if he'd stayed home to start with we'd have control of this whole country by now and we'd all be home."

"Yes, sir." Carroll knew to give General Jackson his head when he ranted so.

"Do you think the Creeks are stupid people, Billy?"

"Sir?" Carroll was surprised at the change to a new subject.

"Think about it, Billy. We oughta been dead by nightfall. Here we are with our butts hanging out for the whole Creek Nation and they ain't nowhere abouts. Least I guess they ain't or they would have jumped us by now. Any half ass military strategist would bring his whole force against a weakened bunch like ours with no provisions and little ordnance."

"Maybe they are unaware of our plight, sir."

"Not likely, but if so, even more unforgivable. They oughta have scouts all over our ass." Jackson winced and rubbed his elbow. The arm that had suffered the pistol wound in Nashville still bothered him. "Hell, if I was commanding the Red Sticks, half those Creeks out there with our boys would be spies."

"Maybe they know we got reinforcements coming."

"If they were smart we'd all be chopped up before any reinforcements got to us. Then, they oughta be ambushing anybody coming in. Besides, we don't know for sure that help is coming, do we?"

"Runners from Fort Deposit have been telling us for the past week that fresh troops are on the way."

"Hell, if they do come, they better bring stores with 'em. We're down to hard biscuit and roasted acorns. Everything else is cleaned out, even most of the fish in the Coosa, it seems."

"We're very low on powder and shot and repair parts, too, sir."

"God damn, Billy, I know that. We're dead for sure if the new units come empty-handed." Jackson's cigar had been chewed into a thin, ugly twist. "Or if they don't come at all. Billy, I want every man inside the stockade for the night. Any Indians, too, that want to come in. And double the guard all around."

"Yes, sir."

"At daybreak send out scout patrols for a thousand yards up and down the river and along all trails and roads. We need to know if those mangy scoundrels have been skulking about."

Troops had been leaving for home over most of the past month.

General Jackson had been able to stand them down for a while, even after enlistments began to expire. He had called them cowards and mutineers and had even threatened to shoot those that deserted him. But when his officers reminded him that the men were within their rights, he had no choice but to let them go.

"Riders on the road!" the sentry on the north road at the edge of the clearing shouted at midmorning the next day. "Large column!"

"Riders on the road!" relayed the stockade guard post. "Alert General Jackson."

A militia colonel rode into the clearing at the head of a company of cavalry. General Jackson, General Coffee, and Colonel Carroll greeted him before the front gate. "Colonel," grouched Jackson, "you certainly took your time. We expected you days ago. Our asses have been exposed here for three days since the last of General Cocke's East Tennessee outfit pulled out."

"Yes, sir." The young officer dismounted and saluted sharply. "I'm Colonel Patrick Highsmith. I bring you compliments from Governor Blount and a detachment of fresh militia."

"How many?"

"There's another company of cavalry on the road no more than a mile back, with a regiment of infantry. Over eight hundred personnel in all."

"Eight hundred!" exploded Jackson. "God damn, Colonel, we need at least three thousand. Haven't Governor Blount and President Madison and the Secretary of War been reading my dispatches?"

"I wouldn't know, sir. The governor says to tell you he's doing his best to recruit adequate forces. We're the first of your replacements."

"Did you bring ample stores? Provisions, tools, ordnance, shot and powder?"

"Yes, sir. We have enough for at least a week."

"A week? Damn, isn't anybody up there thinking with half a brain? Colonel, we need a month of reserve supplies. We're on the verge of starvation here."

A new shout came from the sentry at the head of the road. "Men on the north road! A large column!"

"That would be the remainder of your brigade, Colonel," sourly spoke Jackson, chomping down on the same mangled cigar of last night. "Get them settled in. Colonel Carroll will direct you. Meeting of staff officers in two hours. You and your second and third in command will be there, of course?"

"Of course, General."

By the time he gathered his officers, Jackson raged hotter than ever. While the eight hundred men rendered him less vulnerable, they didn't come close to the number he thought he needed to defeat the Creeks. His personal military strategy had always been to assure himself the advantage of overwhelming force before challenging an enemy. But Blount was falling short of recruiting the militia he needed and the Secretary of War continued to ignore his pleas for a Regular Army brigade.

General Jackson decided he had no choice. He had made up his mind.

"Gentlemen," he began the staff meeting, "we've been holed up here for two months, helpless, while the Red Sticks have been gathering forces. While we don't have the troops we had hoped for, I believe we must act now with what we do have." He studied each officer's face and saw that he had their attention. "Our friendly Creeks have learned that the Red Sticks are massing on the upper Tallapoosa, building a new town there, a big one. They supposedly are putting up some kind of fortress. We cannot allow them to centralize their forces; we have to keep them split up."

"You aim to go after them, General?" asked Coffee.

"Damn right. We ain't got the proper numbers, but if more help ain't here in a week, we can't wait any longer. We're close to starvation already and it's only gonna get worse. And the Creeks are only gonna get stronger. So, Colonel Highsmith, you have maybe five days to drill your men and learn about the Creeks' fighting ways from our boys. Then, weather permitting, we march. We have to go after the murdering bastards. Now let me show you what I have in mind."

General Jackson unfolded a large roll of rough paper on which he had drawn a crude map. "This is the territory east of the Coosa. We actually know very little of the lay of the land between the Coosa and the Chattahoochee. What you see here is what we've learned so far. Here we are, here is the Tallapoosa. We know about Hillabi Creek; it is along here. General Cocke's route from Knoxville to get here took him across Hillabi. That's where the damn fool decided he had to rip those savages that was about to give up to us. The rotten incompetent son of a bitch! Anyway, we will march along his road to about here," Jackson stabbed a finger at the map, "and then cut east until we are about ten miles due north of where the Red Sticks are. There's a little creek we should be able to follow down to the Tallapoosa that'll bring us right on top of 'em. If they don't do a better job of scouting than they've done till now, we may even jump 'em by surprise."

Each officer scrutinized the map, asked questions, offered suggestions. After another hour, they were unanimous in approving General Jackson's scheme.

"Gentlemen, we have a few days to refine the plan and to prepare the men." Jackson scowled. "And if more reinforcements haven't arrived, then by god, we'll whip the Red Sticks' rotten asses by ourselves."

20

The Murph settlement, January, 1814

The week-old Murph baby still had no name.

"Cousin Josephus back in Virginia," Cal philosophied, "went six months before they named him."

"Hell, Cal," retorted Saul, "this baby will go nameless her whole life if we can't come up with something better than Josephus."

Adelin thought it wonderful that the baby was a girl. "The women here now outnumber the men," she gloated. "What do you fellows think of that?"

No work whatsoever beyond essential chores had been done around the compound since the coming of the baby. Nothing, anyway, except caring for the infant and Soosquana. She was on her feet the day after the birth, and had now returned to full household duties plus the joyous, consuming task of new motherhood. The others would not leave her alone for long. When they weren't ogling the baby they were volunteering to do something for her.

Saul had almost lost his fear of handling his daughter. He still lifted her and held her with overbearing care, but Adelin and Soosquana, amused at his caution, congratulated him on his progress.

"You're getting better at this, Saul," encouraged Adelin. "You are going to be a great father."

Adelin even coaxed Cal into holding the baby. As Adelin settled her into his lap, Cal sensed that he dare not move an eyelash, lest he risk grave harm. After less than a minute with the baby in his lap, sweat lined his forehead.

"Some brave backwoodsman you are!" chastised Adelin as she retrieved the baby and laid her back in the sturdy cradle that Soosquana had built. "You'll face down angry hostiles or march a hundred miles over virgin lands without even thinking about it, but you are a big coward when it comes to women and babies."

"Ha! I married you, didn't I?"

"It wasn't the easiest thing you've ever done, if you recall. You were almost as scared then as you are of this baby."

"Yeah, I reckon that was worse than wrestling a mad black bear."

"You've never wrestled a bear," Adelin scoffed. She leaned over and looked into her husband's eyes. "What do you think, Cal? Would you like one of these?"

"What!? Whaddya mean? No! Are you daft? Why do you ask? What? You got something to tell?"

Adelin couldn't control her laughter. Soosquana, who had been listening across the room, laughed with her. Adelin could only shake her head as she started for the door. "Some day," she managed, with a shakened Cal following her into the yard. "Maybe some day soon."

Debate over the child's name continued. Saul thought she should have a Muskogi name and pressured Soosquana to select one. She disagreed, with perhaps more head than heart. Her main argument sounded unusually wise and thoughtful.

"This child will surely not grow up in Muskogi culture, if the Muskogi Nation still exists for her. She will be part of the white man's world. So she needs a name from the white man's culture."

"But she will always be Muskogi, Soos. We won't ever let her forget that."

"I know. And she will always be proud, as I am proud. But you and yours will be her people. You are my people now also, even as I will forever remain Muskogi. I think she must have an American name."

Neither parent would yield, so the friendly stalemate continued for several more days. Life at the compound gradually returned to near normal. The animals were let out for daily exercise. Mounds of firewood accumulated under assault from a busy ax. Several good catches of large catfish were taken from below the shoals.

Traffic along the river had subsided to near nothing. The few travelers that did come along were Red Stick warriors heading north, but they showed no hostility. No women at all, no children, no families. It seemed that the whole of the Muskogi Nation had gone into hibernation for the winter.

Finally, one evening at supper, almost two weeks after the baby had been born, Soosquana sought to break the name standoff.

"Did you know that Adelin has another name?" she asked Saul and Cal.

Saul looked at her. "What?"

"Yeah," said Cal. "You mean her middle name?"

"Adelin's other name is Anna," Soosquana continued. She addressed Saul. "You want me to give the baby a Muskogi name? Adelin is my Muskogi sister, is she not? So I pick Anna as our baby's Muskogi name."

"Can't argue with reasoning like that, big brother," offered Cal.

"Why, Soos, how nice," said Adelin, thrilled. "I'm flattered, but I'm sure you can . . . ."

"Anna it is," persisted Soosquana. "Anna Murph. You like it, Saul?" She smiled happily at him.

Saul only stared, lost in thought. "Why not?" he finally relented. "Yeah. Anna Murph. I like it, I have to admit. I like it a lot. Does everybody agree?"

All agreed. The remainder of the meal became a celebration of the life and future conquests of baby Anna Murph . . . American . . . Muskogi . . . of the Tallapoosa River country of the Mississippi Territory.

21

Near Enitachopco Creek, January 24, 1814

The ragtag infantry company arrayed itself across the top of the slope leading down to the creek, a quarter mile below. "Captain, you must hold this line!" Colonel Billy Carroll stressed to the officer in charge. "It'll take at least a half hour to get the column across. Keep a sharp eye and don't flinch if hostiles show."

Carroll knew that the supply wagons, cannon carriages, and wounded would require substantial time and work to ford the stream. The infantry unit, as a rear guard, must protect the operation. What remained of one cavalry company had been sent ahead to scout the far slope and secure positions atop it. Besides the advance group, the rest of the cavalry, most on foot, scattered through the column to assist with the wounded and in moving along the cannons and supply wagons.

"Step lively there! Get that wagon across the creek!" yelled General Jackson, not bothering to disguise his impatience and annoyance. He sat on his horse on the opposite bank of Enitachopco Creek, the main tributary of Hillabi Creek, and watched his undermanned, inexperienced, and dispirited army stagger through the narrow ford and up the slope.

The improvised role of cavalry personnel was made necessary by the depletion of horses. Twenty-three seriously wounded soldiers rode on litters fashioned partially from the hides of horses killed in the fighting of two days before, and dragged by other horses commandeered from cavalrymen.

Jackson's plan to attack the Red Sticks at their new stronghold on the upper Tallapoosa had gone as he had hoped until he reached Emuckfau Creek. He had marched his army down the Coosa, turned east through Hillabi country and crossed at this same ford of the Enitachopco on the morning of the twenty-first. Though it was known that at least one Hillabi village lay nearby, the army had encountered no sign of the enemy. Jackson was sure the Creeks knew he maneuvered in the vicinity, but hoped they would not guess his intention.

Reaching the Emuckfau late in the day, Jackson elected to camp for the night and make his final push down the creek to the Tallapoosa on the morning of the twenty-second, hopefully to break the back of the Red Sticks' power.

Jackson reckoned that he could be no more than ten miles from the river. He set out following the course of the creek at daybreak, hoping to finish a victorious campaign by midafternoon.

Less than a mile along, musket balls and arrows suddenly rained from the slopes above both sides of the stream. Soldiers and horses fell before a punishing onslaught. Men dived for cover in the creek bed and behind trees and logs, and began a steady barrage of musket fire in return. After a short time, the Americans' superior firepower and marksmanship had neutralized the battle, but they remained pinned down for most of the day. Finally, near dusk, with the Red Stick attack considerably lessened, General Jackson and General Coffee rallied their forces from the creek bed and charged to the crests of both slopes. The Red Sticks fled, but they had accomplished their mission. Jackson's foray had surely been thwarted and his entire campaign seriously weakened. However, many lives had been lost on both sides of the bloody battle.

General Jackson used the cover of darkness to collect his wounded and his able-bodied forces and to reorganize them. Sapling frames covered with the hides of dead horses made up litters hitched behind cavalrymen's mounts to transport the seriously injured. Fearing another attack if they stayed until morning, the general decided to retreat before dawn. He camped at midday on a defensible ridge halfway between Emuckfau and Enitachopco Creeks to treat wounds and rest the troops and horses. There he remained until setting out again for Fort Strother on the morning of the twenty fourth.

General Jackson and his chief scout, a Tennessee backwoods hunter named David Crockett, were positive the Red Sticks had stalked them all the way from the Emuckfau. They feared an attack could come at any time. Looking ahead, they anticipated that the Enitachopco ford offered as likely a site for an ambush as any point on their route. Even beyond there, they would not feel safe until they reached the Coosa.

"Lieutenant Armstrong!" barked Jackson as he monitored the crossing of the Enitachopco from astride his mount. His mood was ill and angry. "What is the trouble with that limber? I suggest that you get it moving! Understand, Lieutenant?"

Cannoneers struggled with the massive six-pounder in the mud and sand of the creek bottom, trying to wrestle it across. As if the Creeks were in close communication with the fears of the Americans, at that moment shots sounded from the eastern ridge.

Red Sticks charged in an all-out frontal attack on the rear guard militiamen. The soldiers, from kneeling and prone stances, fired a withering volley, dropping a score or more of the attackers. They frantically sought to reload, but realizing their barrage had not stopped the Indians' charge, they backed down the hill, trying to maintain a skirmish line. Then, before the Indians' muskets, arrows, and threatening red war clubs, most turned and ran. Three hundred painted warriors, screaming threats and curses at a shrill staccato, poured over the lip of the ridge and down the slope in pursuit.

Indians also attacked from upstream and downstream of the creek, leaving the troops at the bottom of the hill and on the other side of the creek powerless to aid the rear guard. Jackson's militia suddenly found themselves surrounded on three sides by a fierce, angry foe.

"Look sharp, men!" yelled Colonel Carroll. "Hold your positions! Load and fire on rhythm! Make certain of your target!" Most of his instructions were lost beneath the clatter of gunfire, boisterous threats of onrushing Red Sticks, and the curses and panicked screams of the militiamen spilling down the hill.

A soldier fell wounded at Colonel Carroll's feet, an arrow in his side. Carroll and another soldier fired simultaneously at a Red Stick that had broken ahead of his band and ran full speed at them, swinging his war club. The man died before he landed, his bowels spilling across the ground as he skidded on the muddy creek bank. Colonel Carroll turned his attention up the slope, seeking to reorganize the retreating rear guard.

The other soldier rapidly reloaded. As he tamped down the musket ball with his ramrod, a loud, shrill yell startled him. He glanced up to sense, more than see, an Indian launch himself straight at him in a dive from five yards away. Instinctively, he pivoted and cocked the musket and pulled the trigger at the same time. Smoke, flame, the flying body, and the warrior's war club engulfed him all at once. The soldier tumbled backward into the water, the enemy body welded to his. He struggled to throw the dead man from him. The ramrod protruded equally from the center of the man's chest and from his back. The soldier scrambled to find his musket and to extract himself from the creek, ignoring the deep, nasty gash that gushed blood from the left side of his head.

Lieutenant Armstrong, the cannoneer commander, still struggled with the six-pounder crew to free the piece from the creek. The limber, the two-wheeled cart by which a two-horse team pulled the cannon carriage, was hopelessly mired in the mud. Colonel Carroll saw their plight and, realizing the importance of the cannon, rallied a company of his infantry to a point up the slope between the creek and the advancing Red Sticks. He directed a systematic pattern of fire, reload, fire, reload, desperately seeking to give the cannoneers a chance to get their weapon into action.

The soldiers unhitched the carriage from the limber and ran a rope from its tongue to the saddle of a cavalryman's horse. Armstrong and a half dozen of his crewmen pushed and pulled and struggled until the cleated carriage wheels rolled from the water and up the western slope to a level outcrop thirty yards above the creek. Other cannoneers had seized the position and with their muskets fired over the heads of Carroll's line of infantry as they grudgingly gave ground back across the creek.

Privates Constantine Perkins and Craven Jackson leveled the cannon at the ford where most of the Red Sticks would storm across, and made ready to load. To their horror, they discovered that the tools for loading and priming the cannon had been left on the marooned limber and that there was no chance to retrieve them.

"Damn, what do we do?" anguished Private Jackson.

Perkins had an idea. "Pass me a cartridge. We'll make it work." He unfixed his bayonet and returned it to its scabbard. He stuffed a cartridge of powder wrapped in flannel into the cannon barrel, followed it with a cluster of grapeshot, and turning over his musket, rammed the charge to the back of the breech with the muzzle end of the weapon.

Craven Jackson followed his cue. With his musket ramrod, he punctured the flannel through the touch hole of the cannon. Then, tearing open a paper powder cartridge, he spilled grains into the touch hole. Someone handed forward a smoldering match cord to ignite the powder.

The roar of the six-pounder and its shower of grapeshot caught a crush of sprinting Red Sticks at midstream. Dead and wounded bodies littered the creek, its water turning red. The cannoneers cheered, already ramming another grapeshot cartridge down the mouth of the big gun.

"Defend the cannon, boys!" roared Carroll. He formed his infantrymen in lines under and abreast of the cannon position and continued the musket barrage at the still coming Red Sticks.

The cannon fired again. Another cluster of bodies splashed into the creek or fell across those that had perished moments before. Then again.

"Reload!" cried Lieutenant Armstrong after each blast. "Keep firing! Keep that ammunition coming!" He had himself joined the line of cannoneers that passed powder cartridges and grapeshot to the gun crew.

The Indians still attacked. The cannon crew with their makeshift loading regimen and protective infantrymen held their ground.

"Damnit!" declared the scout Crockett, loading and firing his musket with skilled precision. "There's Indians behind every tree. They just keep coming!"

The Americans gained control of the western bank, thanks to the cannoneers. The Indians could advance no farther than the creek and finally withdrew to positions halfway up the eastern slope.

General Jackson took advantage of the lull. "Colonel Carroll, advance to the opposite creek bank and establish a defense line," he ordered. "Then assign details to retrieve the wounded. Lieutenant

Armstrong, send a detachment down to the creek and rescue that limber."

The column eventually assembled and reorganized at the crest of the ridge above the west bank of the Enitachopco. More than twenty soldiers had been killed at Emuckfau and Enitachopco combined and close to a hundred wounded. The limp back to Fort Strother over more than fifty torturous miles lay ahead.

Though General Jackson expected to be harassed all the way back to Fort Strother, the remainder of the retreat passed without further incident. The general swore vengeance while he tended his wounds and awaited the badly needed reinforcements still being promised.

Jackson's venture with an undermanned force had failed. He had tragically proven that a garrison of only nine hundred volunteer soldiers and two hundred Cherokee allies were sadly inadequate to defeat an Indian nation fighting for their homeland. He needed more militia, lots more, especially trained infantry units. He would need help to free the Alabama country and the Mississippi Territory from the savage Red Sticks and make the land safe for American farmers and hunters. General Jackson anxiously awaited militia reinforcements and the regiment of regulars promised him by Governor Blount.

22

THE MURPH SETTLEMENT, LATE JANUARY, 1814

The weather turned cold, very cold. The Murphs had discovered that most of an Alabama winter was relatively mild, but several periods of a few days to two weeks each could be quite bitter. Late January and early February was the usual time for the worst. Following the normal pattern, the current cold front had come on suddenly and dropped daytime temperatures to near freezing and to hard freezes overnight.

The cold weather provided the right opportunity to go after prize bucks for hides and meat. The Murphs needed them for barter at the trading post next summer. Traders would take every hide, as there was a rich market for fine deerskin back east. There was something special, it seemed, about the unspoiled skins from the virgin Alabama wilderness. The traders would also take a certain amount of smoked venison, so the excess meat above the Murphs' needs would not go to waste.

"Cal and I will go again," Adelin volunteered before Cal had a chance to respond to Saul's suggestion.

"I believe I have been commandeered," Cal conceded.

"Don't go too far," Saul cautioned. "Things seem to have settled down a little now — let's hope for good — but we need to be careful. There are still too many mad Red Sticks about and too many blood-crazed soldiers."

Cal and Adelin hitched George to the empty cart and led him up the road. Their new rabbit-fur parkas warmed them against the icy morning. Less than three miles out they turned down into a hollow where Cal was certain a small herd of superior specimens roamed.

Sure enough, they had three giant bucks by midday. Carrying them back to the cart proved the toughest job of the hunt. The front feet of each carcass had to be lashed together; likewise the back feet. A strong staff was passed through the tethers and shouldered by the hunters, one in front and one at the rear. Cal and Adelin struggled under the weight of each kill. The bucks, they speculated, must certainly be among the heaviest in all of the Mississippi Territory.

Cal and Adelin agreed that two more would be enough, maybe only one. It would take several days to dress the meat and cure the skins they already had. Besides, they sympathized, that's about all that poor old George could be expected to haul in such frigid weather.

"Be patient, George," consoled Adelin, petting the mule, "we'll be going home soon." George contentedly grazed near the cart, having been staked out when they arrived in the hollow.

Cal and Adelin resumed the hunt, tracking their prey in a small branch bottom, careful to stay downwind from the buck's suspected location. They had caught a glimpse of him once from about two hundred yards distance.

"There," whispered Cal, pointing to an outcrop fifty yards ahead. Adelin nodded. "He's gotta be around that knob."

They approached the granite outcrop. Adelin crept over the top while Cal eased around the low side. No deer.

"Where did he go?" pondered Cal, disappointed. "I just know he was here."

"Must have gotten wind of us somehow. Let's keep after him." Adelin jumped from the rock and fell in beside Cal as they continued along the burn.

They stopped dead still. Thirty yards ahead, from around the next outcrop, strolled four painted Red Sticks. The Creeks saw Cal and Adelin at the same time. They, too, stopped and stared, indecisive.

"Don't move," cautioned Cal.

"Now we know what spooked the buck, don't we?" said Adelin.

The Red Sticks each carried a bright red war club. Only one held a musket, the others bows. Their appearance was that of angry warriors, definitely not of congenial neighbors.

Cal tried anyway. He raised an arm with an open palm. "Peace." A pause. "Friends?"

Threats and curses in angry Muskogean met his overture. The Indians brandished their clubs as they spread out in a line.

"Back away. Slowly," said Cal, pushing Adelin behind him. "Don't take your eyes off them."

They inched toward the rock they had just left. The Creeks held their ground. The one with the musket fidgeted with it.

"Are we going to have to fight them?" asked Adelin.

"I don't know. That old short barreled musket he's got won't hit anything past his arm. It looks like it might not even fire. The ones with the bows are probably more dangerous."

They reached the rock and ducked behind it. They showed their muskets, pulled the flintlocks to full cock, and positioned the steel strikes. The Red Sticks had not advanced but had widened their separation.

An arrow grazed the top of the rock, skipped high, and pierced the ground ten yards behind them.

"Hey!" shrieked Adelin. "That was close!"

"Don't shoot," said Cal. "Hold steady. They may just be bluffing." Noting the Creeks' indecision, he had an idea. "Let me try something. You keep your musket primed."

Cal aimed and fired. The pan of his musket flashed, the muzzle thundered flame and smoke. A musket ball crashed into the pine tree behind the Indian with the musket, who seemed to be the leader. He ducked away, glanced at the tree, saw that the gash was only inches above his head. He yelled and shook the gun in one hand and his club in the other at Cal.

The Red Stick barked something to his companions, then turned again to Cal with more curses. The other warriors backed off. He followed, still threatening, still jeering, angrier than ever. They disappeared around the far outcrop.

Cal finished reloading. He breathed relief. "Glad that worked. If we had to shoot any of them, they would be all over us back at the river. If we made it back to the river, that is." He visibly sweated from the ordeal, even in the cold. "Let's get back to George and hurry home. I think we have enough venison for now."

Adelin already scurried ahead of him. "I certainly have to agree with that. I've had enough deer hunting for one day. And enough Indian fighting for a lifetime."

23

KNOXVILLE, TENNESSEE, JANUARY 29, 1814

Judge Hugh Lawson White had been back in Knoxville less than a week and, he felt certain, the town made fine sport about his misadventure. He thought it not so humorous, and neither would his fellow citizens if they only knew the danger to his father, General James White.

Three weeks earlier, Judge White, the Chief Justice of the Tennessee Supreme Court, received news of his sixty-six-year-old father's exploits in Alabama country fighting the vicious Creek Indians. Word was that he had fought bitter battles with a faction of the savages and, though he had been victorious, his regiment had suffered numerous casualties. Further, he and his superior officer, Major General John Cocke, had joined forces with General Andrew Jackson, the Major General of the Tennessee State Militia, who had been campaigning in Alabama since October. White figured that Jackson, whom he mistrusted, could only lead his father and his troops into more danger and hardship, and that was no place for an elderly man.

James White, the founding father of Knoxville, had served honorably as a captain of militia in the Revolutionary War. Later, he had been a North Carolina legislator where he had voted to ratify the new United States Constitution. He had moved gradually west until he settled at the site of Knoxville, naming the new settlement

White's Fort. White's Fort served as the territorial capital and, after being renamed Knoxville by White himself, was the first capital of the State of Tennessee, remaining so until 1812. White had been elected to the senate of the new state and had served briefly as the speaker. He had been appointed major in the state militia, then lieutenant colonel, and finally brigadier general, a commission he had held for a decade and a half. When the Creek troubles began in the Mississippi Territory, General White felt young again and itched to go to war. He set about growing his militia command to a thousand men.

"What the hell do you think you can do, Father?" scolded Justice Hugh Lawson White, his oldest son. "You're sixty-six. You have no business commanding a regiment of active militia. And you damn sure shouldn't go off fighting godless, barbaric Indians in an infested wilderness."

"Son, I'm fitter than I've ever been. My men need me, and I hear the call. I can't let my country down."

"Horse hooves! You've served your country over and over, more than mortal man can be expected to. General Cocke should be flogged for asking you to raise a regiment and join him in his reckless venture."

Judge White could not dissuade the stubborn old man and so, in early November after raising an army, Major General John Cocke marched south with Brigadier James White in command of one of his infantry regiments. Young General Cocke relished the glory he expected to receive but complained bitterly that General Jackson had beaten him to the field. After the Fort Mims massacre had beckoned to patriots of the State of Tennessee, Cocke had thought that none other than Cocke himself should lead the charge to Alabama country.

Judge White had no doubts that Cocke purposefully targeted his father to join his campaign because of the political muscle the old man could wield. As an ally and a confidant of both Blounts, Willie and his late brother William, and John Sevier, James White had laid in reserve hefty stores of influence. General Cocke knew this and would not hesitate to draw on it to enhance his own military exploits or to promote himself in an expected rivalry with General Jackson.

Alarmed at the news from Alabama, Judge Hugh Lawson White knew he had to get his father out. Nothing had worked to keep the old man from going but, by god, the younger White would go after him and drag him back by force if necessary!

White and two of his aides set off on horseback, thinking they could reach the middle stretches of the Coosa River where his father supposedly camped with General Jackson and General Cocke. They followed the Tennessee River to the southwest until they were sure they had entered the Mississippi Territory, then struck due south across a wide table top mountain, thinking to intersect the upper Coosa and follow it into the wilderness. They soon found themselves lost. With no roads and having no guide familiar with the region, and inadequately equipped and provisioned, Judge White admitted the folly of his scheme and turned back toward Knoxville.

His homecoming was less than glorious. No one chided him to his face, but he knew there was talk. He would have talked, too, he supposed, for someone in his position should have acted more rationally. However, his reputation would survive; and he wasn't finished attempting to retrieve his father from the jaws of the murdering Creeks in the Alabama wilderness.

Hugh Lawson White enjoyed considerable political leverage himself, independent of his father's influence, and now was the time to use it. He knew that General Jackson had been clamoring for

President Madison and Secretary of War Armstrong to assign him regular troops to use against the Creeks. By a happenstance, the Thirty-Ninth Infantry, commanded by White's brother-in-law, Colonel John Williams, was quartered near Knoxville awaiting orders for New Orleans. Justice White had already sent dispatches to Armstrong and Congressman Sevier requesting that the Thirty-Ninth be temporarily placed under his jurisdiction. He lobbied Governor Blount to increase his own efforts for the services of the Thirty-Ninth. Peppered through his arguments to all were more than subtle hints and promises of future political favors.

Soon, authorization to temporarily assign the Thirty-Ninth as he saw fit reached Justice White. His next step was to convince Colonel Williams, for without his accord the campaign could not succeed.

"Hugh, I welcome the challenge," agreed Williams as he and Judge White strolled the grounds of the new administration and lecture building of Blount College. James White had donated the land for the school and was a member of the original Board of Trustees that chartered it in 1794. "You knew I would."

"Yes. But I had to present to you a formal request."

"You need have no qualms about the motivations of my men. I feel certain that they would rather journey to Alabama country and fight the Creeks than to engage the British at New Orleans. They shall perform with distinction, have no doubts."

"I know your regiment is among the finest trained in the entire army. And I know you to be a superb commander. I have every confidence in your prospects of success." The two paused to appreciate the vista of the Tennessee River that lay before them. "Incidentally, congratulations. Best of fortune on your birthday. Melinda reminded me that today is your thirty-sixth."

Melinda was Hugh White's sister, married to Colonel Williams. "Yes, she does talk, doesn't she? But thank you for your sentiments."

"When I talked with her yesterday, she was as worried as I about Father. But she didn't particularly embrace the idea of you going to his rescue."

"She accepts that I am a soldier. It's been a year since I returned from Florida. With my new commission, she knew I would be assigned a campaign soon, probably New Orleans. I think that in spite of her protests she would prefer that I pursue her father in Alabama than to embark on an impersonal adventure to Louisiana."

Williams had begun his military career as a U.S. Army infantry captain at age twenty-one, but after two years of service had resigned and become a lawyer in Knoxville. When the new war with England broke out he raised a cavalry force of two hundred volunteers and led them to Florida as their colonel. His troop devastated the Seminole opposition and they returned as glorious victors. Soon after, Williams accepted a commission as colonel in command of the Thirty-Ninth United States Army Infantry Regiment. He had recruited, equipped, and trained his regiment to an elite force of six hundred crack soldiers eager to prove themselves.

"I'm humbled by your confidence in me and my men." Williams, a modest man, savored White's praise but felt compelled to share it. "For sure, I have under my command a collection of some of the finest young officers in the U.S. military. I'm very proud of them. In Alabama, New Orleans, wherever, they are destined to cover themselves with glory. They and a fine enlisted cadre make it easy for me to be a successful officer."

"Little argument that General Jackson will welcome you; by the way, I alerted Governor Blount to send a dispatch to him two weeks ago that he might soon expect your services."

"Confident of your persuasive ability, weren't you, brother-in-law?" chuckled the colonel.

"Just confident of the politics involved, that's all," White smiled slyly. "A man helps his cause if he knows which chain to pull and when to pull it. When will you leave?"

"Two days, I think. It'll take about a week of forced march to reach Jackson's encampment. If your father is still there, my first act will be to request that his superiors order him home."

24

Muskets in one hand and fishing spears and rawhide nets in the other, Cal and Adelin picked their way down the trail of loose stones and ruts. Below, Saul already fished from the rocks in the middle of the river. Soosquana sat in a chair at the edge of the bluff near the oak tree, nursing baby Anna.

"I saw a mouse this morning, Cal. Next to the fireplace."

"Did you kill it?"

"Couldn't catch it. He got away through that big crack behind the bottom stone."

"I have to patch that."

"Yes, you do. And I think we need a cat."

"What?"

Adelin laughed at Cal's surprised reaction. "A cat. A mouse catcher. You've heard of cats, haven't you?"

"And where are we gonna get a cat?"

"We can get one from the farm when we journey up there this summer. A kitten. Maybe two. Anna's gonna need a pet soon, anyway."

"How about a puppy while we're at it?"

"Yeah. Why not? The more the better."

"You're hard to live with," he scolded as Adelin giggled.

"'Bout time y'all got here," greeted Saul as the couple stepped lightly across the slippery rocks after leaving their muskets and pouches propped against a big boulder on the river bank. "I already have two. See?" He held up a string with two nice catfish attached.

After a half hour, three strings held several fish each. A spirited competition developed, but Saul's skill kept him well ahead. He grinned happily at each success as his two rivals screamed at him.

"Saul!" Soosquana, from atop the bluff, did not make herself heard at first. "Saul!" she yelled louder.

She pointed upriver. Saul stooped to clear an overhanging limb from his line of sight. Cal and Adelin also sought unobstructed views. They saw a blob heading toward them, surely a canoe though not quite yet discernible.

As the canoe came into focus, another cleared the bend behind it, then another. The two latter ones seemed to be chasing the first. As the first one closed to within a hundred and fifty yards, a puff of smoke erupted from the second canoe. The clap of a musket rolled down the river.

"Hey!" yelped a surprised Cal. "What's going on?"

"We better move aside," understated Saul. All three were already scurrying toward the bank and their muskets.

Since they would not have time to make it all the way up the trail, Saul, Adelin, and Cal hid in the brush a few yards up the bluff. Saul looked anxiously for Soosquana. He didn't see her, but he knew he wouldn't. He was sure she had taken the baby to the safety of their cabin. He looked back to the drama before him.

The lead canoe was close enough to see that its occupants included a strapping warrior, probably a Hillabi, in the stern. A young boy, barely a teenager, frantically paddled from the bow. Between them a woman crouched as low as possible, protecting with her body what apparently was a small child. The trailing boats each carried two warriors, paddling hard and screaming and cursing. They wore the red paint of Red Sticks and they gained fast on their quarry as the shoals loomed ahead.

The warrior with the family aimed his canoe's bow toward the deepest opening between rocks, one of many where the flow of the river converged to narrow slots and thus accelerated to cascade wildly through the maze of boulders and eddies of the shoals. He skillfully hit the opening dead center, with scant inches of clearance on either side. He rode the current dizzily, controlling his bow as best he could with his paddle as a rudder, until he again hit flat water forty yards along the trace. The current remained swift but he now had full control.

The first pursuer spilled through the same gap and skidded toward the fleeing boat. As the two occupants fought for control, the warrior powering the pursued canoe suddenly back paddled, furiously turning his craft sideways to slow it in the fast current. The chasing canoe caught up quickly and was about to slide past just as the two warriors regained steerage and began to react to the surprising maneuver.

Too late! The first warrior twisted his body and raised his paddle in both hands as he would wield an ax and swung it full into the face of the other vessel's bowman as it raced alongside. The splat of the paddle against his mouth interrupted the man's scream. The blow knocked him sideways. He grabbed the gunwale of the canoe in a desperate effort to stay aboard. Unsuccessful, he tumbled into the water, turning the boat over behind him as he continued to hang on. His partner leaped clear with an angry curse.

While the first canoe turned straight to race away downriver, the third one slid through the shoals out of control. Its sternman saw the overturned shell but was powerless to avoid it. It hit broadside and rode up over the upside down hull. The two startled warriors tried to balance their boat with its suddenly dry bow now pointing skyward and its stern deep in the water. As they struggled, water poured in until finally they had no choice but to jump overboard lest their canoe should fill completely and sink or overturn.

The four swimming Red Sticks fought to untangle their crafts and pull them to shallow water near the eastern bank, opposite the Murphs. They stood in waist deep water and looked downriver just in time to see their quarry escape around the far bend. They angrily shook their fists and cursed loudly at the fleeing family.

Saul, Cal, and Adelin fought to repress their amusement. They didn't dare reveal themselves. The embarrassed warriors would surely welcome a spat with a substitute foe and the Murphs did not wish to volunteer. But, oh, how hard it was to muffle their mirth! For now they managed somehow, though they would laugh about the incident for days.

It took the four vanquished warriors more than half an hour to wrestle their two canoes to the bank, empty them, and portage them upriver around the shoals. Considerable time and effort had to be spent retrieving the two paddles that had floated a good way downriver before lodging one against a rock and the other on a sandbar.

As the images of the two canoes grew small near the upriver bend, the secluded Murphs could finally stand up and laugh aloud.

"Have you ever seen a band of more flustered fellows?" mused Cal.

"If that was an example of the Creeks' fights with each other, then I dare say both sides are safe," ventured Saul.

"It's sad that they all don't turn out as well, isn't it?" said Adelin.

The three enjoyed another chuckle at the comedy they had witnessed, then turned to their own business.

"Come," suggested Saul, a little concerned. "Let's check on Soos and the baby. We have enough fish for a king's banquet. We should leave some for another day."

The three gathered their weapons and gear and impressive catch and climbed the trail.

Adelin held her string of fish against the larger one of Saul. "We'll get you next time, Saul. You can't always win."

"I would've beat him today if our clumsy friends hadn't scared off all my fish by crashing their canoes together," claimed Cal.

They laughed again as they happily reached the top of their bluff above the river.

25

FORT STROTHER, FEBRUARY 6, 1814

"No, Colonel, he isn't here. General White left with General Cocke's militia a month ago." Andrew Jackson scowled. "Good riddance to the lot of 'em, too, except that their departure left us woefully short of men. Why do you ask?"

"Well, sir," explained Colonel John Williams, "I promised his family that I would inquire of him as soon as I arrived here and try to expedite his return home. He is a little aged, I believe you'll agree, for this duty. The family is worried about him, especially Judge White and my wife. I must confess, General, that General White is my father-in-law."

"I see. I mean no disrespect, but you are right. His age should have disqualified him for this campaign. And, too, why he would ever want to serve with that pompous fool, Cocke, is a mystery."

"Yes, sir."

"Judge White, you say? I take it that Judge Hugh White is your brother-in-law? General White's son?"

"Yes, sir."

"I hadn't made the connection before. According to the letter you brought with you, Judge White is responsible for your regiment being here."

"I believe he is, sir."

"Then I shall forever be in his debt. And in yours, Colonel.

156

Quality fighting soldiers have been at a premium around here and our junior officers have been mostly untrained volunteers on short terms of service themselves. Your regular army fellows will do us proud, I'm certain."

"We hope to justify your confidence, General."

"Now let's have a look at your regiment."

General Jackson and Colonel Williams strode across the stockade yard and out the front gate. The Thirty-Ninth had begun to establish camp at the far end of the clearing. Soldiers busied themselves around campfires and newly pitched tents as they attempted to purge the mud and dust and fatigue of a week-long accelerated march.

Colonel Williams and his regiment of more than six hundred army regulars had arrived shortly after noon. While Colonel Billy Carroll had guided the company commanders to appropriate camp-sites, General Jackson had conducted Colonel Williams on a tour of the fort and briefed him on the status of the Fort Strother garrison.

Now, hours after the Thirty-Ninth's arrival, Jackson and Williams walked slowly across the clearing, surveying the newly arrived regulars before them and the militia infantry and cavalry quartered to either side.

"Regrettably, Colonel, our force had fallen to less than eight hundred total men, and before the last contingent of militia arrived, to less than fifty at one point. Very few are real soldiers and, like most others we have had with us, many will soon leave for home when their enlistments expire. Yours is a most welcome arrival, to be sure, but I'm afraid we still need additional reinforcements to defeat the Creeks. Did you receive any word from Governor Blount, or perhaps from Judge White, regarding fresh militia?"

"Not directly, sir. But Judge White insists that the Governor is continuing to recruit new units as a high priority. I would think, sir, with confidence, that you should soon have adequate troops."

"And adequate supplies, I should hope. We aren't far from starvation here. It hasn't been a kind winter and we were ill prepared for its privations. I would appreciate an inventory of the stores you brought, Colonel."

"I'm afraid they are sufficient for only a short time. They didn't spare us a surplus, but did promise to ship down additional stores as they could muster them."

"Ordnance? I notice that you towed no cannon."

"No, sir. We have two full wagons of shot, powder, and new muskets. Also, having been told that you have a six- and a three-pounder, we loaded on cartridges, round shot, and grape shot. I hope we were not misled."

They had reached the end of the clearing and stood watching the soldiers. Many were as young as the average militia recruit, barely out of their teens if that. Most had doffed the tall shakos with the loose fitting chin straps, and other items of uniform. The few that were still fully dressed wore coarse cotton pants of a light color, calf-length boots, and blue waist jackets. Over each jacket were draped crossed belts suspended at the shoulders and fastened together in the middle of the chest with a large brass buckle. Suspended from one of the belts, hanging at the soldier's right side, was his kit containing shot, paper powder cartridges, loose powder, spare flints, and tools for repair and cleaning. On the soldier's left hip, fastened to the other belt, was a leather scabbard containing a foot-long bayonet with a triangular blade tapered to a point, a formidable weapon in close combat.

Muskets were stacked in front of the tents, three and four clipped together at the middle band of the upraised barrels, stock butts to the ground. Tents were aligned as the lay of the land permitted, and those of squads and companies grouped together. Jackson's ill-

LARRY WILLIAMSON / 159

trained militiamen stood watching from a respectful distance, grudgingly admiring the efficiency and discipline of the regulars.

"Begging the Colonel's pardon, sir." A tall, sturdy officer, fully dressed, snapped to attention at Colonel Williams' side. He saluted smartly. "General."

"At ease, Major." Williams returned the salute.

"Sir, I'm pleased to report the regiment has established camp. Our state of readiness remains immediate. Your orders, sir?"

Instead of answering, Williams turned to Jackson. "General, permit me the pleasure of introducing a fine soldier. This is Major Lemuel Montgomery. Major, General Andrew Jackson."

Montgomery clicked his heels and saluted. "My pleasure and honor, General Jackson. At your service, sir."

"Major," Jackson acknowledged.

"Major," instructed Williams, "I trust your discretion to see to the organization of the encampment, set sentries as you deem appropriate, and issue orders as necessary. Subject to the General's approval, of course." He glanced at Jackson, who nodded favorably.

"Yes, sir." Montgomery snapped another salute, about faced, and strode away.

"General," said Colonel Williams with an obvious tone of pride, "you have just met my best soldier. I would dare say further that Major Montgomery is probably the finest infantry soldier I have encountered in my years of service."

"He is indeed impressive, Colonel. He seems well-spoken and to have much poise about him."

"I should like for him to serve only as my adjutant, but he is such an extraordinary combat commander that I am compelled to also place him at the head of my most able company. The men look up to him and, I dare say, would storm through the portals of hell should Major Montgomery lead them."

The two continued their tour. General Jackson showed the colonel his militia forces and their equipment and weapons, many of which were aged and in various stages of disrepair.

"General Coffee's cavalry regiment, as depleted as it is, is my best unit. Has been from the outset. However, in the wilderness, where fighting is most often tree to tree, cavalry is limited. One must have expert infantry units to succeed in this country. Cavalry can only support the foot soldier until we can catch the enemy on an open theater. Also, artillery is not as effective as one might suppose. I'm afraid we have knocked down more trees than Creeks with our two meager weapons."

Colonel Williams smiled at that observation. "Is it the enemy's tactics to stand and fight, General, line versus line?"

"Unfortunately, no. The Creek warrior is a moving target, often confused with the bushes. They are a savage lot, though. They will face you down and come at you head-on when cornered. Your bayonet may prove to be your best weapon, Colonel."

"Yes, sir. We are well drilled in close-order tactics. If I may say so, sir, it seems that my regiment may be precisely the kind of soldiers you have needed."

"My point exactly, Colonel, that I have tried to make with our leaders. Damnit, if they could only be here and see the challenge for themselves." They had reached the front gate of the stockade. "Colonel, you had best see to your men and to your own comfort. A hut is available to you within the stockade as your personal quarters and your office."

"Thank you, General, you're very kind."

"Colonel, we shall meet in two hours. I and my staff will brief you fully on our progress to date and our shortcomings. You will receive a full status report and your frank opinions and suggestions will most certainly be solicited. It is urgent that we lay out correct strategies as spring approaches so that we may successfully conclude this abominable campaign in due time."

"Yes, sir."

"And, Colonel, make certain that your Major Montgomery attends with you. And other officers of your choosing, of course."

That evening, General Jackson, General Coffee, and Colonel Carroll related to the officers of the Thirty-Ninth Infantry the stories of Tallashatchi, Talatigi, Hillabi Creek, Emuckfau, and Enitachopco. They detailed the tactics of the Indians and delineated what had worked against them and what had not. Jackson chose to focus on the Emuckfau Creek incident.

"We made tactical mistakes, that's obvious. We moved without adequate forces. We thought we could surprise them. We should have known better; this is their native environment. Our route of march was too long and our withdrawal too exposed. We are determined, gentlemen, not to repeat those errors."

"Your plan, General?" inquired Colonel Williams.

"That fortress of theirs on the upper Tallapoosa seems of paramount importance. We cannot permit the Creeks to concentrate their forces; we have to keep them splintered. Therefore, as soon as further reinforcements and supplies reach us, and weather is favorable, we must make another attempt on that facility. But not as before. I think we must have an outpost, much closer than Fort Strother, from which to operate. General Coffee and I have been discussing the feasibility of moving down the Coosa and setting up such a post. From there we can cut a trail east to the Tallapoosa. It is still a long way to string an army, but I see no better choice as yet. Also, with an outpost on the Coosa, perhaps we can float supplies down by barge more easily than over land. We anticipate that spring rains will swell the river and make that possible."

"Will such maneuvers not tip our hand, General?"

"Certainly. But we have learned that it matters little. Since we possess superior weaponry and, perhaps soon, imposing numbers, it is only important that we arrive on the field with the greater force and the greater resolve. Gentlemen, let us prepare."

26

The council fire shone as a beacon in the clear winter twilight. Scalding rhetoric turned angry men angrier.

Tukabatchi, the capital of all the Muskogis, Upper and Lower, lay on a wide, flat plain in the crook of the Tallapoosa where the river turned west to meet the Coosa. Four miles to the north thundered the great falls of the Tallapoosa, marking the fall line that began the coastal plain running to the Gulf of Mexico.

Annually, and more often when necessary, the chiefs met in council. The Great Council Tree, sacred to the Muskogis, provided the aura by which the chiefs could call upon the Maker of Breath and other Spirits. Somewhere beneath the Great Tree were safely buried the seven sacred brass plates, handed down from the ancients.

Across the river to the east lay Talisi, and on the southern bank Atasi, both important warrior towns dominated by Red Sticks. Until the attack on them by the Georgia militia, however, their leaders had not been willing to oppose the American invaders. Since, militant Red Sticks held the power and virtually all villages on the Tallapoosa were ready to fight the whites. Even the Upper Muskogis of Tukabatchi, who had formerly advocated trust and compromise, were now resigned to bloodshed.

The Lower tribes, mostly from the environs of the Chattahoochee

River, and particularly the important towns of Cusseta and Coweta, favored acceptance of the American culture rather than open opposition to the settlers. They still held out, as they had suffered few violent incidents themselves. Their position only opened the rift wider with the Upper villages, with whom they were already in a state of civil war.

"You will fight on the side of the whites?" angrily accused a Red Stick chief.

"No. But we do not fight against them, either. You know we cannot defeat the whites."

"Then we die!"

"You will die," agreed the Cusseta chief. "If you fight, you die. Why will you not bend to their wishes? We survive, and we keep most of our land.

"The white man cannot be trusted! Look what they did at Atasi! Look what they did at Talisi!"

The large fire crackled. Sap from green pine logs boiled and popped, sending live embers high into the darkness astride heated updrafts. Chiefs from all the Muskogi towns and villages sat on the ground in a wide circle ringing the fire. Hundreds of other Muskogis sat in near concentric circles extending many yards in radius.

Another chief arose. "I am from the Hillabi villages. We had hoped to make truce with the American army, but they betrayed our trust and slaughtered our people. We can do nothing now but fight. Dying before the muzzles of their muskets will be more honorable than dying in the face of their lies."

"Your talk is foolish," said a Coweta chief. "All the Americans want are roads across our hunting grounds and safe passage to float our streams for their trade."

"You, chief of Coweta, are the one who speaks foolish!" yelled a chief from Ipisoga. "Do the Lower tribes forget that the Georgia whites took your land between the Oconee and the Ocmulgee, promising to come no farther? But they kept coming till they crossed the river they call the Flint, and now they threaten the Chattahoochee. Are you too blind to see that words will not stop them?"

"Your war clubs and arrows will not turn aside their cannon and muskets."

"We have muskets!"

"How many muskets? One for every two warriors? One for every three? How good are they? Do you have enough powder and shot?"

"They cannot harm us when we stand on sacred grounds. The shamans tell us so. With the help of the sacred prophets, we shall triumph!"

"Your shamans and your prophets cannot protect you. Wise counsel will. Allow the Americans their road!"

"No! You permitted a road through your lands into our southern reaches. It extended to the white man's ships on the great ocean gulf. What has that brought? Our people were massacred at the Burnt Corn."

"Our road did not cause that attack."

"We must not tempt the white man's greed. I say, no road, no passage!"

Another Red Stick chief stood. "I took up arms against the American army at Emuckfau Creek when they marched on Cholocco Litabixi. Chief Menawa and the prophet Monahi led us then in victory and vengeance and are there now preparing to defend again our sacred heritage. Men of Cusseta and Coweta, I ask you why warriors of your tribes fought alongside the Americans against us? Have you no loyalty to your ancestors?"

"You are my brother," retorted the Coweta chief. "I do not question your loyalties, you do not question mine. I will not fight against the whites, but I will never dishonor my ancestors or betray my people by fighting on the side of the American soldiers. Some of our young men, I am sad to say, have enlisted with the Americans. They are condemned. They are no longer welcome in their own villages."

A very old man arose from his seat at the head of the circle. He was Tustunnuggee Thlucco, or Big Warrior, the head chief of Tukabatchi, loosely the First Chief of the Muskogi Nation, and once the most respected man of the land. He lifted both arms to chest level with palms down, signaling for quiet. Arguments trailed to silence. For nearly a minute, the only sound was the crackling of the fire.

"These council grounds are holy," Big Warrior began. "That is why you argue in truce tonight, though you may revert to bloodshed one against the other tomorrow. You, as your fathers did, have often thought of me as wise and have sought my counsel. I have given to you my best always. I love my Muskogi land and I cherish my Muskogi heritage. I love my people; all of them. Though I am of the Upper tribes, I have equal devotion to those of you from the Chattahoochee.

"I have long advocated peace with the white settlers and have worked hard to achieve accord. I have trusted the American agent Hawkins, trusted him to be the bridge between the Muskogis and the Americans. Many of you, my brothers, held the same counsel, fearing that the alternative would be that our people would perish before their plows if not their guns."

Big Warrior paused. He cast around the circle for some expression of dissent. Dead silence; his people still valued his counsel.

"We have disagreed for years. We have openly and foolishly fought each other since last summer. I have held Tukabatchi open to all as a sanctuary. We have accepted your women and children while you fought each other. We took in all refugees when Talisi and Atasi were overrun. We feared that we, too, might be attacked, yet we made no defense.

"Many of you have urged me for months to declare war on the Americans. Others have advised me to accede to the Americans' demands. I have done neither. As for myself, I still will do neither. I am an old man; I cannot fight and I will not betray my heritage. But we must recognize that we have reached a crisis. Every Muskogi must follow his heart. As for me, I must conclude from recent events that the Americans can no longer be trusted. I urge those of you that still hold them in your confidence to be very careful. They have ignored every treaty and broken each promise. Likewise, I urge those of you that think it honorable to fight the whites also to be very careful. We are at an overwhelming disadvantage. We not only stand to lose our lives, but if we do not win, we lose our nation. If they are the victors, they will show no mercy, I fear."

Big Warrior sat down, his movement betraying his age. The silence slowly gave way to mumbled comments, then muted discussions, and finally back to shouted challenges. Each side contended that the wise old chief supported its respective view.

The debate continued for another two hours until a Red Stick chief, feeling that his militants were in the majority, stood for a declaration.

"Let this council be concluded and all that would hide in their houses among their women be dismissed. Let all that will bravely take up arms to repel the invaders respect the Dance of the Lakes."

At that, a dozen painted warriors leaped to their feet and began the war dance of the Shawnee, learned from Tecumseh and his followers more than two years before. The dancers slowly circled the fire, enacting the hunt and the kill. They voiced the sounds of pursuit and conflict. For fifteen minutes they danced, then suddenly with a frightening whoop, they stopped and sat down. One of their number stood again and revived the ritual, this time with more animation and more voice. His solo dance evolved to a fury as he simulated stalking an enemy and gaining victory over him. As suddenly as the first phase of the dance had ended, so did this one. Then the entire troupe furiously leaped forward and, in a frenzy, urged each man in the audience to join them. For another fifteen or twenty minutes the dance continued. More than a hundred warriors rehearsed their plans to defeat the enemy; they would drive them away under waves of passion, noise, and blood.

On the outer edge of the campfire circle, a lone warrior had sat quietly and listened intently during the entire debate. He watched the last of the Dance of the Lakes, knowing that it meant unrestricted war. He had not danced himself, but knew on which side he must fight.

Pokkataw pulled himself to his feet and walked north through the night, up the Tallapoosa.

27

THE MURPH SETTLEMENT, FEBRUARY, 1814

"Anna, you are so beautiful." Adelin sat in the yard with the baby lying face up on her lap. She cooed and made faces at Anna, trying to provoke a giggle or a squeal. She happily settled for a gurgle and what she was sure was a smile. "You are the prettiest baby in the whole Mississippi Territory."

In spite of cool weather, Soosquana had agreed that a few minutes of fresh air in the noonday sun would be good for Anna. Adelin bundled her up and took her to a spot near the edge of the bluff. With no wind to mind and no one else around, she soon became totally immersed in the joy of entertaining the baby.

Adelin loved playing with Anna and caring for her, and Soosquana appreciated the breaks. Adelin never thought of herself as the motherly type, but she couldn't remember anything quite as joyous as tending this infant. Maybe someday soon it would be her turn.

"Look, Anna, look," Adelin babbled as she shook a leather toy above the baby's face. Anna's large, bright eyes followed the toy in fascinated awe. She gurgled again and Adelin laughed.

Something in Adelin's peripheral vision suddenly seemed different. She looked up and rapidly scanned the compound. There, at the head of the trail leading to the river ford, stood a band of fully armed Red Sticks.

Adelin snatched Anna from her lap, hugged her blanket tightly around her, and ran for the cabin, yelling for Cal and Saul. She laid Anna on the bed, grabbed her musket, and cocked the flint and checked the flash pan. She slowly cracked the door. The Indians had not moved.

Cal and Saul dashed around the corner of the cabin together, muskets at the ready. Cal went to a kneeling position while Saul braced his musket against the corner post of the porch. The Red Sticks did not react, maintaining the same stance. Then the one in front raised a hand, palm forward.

"Hold it," said Saul in recognition, relaxing but still aiming his musket. "It's Pokkataw. But I don't know the others." He lowered his musket and stepped away from the porch. "Stay here, Cal, and cover me. I'll find out if they are friendly or otherwise."

As Saul started toward the group, Pokkataw separated himself from the band and walked forward. The two friends greeted each other.

"Friend." Pokkataw grinned. "Long time."

"Welcome, brother. You scared us for a moment. We weren't expecting you."

"Sorry. Too quiet."

"Who are your friends? We haven't seen them before, have we?"

"From Saugahatchi. No harm. Good friends."

"Then they, too, are welcome." Saul turned and signaled to Cal to relax. "We are happy to see you again after many weeks. Come over to the cabin. The others are anxious to see you."

The two walked together to Cal's and Adelin's front yard. Soosquana came from her cabin and the two Muskogi friends greeted each other warmly.

Adelin stood waiting for the group on her porch, Anna cradled in her arms.

"You must see our baby!" Soosquana offered. "You have not been here since she was born."

Soosquana received the baby from Adelin, turned, and showed her proudly to Pokkataw. He stared and smiled, then raised his eyes to Soosquana.

"She beautiful. Your eyes. Strong baby. Name?"

"She is Anna. That is Adelin's other name. We named Anna for her."

"Pretty name. Fine baby."

"Would you like to hold her?" Soosquana urged.

Soosquana placed the bundle in Pokkataw's arms. He looked at Anna, smiled wider than before, then tenderly hugged her to him. Soosquana beamed.

Adelin elbowed Cal in the ribs. "See, scaredy, all men aren't afraid of babies."

Pokkataw lingered a long time over Anna. His mood slowly turned somber and his eyes moistened.

"Muskogi child," he said softly. "No future. American child. Peace. Much fortune."

He gave Anna back into Soosquana's arms, looking regretful to do so. His four friends all seemed puzzled by his cryptic words. He still stared longingly at the baby.

Adelin yet stood on the porch. "Pokkataw," she said, "ask your friends to come over." She had noticed that they had not moved. It could be seen now that there were four of them, all sturdy young warriors.

Pokkataw walked a few steps toward them and called out in Muskogean. One of the men answered back but none moved. Pokkataw exchanged a few more comments with them.

"They don't trust us," said Soosquana to Saul. "They refuse to come closer."

Pokkataw returned. "They stay. Not trusting."

"It's all right," said Saul. "We understand."

"Tell us, Pokkataw," asked Cal, "where have you been? What has been happening?"

Pokkataw began to relate events of the three months since he had last visited in November after the Hillabi Creek raids. Uncomfortable and still awkward with English, he quickly lapsed into Muskogean with Soosquana as interpreter. She handed the baby back to Adelin. The two Muskogi natives spent long minutes discussing new details from Talisi and Atasi, with little interpretation being shared with the others. He had news of Soosquana's mother and sisters, and told of how the towns were recovering. He told what he knew of the American army, and related the stories of the fights at Emuckfau and Enitachopco Creeks. The Murphs had not previously learned of those incidents. They were stunned as Soosquana's interpretation came through.

"I was at Enitachopco," Pokkataw told Soosquana, and she relayed it in English, "but I wielded no weapons to fight. But now I pick up my arms against the American hostiles. With my brothers." He gestured to the four warriors.

"What will you do?" asked Cal.

Pokkataw stayed with Muskogean, speaking directly to Soosquana. He told of the Council of Chiefs at Tukabatchi two nights before. "We go now to the Hillabi villages to talk with friends and my kinsmen, who will join me and these men of Saugahatchi. We go from there to ally with Chief Menawa at Cholocco Litabixi."

"That may be where my brothers are," offered Soosquana.

"I have been told that is true."

"Cholocco Litabixi?" asked Cal.

"Horse. Flat foot," Pokkataw attempted to answer in English. He tried a better explanation in Muskogean.

"Horse's flat foot," Soosquana relayed. "Or maybe horseshoe. That is a shape in the river a long day's walk north. Chief Menawa is massing Muskogi warriors and building a new village. Perhaps there warriors and Muskogi families can be protected and will live in peace and safety. It is to be a refuge from the soldiers, some say. The army has already been driven from it once. Others wish it to be an alliance to drive unwelcome Americans from our land for good."

"Sounds to me like things have gotten worse," said Saul. "No turning back on a bad situation unless the army decides to leave."

"We can only hope they will," offered Adelin. "They should not be here."

"Looks like the Creeks aren't going to give in, that's certain," observed Cal.

"If you see my brothers, Tolokika and Ettepti-lopa," asked Soosquana, "will you tell them you saw us? Tell them I love them and that my wish is for them to visit to see my baby and me. You will tell them about the baby, won't you?"

Pokkataw smiled and patted her shoulder. "For certain. I will tell them what a beautiful daughter you have and how fortunate they are to be uncles."

"And tell them to be cautious. I know they are determined to fight, as you now seem to be. All of you must take care. Spill no unnecessary blood," pleaded Soosquana sadly and with fear in her voice. "I beg of the Spirits that no enemy will spill yours."

"I leave," Pokkataw announced. "We hurry. Peace." He shook hands with everyone, hugged Soosquana, and touched a gentle finger to Anna's cheek and lingered there with a regretful look on his face.

He then hurried to rejoin his Red Stick compatriots, declining the Murphs' urging for him and his friends to stay longer and to share a meal.

He led his party along the edge of the bluff to the trail down to the shoals. The Murphs walked to the top of the path and watched the five Red Sticks skip across the rocks to the other side of the river and disappear into the woods to the north.

No one said it, but each Murph had the same thought. They feared they might never see their friend Pokkataw again.

28

The edge of the clearing and adjacent woods overflowed with campsites of American soldiers. Two thousand militiamen under the command of Brigadier General Thomas Johnson had arrived at Fort Strother from Nashville. Complementing the two thousand were two thousand more brought by Brigadier General George Doherty from Knoxville two days earlier. With both contingents came sufficient supplies, arms, and rations for a month.

General Jackson was ecstatic. With more than four thousand six hundred soldiers and six hundred Cherokees and friendly Lower Creeks in camp, he felt he could now go after the heart of the Creek Nation.

"Gentlemen," he announced at an evening staff meeting, "spring will soon arrive. We must be ready. We have little time to settle on correct strategies and join together our units. We will push forward with plans to establish an outpost farther south on the Coosa. We have the manpower to send down a construction crew and protect and supply them."

"General, have you determined a site?"

"We have. We've selected a location about fifty miles down, on the west bank. That will place our forces only another fifty miles, by dead reckoning, from the Creeks' fortress on the Tallapoosa. That fortress, gentlemen, remains our objective."

"Why the west bank, sir?"

"Same as for here, General Doherty. The hostiles lie to the east, very few to our west. The river provides a natural defense. Why not place it between us and the enemy? I've also selected a name for the outpost. It will be Fort Williams. Colonel Williams and his regiment have been on the field for just a few weeks; they've made a difference. The Thirty-Ninth will be at the point of our offensive to the Tallapoosa. It's fitting that we honor Colonel Williams this way."

At the far edge of the clearing one soldier, no more than twenty years old, sat alone on a stump, balancing a small writing board on his lap. The stubby quill between his fingers moved with a scratchy sound across the coarse paper pinned to his board.

Dearest Elsa— I cannot help myself but to address you once again. You never leave my thoughts. I know that you forever share my love. I rue the day and the hour that I took leave of your sweet arms. But I felt then as I do now that I must answer the call of our country and our state. General Johnson has brought us to the service of General Jackson. They promise a timely end to this campaign, an adventure that I know we shall be most proud of. But such a promise pales to the promise of returning to you and our life together. Once again I beg your forgiveness for leaving you only a month after our wedding . . . .

"Writing another letter, Virgil Tom?" asked another young militiaman as he strolled up. "That little wife of yours must be awful special. You're always writing to her."

"I do miss her, Ethan. Very much." Private Virgil Tom Ottis instinctively patted the packet of papers in the oilskin wrapper under his jacket. "I wish I had some way to post my letters. The couriers will only carry official dispatches from officers."

"Never you mind. We'll be through with this business and away from here soon and back in Nashville. Your lucky lady will be purring in your ear again."

Virgil Tom smiled at Ethan's sentiment. He lost himself in a momentary daydream as Ethan walked on, then dipped the quill in his small vial of ink made from blueberry juice and spirits. He resumed writing.

> . . . My friend Ethan also thinks we shall quickly finish this war. My love, I pray so daily. This wilderness is a beautiful place but a terrible one without you at my side. I miss you every minute. Be well, dearest, and keep me always in your thoughts. Dream of me each night as I do of you. Your loving husband, Virgil Tom.

The next morning Private Virgil Tom Ottis remained behind as a detachment of several hundred militiamen set off south. They carried tools and equipment to clear land and build a small stockade. Three companies of cavalry accompanied them, dropping off patrols at strategic points to secure the route. A hundred more soldiers were assigned to build flatboats to float supplies down the Coosa to Fort Williams.

Tactical drills with combat troops began in earnest and continued until sunset each day. The tentative scheme called for General Coffee's cavalry regiment to be used in a reserve or support role, the nature not yet determined. Horsemen, it was supposed, would be of limited value in a direct attack on a river wilderness emplacement. Colonel Williams and the Thirty-Ninth would center any direct assault, with General Doherty's militia infantry on one flank and General Johnson's on the other. General Jackson himself, along with his adjutant, Colonel Billy Carroll, would oversee Lieutenant

Armstrong's cannoneers. Officers calculated that the two light artillery pieces could be pulled overland to the battlefield. The cannon offered limited firepower but Jackson hoped they could splinter the Red Stick barricade before he had to send the infantry to the fore.

Jackson's confidence was tempered only by the lack of sufficient intelligence. Cherokee and friendly Creek scouts would have to be dispatched ahead of the column when the march began. The general thought it imperative that he have the layout of the Creek fortress and the lay of the land and nature of the river adjacent to it. He also needed an assessment of the Creek garrison and their weaponry.

The newly arrived troops, even the disciplined regulars, were anxious to fight. The few that had been on the scene since autumn had sickened of winter and its sparse activity, and they remained bitter about Emuckfau and Enitachopco. They craved revenge and in no small way blamed the newcomer soldiers for not being with them earlier. That's why they were undermanned, they reasoned. The mixture of men and attitudes stirred a volatile brew. Daily fights, in the evening and even in the midst of training drills, became common.

"You fancy sonofabitch!" snarled a militia ranger sergeant after decking a Thirty-Ninth Infantry enlistee with one punch. The ranger chewed a wad of tobacco, a few strands of which dribbled out the corner of his mouth, floating on a rivulet of juice. "You bring your stuffy uniforms and your high-handed marching drills down here and think that's gonna scare them Indians. Hell! I've killed more of them stinking savages than you've ever seen."

The soldier slowly picked himself up. The sergeant made a run at him to continue the assault, but the other man parried his punch and shoved him off balance. The smaller soldier kicked the big militiaman on the shin, then stepped aside and punched him hard in the head as he stumbled past. The sergeant went down with a thump and skidded across the bare, packed dirt, all foliage having long ago worn away.

The sergeant jumped up, cursing and spitting out mud mixed from a mouthful of dirt and thick brown tobacco saliva. "You bastard, god damn you! I'll kill you, you mule turd!"

Another man stepped between them, catching the full force of the sergeant's brawny body. The interloper almost went down himself, but he had stopped the charge. All regained their balance and their composure.

The regular snapped to attention. "Beg your forgiveness, Colonel Carroll. My apologies."

"What the hell are you idiots doing? Wai . . . Stand at ease, damn it! Wait and kill some Indians, not each other!"

"That sonabitch started it, Colonel. These pretty boys think they can . . . ."

"God dammit, Sergeant Barnes! Always something with you. Can't you just be a good soldier?"

"I am a good soldier. Damn good!"

"Away from the post, maybe. With someone to shoot at. Hell, you've been here all winter, haven't you?"

Pride flickered across Sergeant Barnes' face. He pulled himself to full height. "Yessir! I've fought some Indians, too."

"But you didn't come down from Nashville with General Jackson, as I recall." Carroll sneered. "You arrived with Cocke's militia."

"Yes, sir. General White's ranger company. We kicked them Indians' asses before the others left!"

"You raided Creek villages that didn't want to fight," Carroll corrected. Barnes gritted his teeth at the insult but didn't dare argue. "Why didn't you return to Knoxville with your unit, sergeant?"

"Hell, I come here to fight Indians. I warn't gonna go back while any of the mangy skunks was still murdering decent Americans. So I stayed and enlisted with General Jackson. Good thing some of us did, too, Colonel, 'cause these damn pretty soldiers don't know a Creek Indian from a billy goat."

Colonel Carroll quickly assessed that the sergeant's opponent and his regular army buddies had drifted away. Another potential brawl that could have been born from Sergeant Barnes's insults was thus averted.

"Well, how about saving your fighting for the Creeks, sergeant? Or for the billy goats? Goddammit! We're having to break up twenty scraps every evening." Colonel Carroll turned and walked off. "Don't kill each other," he called back over his shoulder. "In due time, I assure you, you'll have your chance again with the Creeks."

Fifty miles down the Coosa, there was scant time or energy for fist fights or other diversions. The construction detachment worked night and day to build Fort Williams. The outpost's mission was to serve primarily as a supply depot. Three thousand soldiers would use it as a stopping off point. Upon their return from the Horseshoe, weary and wounded men would rest and recover under the post's protection.

The site had been selected near a stretch of the river that was wide and shallow and swift. A reasonable ford for horses crossed a half mile downriver. Adjacent to the rising stockade, workers set up a blacksmith shop and a forge.

On the river, craftsmen built a large, flat barge to ferry troops and wagons. The design of the ferry followed closely that of the one spanning the river at Fort Strother. Two thick, strong ropes looped through metal grommets atop the rails running the full length of either side of the barge. With the parallel ropes stretched taut and anchored to either bank of the river, the vessel would maintain a nearly straight course as its grommets slid along the ropes.

Another massive rope was attached to the midpoint of one end of the ferry and ran through a pulley anchored to the trunk of a large tree on one bank. From there it doubled back to pass through two pulleys on the centerline of the barge, one at each end, on to a pulley at the base of a tree on the opposite shore, and finally back to be secured at the midpoint of the other end of the barge. A dozen men on deck would pull on the middle rope to convey the ferry from one side of the Coosa to the other, slowly but effectively. A hundred men or four wagons, less their mules, could ride on each crossing.

As with other phases of the project, the river crossing sparked dozens of mishaps. The cold water claimed several dunking victims each day.

"Aiieee!" The scream signaled another involuntary plunge as one of the ropes unexpectedly snapped tight and propelled a surprised soldier working at one of the barge rails high into the air and over the side. He landed with a dramatic splash and was immediately caught by the current. The canoe that shuttled tools and materials between the river banks pulled alongside.

"You all right there, mate?"

"Hell no, I'm not all right! I'm freezing in this damnable river." The man shivered and his teeth chattered as he struggled to stay afloat. "Get me in your boat."

"Nay. You'll tip us over. Swim for the bank and dry yourself by the fire."

"Damn you! I'm trying to swim, you fool."

"Then swim harder."

He did and finally attained the eastern bank, exhausted, cold, angry, and a quarter mile downstream. He struggled back to the landing and the blazing fire, feeling more dead than alive. He stripped naked and proceeded to dry his clothes and revive his blood circulation. A half hour later he was back on the barge finishing his work on the rail.

On the east bank workers cleared a large staging area, and also the first mile of road leading eastward into the wilderness. Cavalry patrolled both sides. Woodsmen cut and hauled logs for the fort and the ferry. Carpenters and craftsmen fashioned the logs into walls, gates, ramps, huts, and the thick deck of the barge.

Campsites settled in on the west side of the river around the stockade. Generally, two or more tents shared a fire, around which the men cooked their sparse meals and dried their clothes. The uncomfortable tents fostered little sleep, but those few hours were nevertheless precious.

In a little more than a week, the commander of the exhausted construction detachment sent a message to Fort Strother:

> "General Jackson, I beg you to accept my compliments and my deepest admiration. It is my satisfying duty to inform you that Fort Williams is fully constructed and ready for the occupancy of your army. We await your good pleasure, sir, and your instructions. With loyalty and devotion, ..."

Every piece of General Jackson's plan had now been assembled. All that remained was for him to fit them together into a devastating, undeniable fighting force.

29

The Murph settlement, March, 1814

Saul reached the end of the row. He straightened and wiped sweat from his brow, despite the chill of this cold day in early March. He set down his pail of seed corn and watched Cal struggle behind the makeshift plow pulled by George as they finished another furrow a few rows over. He leaned on the hickory staff he used to punch holes in the turned soil to receive the kernels of corn.

"You watch," pronounced Saul. "Shoots will poke through in a week if we get a little rain and it doesn't turn colder. We'll be eating corn from this field in two months."

"If we don't get another hard freeze, you mean." Cal wiped his own sweat as George maneuvered around to head in the opposite direction. "What then?"

"We just replant. We got plenty of seed."

"I still say we're planting too early."

"I ain't been wrong yet, have I, since we've been here?"

"Dumb luck, big brother. But still, that early summer corn sure tastes good. And the onions, and the beans, and all the other stuff."

"Pa always tried to plant early back in Virginia. You were too young to care then. The weather wasn't always agreeable and the soil was more suited for orchards than vegetables. But he made it work somehow." Saul retrieved his pail and stepped over to the next fresh furrow. "Not like here, though. This dirt can grow anything."

"You think we need to break extra ground? We do have two more people now than we had this time last year."

"Naw. We already been growing more than we need or can give to the Creeks." He snickered. "Don't think Anna's gonna eat much anyway. This patch of corn will be more than enough for us and the animals and plenty of seed for next year. Double if we get good growing weather."

"Yeah, I guess. How many more rows then, you think?"

"You just keep up with George. He'll know when to quit."

At the end of the next row Adelin met them with a wooden bucket half full of water, and a gourd dipper.

"What are you ladies doing this morning?" asked Saul as he drank. He handed the gourd to Cal.

"The three of us are having a fine time. I refuse to tell you what we're doing, though," Adelin teased.

"Another one of your secrets, is it?" asked Cal.

"No. It just might not be any of your business. Tell you what is your business; you promised to patch that leak in the roof today. Next time it rains we might get floated out if you don't get to it."

"All right, Miss Nag. I'll do it this afternoon when we get through here."

"Look!" Adelin whispered, pointing to the edge of the woods. A fawn, scant weeks old and still on wobbly legs, had wandered a few yards onto the field. He stopped when he saw the strangers, stared a minute, then yielded to curiosity and took a few more steps toward them.

"His mama has to be close around," said Cal.

"He's beautiful!" Adelin marveled, then added sadly, "Too bad he has to grow up."

The fawn turned and ran back into the forest. Adelin held the bucket for George to drink the remainder of the water. She caressed the mule's cheek and gave him a playful nuzzle with her forehead, then returned to the cabins. The men and George resumed their work.

Saul and Cal would plant onions and peppers in the next few days, then butterbeans and field peas in a couple of weeks. Potatoes and several kinds of greens and a few other crops would follow later. Each year so far they had harvested a bounty and had plenty extra to store away for the winter and to trade with the Creeks, or to just give away. Saul prided himself on his farming skill. Someday, he often confided to the others, he might like to oversee a large plantation. That is, he would always add, if he ever left his river paradise, and he reckoned that might never happen.

Later, Cal straddled the peak of the cabin roof replacing three shingles that had cracked. The shingles were wide slabs of green pine, split from thick logs. They were fitted tightly together on the roof and the seams sealed with thick mud made from red clay of a consistency that, when cured, would allow no seepage.

A distant movement caught Cal's eye. He could not see the river from his perch but he could see the eastern bank over the lip of the bluff. Someone moved along the foot path, going north. He caught glimpses through the brush that hid the trail, but could not see the travelers clearly until they passed adjacent to the head rocks of the shoals.

Several painted, fully armed Red Sticks hurried along the path. Cal watched them carefully for any sign of hostile intent. However, the warriors never glanced his way, as if unaware that the Murphs were there. He continued to watch long after they had disappeared on the north trail.

There go more of them, he thought. The river traffic since Pokkataw was here has been all north, none going south. I guess they are heading for wherever it was that Pokkataw said he was going, Cal pondered further, someplace named for a horse, or a horse hoof, or something.

Cal asked the others about it at supper, telling what he had seen. Soosquana, who often sat or strolled with Anna near the edge of the bluff, confirmed his observation.

"Cholocco Litabixi," she corrected, giggling at Cal's mispronunciation. "It means the horse's hoofprint. Yes, I have seen many. They never stop, they never look up like some used to do when they passed. They seem very troubled and are in much of a hurry."

"Pokkataw and his friends were in a nasty mood when they stopped by," said Saul. "Something surely is happening or is about to happen, I'm afraid."

"I've not seen any warriors going south. Have you, Soos?" asked Adelin, who also walked with the baby at the bluff at least once a day.

"Only mothers with children sometime. No warriors go south. Cholocco Litabixi is where my brothers are, I am certain."

"All the men we see are from the south river towns, don't you think, Soos?" asked Cal. She grunted and nodded yes. "If they are going to the Horseshoe place, there must be even more on the move from Oakfuski and the Hillabi villages and from other places. What are they up to, reckon?"

"Can't be good." Saul turned somber. "They must know something about Mr. Jackson's army. Something bad. Can't understand, though, what could be going on that far up the river."

30

Cholocco Litabixi, the Horseshoe, March, 1814

Pokkataw, the Saugahatchis, and a half dozen warriors from the Hillabi villages had been at Cholocco Litabixi almost a week. Nearly a thousand Red Sticks had gathered with more arriving each day. Three hundred women and children were also present, which indicated confidence in the shamans' declaration that this peculiar stretch of the Tallapoosa River constituted holy ground and could not be defiled by the ungodly.

The river flowed in from the northeast, made a slight turn south and gently curved right for nearly a half mile. The curvature increased as the river looped around a semicircular bend for more than a quarter mile. It then coursed north for another half mile until it encountered a large island. At that point the bend had traversed a total of more than one hundred eighty degrees. Only a narrow neck of three hundred yards separated the river from itself where the bend began. At the island in the curve of the river where it turns away from the peninsula, the current spun around its right side in treacherous eddies while the channel past its back side was narrow and rocky and shallow. The two forks rejoined and worked westward before gradually bending to the southwest.

The peninsula-like spit of land thus surrounded by the river provided a natural fortress, protected by the fifty to one hundred yards wide river on all but the narrow land end. The interior of the peninsula was a tableland, which dropped off modest slopes to flats leading to the river banks. The flats around most of the bend were from ten to forty yards wide, but at the vertex they broadened to two hundred yards, forming a spacious, open plain hosting many mature pines and hardwoods and overlooked by a wooded knoll. On this plain had been established the new village of Tohopeka, in which most of the warriors and all the women and children lived. A few small, long established villages thrived along a stretch of a few miles on the other side of the river.

Chief Menawa, a warrior of Oakfuski and a mighty leader of past battles against enemy Cherokee tribes and renegade raiders in Georgia, had constructed a massive log barricade across the neck of the peninsula. It zigzagged over the flat of an open field, with an unobstructed view for several hundred yards out front, and along its length until it dropped down either slope to the river. The structure consisted of double layers of large logs built to more than the height of a man. Two levels of ports for sharpshooters' muskets dotted its face. Risers climbed the backside of the barricade to platforms so that defenders could fire muskets or arrows over the top. By way of the risers, warriors could also mount the breastwork to rebut a direct assault with clubs and spears and knives and bare hands. Mud was packed into every unneeded crevice and dried hard. Work continued; builders would keep improving the fortress indefinitely, or until the soldiers came, if they ever did.

An imposing wooded hill lay only fifty yards in front of the barricade. It was this eminence that Pokkataw and others most noticed, but also the total lack of defenses other than the wall. Pokkataw sought council with Menawa.

"Chief Menawa, the hill concerns us. Why do we concede it to the side of the field to be occupied by the enemy?"

"Pokkataw, I know you. We both were nourished from our

youth by the waters of Hillabi Creek. I know of your feats of bravery and of your deeds of diplomacy and good will. Why do you question the wisdom of the prophets?"

"Is it the prophets that have advised you to ignore such a strategic position?"

"The prophets tell me that it is of little value to our cause, and that should the enemy occupy it they will suffer certain death by the anger of the Spirits. The Maker of Breath will permit us no harm from the hill. And since our fortress cannot be breached we will be kept safe from harm by the Spirits."

"Chief Menawa, I know of the whites and of their ways. They do not recognize or honor our Spirits. They will defy any curse and will happily possess the hill. It will be of much use to them. From there they can see into our numbers and can fire their muskets from a high angle. We could suffer greatly. Also, the soldiers seek high ground for their cannon. At Enitachopco Creek their cannon did us grave harm and they had not so good a position on which to mount them. They surely will place their pieces on that hill and our emplacements will lie within their range."

"They cannot penetrate our wall!"

"That may be. Or maybe they can if they have guns big enough. Whatever their weapons, they have much advantage by firing on our warriors so that we do not defend the wall as well as we might. If we concede the hill, Chief Menawa, we will suffer by it."

"I shall trust the counsel of Monahi and the other prophets. They assure me that the Spirits will not betray us, that we cannot be defeated."

"Hear me, Chief Menawa, Mad Jackson's army will number many more men than we Muskogis can gather. They have superior weapons. I tell you, as great as our warriors and our Spirits are, we will be defeated if we do not prepare every possible defense. I beg of you to enclose the hill within our ground, and to set defenses along the river."

"The river, Pokkataw?" Chief Menawa showed impatience. He thought he had concluded the respected warrior's consultation. "The river is its own barrier. The army has no canoes. They cannot wade the waters. No, their soldiers can only reach us across the barricade, and that the Spirits will not permit. Never will we be defeated if the American chief Jackson's army is foolish enough to attack us on this holy ground." Menawa flashed anger. "The prophets have spoken, and I have spoken with them!"

Later, a troubled Pokkataw walked the river bank the entire length of the bend, a distance of over two miles. He studied the landscape on both sides with an eye toward military tactics. The river around the peninsula was indeed deep and the current more than moderate. While its width was not forbidding, it would be difficult for the Americans to stage an invasion from the opposite shore. But the bluffs on that side might provide an advantage for their artillery pieces should they wish to mount them there, making the village of Tohopeka especially vulnerable. Jackson will surely cover the other bank, Pokkataw thought, as any good military commander would, with reserve forces even if he chooses not to attack from there. He didn't wish to doubt a man as great as Menawa, but he feared the weaknesses in the Muskogi positions.

Pokkataw stood pensively on the river bank at the canoe landing, located on the back side of the bend at the end of the wide flats. More than twenty canoes lined the bank. Some were heavy scooped out logs while the more servicable crafts were constructed of sapling frames with deerskin coverings sealed with pine resin. The level corridor between the river and the tableland narrowed to the north, while the flat plain of Tohopeka at the vertex of the peninsula opened before him to the east. Smoke and smells from campfires filled the air as women preparing food scurried among tents and huts. Laughing children chased each other among the trees.

He studied the river current, for it was just past the canoe landing that it began to accelerate toward the swift eddies around the island. At the moment the water level seemed dangerously low. An enemy would have an easy time crossing, mainly because of the subdued flow. A vigorous current was mandatory for the river to serve at its maximum as a natural deterrent.

A voice hailed from behind.

"Pokkataw."

He turned to face two strong warriors. He judged from their body paint designs that they were natives of one of the towns on the lower Tallapoosa river.

"Pokkataw, you are friend of Soosquana? I am Tolokika and he is Ettepti-lopa. We are brothers of Soosquana."

Pokkataw greeted the brothers warmly. He had looked for them since his arrival and, failing, he had decided that they were not there.

"We have been hunting, gathering food for the village. You have seen Soosquana? She is well? Tell us of her little one."

"Soosquana is well and she is happy. She has a strong baby girl that she has named Anna. She asked me to find you and to pass on to you her devotion. Soosquana was certain you must be here. She told me of your family misfortune, for which I mourn with you. She also spoke of your anger."

Scattered drops of rain began to fall. The men didn't seem to notice as they continued to talk of Soosquana's baby and of making war. They climbed the near slope to the tableland and walked across to the wooded knoll that overlooked Tohopeka. The rain increased.

"This position should also be defended," Pokkataw contended, "even if it is well within our bounds." The brothers did not disagree but didn't seem to fully grasp the strategy.

Pokkataw explained. "If we are invaded from across the river, this elevation offers clear view of the river and of Tohopeka. It would be of great advantage in repelling such an attack. And if the soldiers break through the barricade and advance from that direction, this little hill with its thick brush will be the last line of defense before the invaders reach Tohopeka. Escape into the river by the women and children might be possible if the soldiers can be delayed here."

"You seem to know much of the white man's way of war, Pokkataw," observed Ettepti-lopa.

"I have learned much. The white soldiers fight differently from the Muskogi. Even when we have their weapons, we do not use them the same."

"We are not a warring people," insisted Tolokika. "This war has been forced on us."

"Yes, and our failure to lay aside the differences of our peoples and join in a unified defense against the whites is to be the death of our homeland. We have yet to learn the strategies of this new enemy and I believe that we shall suffer from our ignorance."

The rain had steadily grown. It now came in torrents, signaling the beginning of needed spring rains. Pokkataw, Tolokika, and Ettepti-lopa walked together the grounds of Cholocco Litabixi, ignoring the downpour as they awaited deadlier storms to follow.

31

The rain continued. Perhaps not as heavy as overnight, but still enough to shut down most operations.

"Damn rain!" snorted General Andrew Jackson. Water streamed from a crease in his hat. He stood with Colonel Billy Carroll watching soldiers unload the flatboats that had docked at the landing that morning. "This holds us up, I fear. I had wanted to begin the march tomorrow."

"At least the rain released the flatboats," observed Carroll.

The boats had been stranded on sandbars two miles upriver for several days on their journey down from Fort Strother. When the rain had begun yesterday morning and continued hard, the boats had loosened and finally broken free during the night. They had docked just past dawn and the process of transferring their stores to nearby tents and from there to wagons had begun immediately.

The ferry had been moving men and goods across the river nonstop since the column had arrived yesterday morning. It was a slow process and the rain made it slower. Three thousand soldiers had to be transported, and the provisions to sustain them for a week. The ordnance to fight a major campaign also awaited conveyance over the river.

On the east bank, teams of woodsmen had been sent to extend

the road into the wilderness so that when the march did begin it would have a reasonable headstart. Companies of soldiers already ferried across camped along the road awaiting orders.

"How much longer till they are all on the other side, Billy?"

"Sometime tomorrow morning, sir. If the ferry holds up, that is. It's being taxed greatly, General, and the current is increasing."

"Coffee's regiment?"

"He plans to take the rest of his men and horses across in the morning."

"See that he does it this afternoon, Billy. The river's rising; he doesn't need to make it harder on the horses."

"Yes, sir."

"And direct him to send his companies to the end of the road that's been cleared so far. Now, Billy, what do our numbers look like? Those for the march, I mean, not counting the garrisons we're leaving to watch the forts."

"Best we can see, General, 'bout two thousand infantry. The Thirty-Ninth and the two new brigades of militia. We have joined what we already had into those. There is General Coffee's cavalry regiment; we added the new horse soldiers to his outfit, bringing him up to about seven hundred. The Indians number six hundred, one hundred of 'em Lower Creeks. Total personnel about three thousand three hundred, sir."

"That's good, Billy. I think we have adequate forces this time." Jackson gritted his teeth at the remembrance of being stopped at Emuckfau Creek in January. "What about the spy teams we sent out last week? I know some of 'em returned. Others turn up this morning?"

"Yes sir. Two more of the Creeks arrived about dawn. They came over on the ferry and are waiting for us in the stockade."

"Good. We need to know more than we do now."

"Two more teams out. They could've been caught."

"Let's see what these two savages can tell us. Find an interpreter for us, Billy."

The two Indians did indeed have information to add to the intelligence already collected. It was known that the Creeks' fortress lay approximately fifty miles due east on a horsehoof-shaped bend of the Tallapoosa. Its natural landscape made it easy to defend. It would be difficult to rout the defenders, according to the spies, especially now that the Creek warriors had grown to a thousand or more. That was approximately twice the number they had expected to encounter there in January.

"What of their leadership?" asked Jackson through the interpreter. The previous spy teams had not been certain who was in charge at the Horseshoe.

"It is Menawa," the interpreter relayed, "and . . . ."

"Who's he?"

The interpreter didn't have to ask the Creek spies. He already knew of Menawa, so he answered the question himself. "Chief Menawa is an important warrior chief of Oakfuski town. He has long been a militant among the Red Sticks. He is a disciple of Tecumseh . . . ."

"Oh, Christ! One of those blood-soaked weasels."

"And he counsels with the Spirits and listens to the prophets." The interpreter returned to the scouts' intelligence information. "He has several prophets with him and it is thought that one named Monahi is his chief aide and adviser."

"Do we know anything about the terrain of that Horseshoe place?" asked Colonel Carroll. "We also need to know of their arms, and their ammunition supply. Have they gotten hold of any of the new weapons the British are pouring in at Pensacola?"

"Also," added Jackson, "we still need to know more about the wall they've built." He turned back to the interpreter. "Can they say more of that?"

The spies could only add minor new details beyond what they first reported. And, no, they knew nothing of the two spy teams not yet heard from.

"Would that rogue Crockett were still here," complained Jackson. The master scout David Crockett had returned home after the skirmishes at Emuckfau and Enitachopco, but had promised to return straightway. "He'd get more out of these sorry fellows that call themselves scouts. They can't even spy decent on their own kind."

"Crockett weighed that he would be back by now," explained Carroll, "but he still wasn't at Fort Strother when the last of us pulled out. Guess he got held up back in Tennessee."

Colonel Carroll toured the post to relay General Jackson's orders. He personally inspected the ferry and carefully instructed the lieutenants and engineers in charge about the importance of preventing trouble. Breakdowns requiring lengthy repairs could not be tolerated, he stressed.

"That doesn't come from me, gentlemen," he hammered at the officers. "That's General Jackson talking!"

Carroll continued on to General Coffee. Aware of the friction between the scout Crockett and Coffee, he told of Jackson's lamentation about Crockett's absence.

"Hell, we don't need that bastard," spat Coffee.

"I knew you'd like that," laughed Carroll.

Coffee always became angry at the mention of Crockett's name. They had feuded since October when the army first approached Ten Islands. Crockett reported an abnormal number of Indians crossing the river and Coffee discounted his alarm as unimportant. But when a militia major observed the same thing the next day,

Coffee treated his report seriously and acted on it. The snub infuriated Crockett and he loudly voiced his complaint. Crockett already distrusted military command, and the incident only accelerated his venom. He and Coffee still had no confidence in each other and avoided contact whenever possible.

"He's a bragger and a liar," continued Coffee. "And very probably a coward. He had a month left on his enlistment, this campaign came up, he paid some poor slob to finish his term, and he took out again for Tennessee. Not the first time he's done that, either. He scrams in the face of most every action."

"He was with us at Emuckfau and Enitachopco," reminded Carroll.

"I've heard him brag about that. I don't think he did half of what he claimed."

"Perhaps not."

"Can't prove by me he was even there. I don't remember seeing him at all. Maybe he hid behind one of those big trees."

Carroll laughed again, left Coffee to start his cavalry across the treacherous Coosa, and continued his rounds.

The rain slackened at noon and stopped completely by midafternoon. The morale of the men heightened as their clothes dried and the chill disappeared beneath a bright sun that came out to finish the day. The troops quickly regained the itch to fight. The work pace increased though the river continued to rise.

"Gentlemen," addressed General Jackson at a staff meeting just before sundown. "We march at dawn day after next. Spend tomorrow organizing your units, seeing them to their sharpest, and preparing your equipment and your ordnance. See that each man is amply supplied with shot and powder and that his musket and bayonet are of good service. Supply your men with field rations for several days' campaign.

"We should arrive at our objective after three days of cutting through the wilderness, hopefully less if the rain hasn't made the going too soft. There are no roads, not even trails, where we venture. I hope, gentlemen, to face the enemy with the dawn on the twenty-seventh."

The patter of soldiers and the hustle of preparing for war resounded clearly from beyond the walls of the Fort Williams stockade. Dozens of fires burned bright on both sides of the Coosa River, to dry and warm men and clothing as much as to cook the supper meal. Trails of wood smoke wafted into a slight breeze, which ushered it to the river channel and turned it downstream into a blanket of fog.

After riding the ferry across the river, Private Virgil Tom Ottis propped his clothes and equipment on sticks before a fire. They would dry in a half hour if he turned or rearranged them often, he thought. He checked to be certain he had properly laid out every item, then picked up the small parcel of leather oilskin next to his pack and sat down on a nearby log.

Virgil Tom gingerly unwrapped the soft buckskin from around his letters. Elsa would love to have these, he thought; I wish I could get them to her. He unfolded a page and read silently, then returned it to the packet and took out another.

I must find time to write again tonight, he vowed. A long one this time, because we leave tomorrow and I may not get another chance for days.

Virgil Tom refolded the letter and stacked it with the others. He carefully rewrapped the oilskin around the treasures, wiped the mist from his eyes, and rose to tend the fire.

Good-spirited goading and cursing broke out as dark settled in, and gambling, and laughter. Crude songs rang above the din. More laughter. More cursing.

Andrew Jackson stood in the gate of the stockade listening, a coffee mug in his hand. He liked what he heard. His army was happy to be finally going to war. We might end it this time, he thought, and open this fine, rich land for our good Tennessee settlers.

32

Baby Anna gurgled with delight as Soosquana wrestled with her in the shallow, swift part of the brook. Soosquana attempted to bathe the naked infant, a task that had developed into an intricate game for both of them. Nearby, in the wash pool of the little stream, Adelin scrubbed clothes and cooking pots.

"Soos," laughed Adelin, "you're having more fun than Anna."

"She is such a funny baby, is she not?"

"How is Saul doing with her?"

Soosquana giggled. "I make Saul get up and rock Anna at night when she cries. He loves it. He fusses, but he loves it," she repeated.

"Wonderful. I knew he would come around." She got up and began to stretch articles of clothing across tables and chairs to dry.

"When are you going to give Cal a little one to rock at night?" teased Soosquana.

"Ha!" scoffed Adelin. "Cal hasn't learned to handle Anna yet. He's still afraid of her. But truth is, Soos, I'm less ready than he is. Maybe soon, I keep saying. Maybe."

"What do you three ladies gossip about?" Saul walked over holding up a string of fish to show off, having just climbed up from the shoals.

"You!" both women chimed, and smiled at their unison.

"And Cal," added Soosquana. She wrapped Anna in a blanket

and began rubbing her dry. "Nice fish. Make a good supper. You clean them," she ordered, and laughed again with Adelin.

"Fine. And what if I eat all of them, too?"

"You not that big a pig!" declared Soosquana. They all laughed again.

"Where's Cal?" asked Saul.

"He's back in the shed tending to the livestock," said Adelin.

Soosquana changed the topic. "Did any warriors pass by today?"

"Not while I was down there. Why?

"I've not seen anyone on the trail or canoeing the river since several days before it rained." Soosquana looked worried. "I thought that when it stopped raining yesterday we would see warriors travel again. It is strange, is it not?"

"Yes, it seems so, Soos," agreed Saul. He didn't want to alarm her as he was certain that something bad was brewing. To avoid further discussion, he held up the fish again. "I have to get these beauties cleaned for my supper."

Adelin finished distributing the clothes for drying and returned to the brook. She scooped up a handful of sand from the bottom of the stream and began scrubbing it into a cooking pot. Caked soot came free under the wet sand and vigorous hand.

"Adelin," Soosquana asked with a troubled voice, "do you think Tolokika and Ettepti-lopa went to Cholocco Litabixi?"

"I don't know, Soos. I suppose they might have. Pokkataw said he was going there. He'll find them and, together, they'll be all right." Adelin paused and nodded reassuredly. "They'll be all right," she repeated, "even if they are with the angriest of the Red Sticks."

"Adelin, my brothers are the angriest!"

Adelin looked at her and read terror in Soosquana's face.

"It is their anger that puts them in much danger," Soosquana continued. "I have already lost my father and one brother. I don't know where my mother and sisters are or how they fare. Now I am in much fear for the fate of my last two brothers."

Adelin fought an aching heart and tried to turn the conversation and Soosquana's thoughts back to baby Anna.

"Anna is really growing, Soos. She's gaining every day."

"Yes, she is twice her weight at birth."

"She is going to be a healthy, happy little girl. I can hardly wait until she starts talking. She will be better with both English and Muskogean together than anyone ever has before."

Soosquana brightened. "Here, Adelin, let me finish the pots. Anna wishes to take you for a walk. Don't disappoint her."

Adelin laughed and eagerly wiped her hands dry on the legs of her britches. She reached for the baby. "I would be delighted, Anna, to go for a walk with you."

A little later, Saul reappeared from his cabin. Cal walked with him. Soosquana had finished the washing chore and sat in a chair under the bright sun. Adelin strolled over, jostling Anna in her arms and talking to her, succeeding once more in provoking a smile from the baby.

"What's that?" asked Adelin, pointing to the implements in Saul's hands.

"It's a bow." Saul thrust the device forward. "From the Hillabi villages. And arrows. Pokkataw gave them to us last summer."

"He thought we might like to learn to hunt like the Creeks," added Cal. "Haven't tried it yet, though."

"So give it a go, big man," teased Adelin.

"Me first," declared Saul, stringing the bow and selecting an arrow. "Put us up a target, brother."

Cal found a scrap of rabbit fur and pressed it against the bark of a pine tree near the river ford trail. "That's only thirty yards, big brother. See what you can do."

Saul notched the arrow and took careful aim. He loosed the projectile and it stuck solid in the tree. The wrong tree, two yards to the right.

Cal doubled over laughing.

"My turn. Let me show you how to hit that old rabbit."

His arrow went past the tree, well into the brush beyond. He couldn't escape a dose of ridicule of his own. Several more shots by each man improved the results but little. The rabbit skin remained safe.

Adelin stopped laughing when Cal thrust the bow at her.

"And now, Miss Sharpshooter, let's see you do your stuff."

Adelin passed Anna off to Soosquana. "All right, I will. I'll show you mighty woodsmen how to do that."

Adelin took the bow, notched an arrow, and pulled on the string. It only moved a few inches before she relaxed her arms. "This thing is hard!" she exclaimed. The men laughed aloud. Adelin turned to try again. "But never fear. I can do it if you big oafs can."

She pulled mightily, getting the arrow to a little more than half cock before releasing it. The arrow flew straight, but weakly. It plunked at the base of the tree, sticking majestically into the soil. Increased laughter and derision.

"I'm not through yet," Adelin pledged. "I'll get it this time."

She put down the bow and reached for her musket leaning against a chair. She stepped up again and looked toward the target. She levered the flint to full cock and set the strike plate. Taking careful aim, she pulled the trigger, bringing a flash at the vent and an explosion of flame, smoke, and noise from the weapon's muzzle. The rabbit fur leaped and fell from the tree, a large, neat hole in its center.

Adelin turned and curtsied amid the cheers, a big smile on her face. "One dead rabbit fur, gentlemen," she said.

They all laughed again, all but Soosquana. She had turned somber once more.

"If the Muskogis must fight the white army," she said, hugging Anna tightly, "I hope they do it with muskets and not with bows shooting arrows."

33

Cal awoke to find Adelin gone from the cabin. He dressed hurriedly and stepped to the porch. He met a bright, brisk morning but no Adelin. Concerned, Cal reached back inside for his musket and pouch and walked into the yard. At the bluff he looked down at the river. Adelin sat in the gravel at the edge of the water with her back to the bluff. She idly picked up a pebble and tossed it into the torrent. Then she sat still for a long minute.

Cal squatted and watched her. He remained silent as she flipped another rock, obviously aiming at nothing. She repeated the ritual several times.

Adelin seemed to be crying.

Cal stirred and softly walked to the path and down. As he reached the river bank, Adelin saw him coming, stood up, and waited. She fell into his arms and sobbed hard against his chest. Cal hugged her tight.

"Cal," she sputtered as she fought for control. She sniffed. "Cal, I miss the farm. I miss my family. Mother, Father, Bess Marie, Zack, my animals."

"I understand," Cal sympathized, and he thought that he did understand, perhaps clearly for the first time. "I'm sorry, Adelin. Maybe I've been unfair to you." Adelin looked up at him, surprised. "Do you want to go home?"

"No, silly," Adelin replied emphatically. "I don't want to go anywhere. This is my home and I love it here." Still reveling in Cal's hug, she squeezed him back. "I love you. I love Soos and Saul, and I adore Anna." She giggled, mixing it with another sniff. "Can't a girl miss her folks and still be happy?"

"Sure you can." Cal held her in a tight embrace for a long time. "Sure you can." He released her and took her hand. "Come on."

Cal led Adelin upstream to the head of the shoals and out onto a large flat boulder near the middle. They sat down, facing each other. Cal reached out and took both of Adelin's hands in his. They stared and smiled at each other in silence for a long time, and then began to talk. The river rushed past, singing its song and isolating them in their private, intimate world.

They talked of little things, of happy memories, of sad ones. They talked about the loved ones at home, at the Holman farm and the Murphs back in Virginia. They shared newly recalled stories and secrets. They laughed at silly thoughts and fond remembrances. Adelin cried again, then laughed about it.

An hour passed easily, without their notice. Finally Cal looked up, suddenly aware of the world. He sighed. "I wish I could stay right here with you all day," he said to Adelin, "but we better get back. Saul and Soos will be worried about us."

Adelin smiled her own regret and reached for Cal to pull her up from her seated position. They stepped across the rocks and walked up the path with their arms around each other.

Saul and Soos weren't worried. Saul had spotted Cal and Adelin from the bluff and knew to leave them alone. Soosquana had experienced the same melancholies shortly after their wedding and several times since. So had Saul and Cal, but they hid it better than the women.

Later, near the conclusion of the noon meal, Saul turned to Cal.

"I think we should walk up the road a piece and look for sign of visitors. With the Red Sticks stirring and the army about, I'd like to know if we're being watched, and if unfriendlies are passing close."

"Good thinking," agreed Cal. "I'll get my musket."

"We'll only go a short way," Saul told the women. "Fire a shot if you need us. We'll be sure to hear."

A hundred yards up the road, Saul asked, "Adelin all right?"

"Yeah. She misses her folks. Can't blame her."

"That's normal. You have to be patient."

"I know. She's a strong woman, and she really does love it here. She'll be all right."

Into the woods, the two spread to either side of the trace to scout for signs that shouldn't be there. Finding nothing unusual, they widened the search to cover several yards into the brush all along the road. About a half mile from the compound, at the bottom of a long hill, Saul was satisfied.

"Looks like nothing here, Cal. I don't think the Red Sticks are interested in us. Let's go back."

Saul and Cal turned together, looked up the hill, and froze. At the top stood a Red Stick, arm raised with palm forward in a signal of peace.

"Who is he?" asked Cal, readying his musket.

"Don't know. Too far to tell."

"He looks friendly. And he seems to be alone."

"Not likely. He probably has friends hidden on both sides of the road."

"What do we do?"

Saul took a deep breath, checked the prime of his weapon, and cradled it across his chest in the crook of his left arm. "We'll go see what he wants." He took the first step forward. "Stay wide."

Halfway up the hill, Cal knew the warrior. "He's the man Adelin and I met on the lake canoeing. He came with Pokkataw once and ate supper with us."

Saul also recognized him. He fought hard to recall his name. He knew the Creeks were usually insulted if strangers didn't remember them by name. Almost there, he had it.

"His name is Meeskapa," Saul said quietly to Cal. Each held an arm high, palm showing, as they approached to within yards of the man.

"Meeskapa. Friend," greeted Saul.

The man returned the greeting in Muskogean. Most of the words were unintelligible to Saul and Cal, but the meaning was clear.

"We're happy to see you again," continued Saul, enhancing his words with crude sign language and gestures. "What is the purpose of your visit?"

Meeskapa, employing signs of his own, launched into a long explanation. Saul and Cal heard "Pokkataw" several times, and picked out the Muskogean for "danger" and several equally ominous words and phrases. They interjected occasionally with grunts and signals of comprehension, and slowly put together the warrior's message. He explained that their great mutual friend Pokkataw, before leaving for Cholocco Litabixi, had requested that Meeskapa and other friends look in often on the Murphs and see that no harm came to them by way of Red Sticks. Pokkataw had made it clear to fellow Hillabi tribesmen that no one was to approach the Murph compound with hostile intent, for these whites were friends of the Muskogis. So Meeskapa had been around for several weeks making certain that Pokkataw's wishes were followed. But he and his companions would leave that evening for the Horseshoe with the remainder of the Hillabi and Oakfuski warriors.

"We are honored that you have watched over us," declared Saul, hoping that his sign language carried his sincerity. "We thank you with all our being. Our brother Pokkataw is truly a great man and a good friend. Please give him our greeting of friendship and admiration when you see him. We wish him and you peace, good fortune, and long lives."

Meeskapa nodded, seeming to understand, and reached for Saul's hand. The men shared a long, strong handshake. Meeskapa, as did Pokkataw, understood the white man's gesture of good will, and he repeated it with Cal. The two moved past the Indian and dropped below the crest of the hill toward the compound. Meeskapa still stood atop the hill following them with his watchful gaze each time Saul and Cal looked back.

The two shared with Soosquana and Adelin the story of their meeting with Meeskapa. The women didn't know whether to be horrified to have been under such close unknown scrutiny, or to be thrilled that their Muskogi neighbors regarded their friendship so richly. All four felt a new appreciation for the humanity of the Muskogi people. Soosquana, considering what the white man's army had done to the Hillabi towns and to her own home village only a few months back, thought that the warriors' protection of them was especially noble.

The remainder of the day passed routinely, and after supper the couples retired to their respective cabins. As soon as Cal closed the door behind him Adelin assaulted him with a vigorous hug and a barrage of kisses.

"What's that for?" Cal managed to ask, breathless.

Adelin laughed. She kissed him again. "Because I love you. And because you're so wonderful." Her attack continued, then she turned sober. "Cal, thank you so much for this morning. You are the best husband in the Mississippi Territory."

At midnight a thunderstorm rolled up the river. Flashes from crashing lightning illuminated lovers content in each other's arms.

34

Near the Tallapoosa River, March 26, 1814

No fires burned on the crests of the two ridges. Instead, sentries, mounted and on foot, patrolled with eyes focused and ears tuned. This would not be a night to be inattentive.

A small creek flowed through the hollow between the ridges. Beside it camped three thousand soldiers of General Jackson's army. A minimum of damped and sheltered campfires burned near the stream to cook paltry bits of bacon or to heat coffee, but mostly the men supped on hard biscuit and water or cold coffee. A thousand cavalry horses and wagon mules stood pastured for the night at an ample downstream clearing, hobbled within a large rope corral so they could find forage to go with the creek water. Scores of wagons containing ammunition, provisions, and surgical supplies sat on a level atop one of the ridges, heavily guarded. Nearby, the two artillery pieces rested on their carriages, still attached to the limbers.

"Double the sentries and change them every half hour," ordered Colonel Billy Carroll, acting on Jackson's instructions. "Patrol both ridges for a full mile, with horsemen riding the whole length. Set sentries in the creek bottom and on the slopes, in both directions, and completely around the livestock corral. Also, post stationary guards overlooking every possible trail of approach. Any movement is to be reported."

"Yes, sir," responded the captain of the guard.

Carroll turned to a young lieutenant. "Gather a squad and walk the perimeter of the encampment. Make certain that all bivouacs are positioned close. No one is to be out of plain sight of others."

The army had hacked its way through dense wilderness and arrived at the camp location shortly past midafternoon. The crude road had linked ridge to ridge to endless ridge since leaving Fort Williams, an arduous three days journey that wearied the troops, not from the difficult task of clearing the way but from impatience at the slow pace. They wished to find the enemy and engage them.

At dusk General Jackson met with his command officers.

"Gentlemen, this is probably our final session for strategy," he began. "I fully expect to meet the enemy in the morning. We still know too little of their strength of arms, and woefully little of the terrain we face."

"Where are we tonight, General, in relation to their position?"

"Our scouts tell us we are camped about six miles northwest of our objective and a few miles north of the Tallapoosa. This creek is perhaps an eastern branch of Hillabi Creek." Jackson beckoned the officers to scan the crude map before him. "We march at daybreak. The main body of the infantry and the artillery will reach Emuckfau Creek and parallel the river from there. That should funnel us into the north of the Horseshoe. From there we will judge the lay of the land for ourselves.

"We will select the best placement for our artillery pieces and, if the stories of their barricade are true, the cannon will knock it down with a barrage of round shot. That wall will be mounds of splinters by midmorning. Then we attack with the infantry, hopefully against a minimum of remaining resistance. As already outlined, Colonel Williams and the regulars will lead from the center, the West Tennessee militia on the left, and the East to the right.

Commanders, deploy your companies on the field as the terrain affords you best advantage.

"General Coffee." Jackson looked around for his friend and trusted associate. "Not knowing beforehand how effective your horsemen will be, we shall deploy you south of the river. Our scouts reported back this afternoon that there are extensive shallows with a reasonable ford about two miles downstream from the mouth of Emuckfau Creek. I propose that you take your cavalry regiment with two companies of rangers and most of the Cherokees and take possession of the south bank of the river. Hold your ground from there and await a proper signal. But permit no escape by way of crossing the river."

"Yes, General," beamed Coffee. "My lads are more than capable." He surmised that his horsemen might yet see more action than first thought. "Drive the savages our way, sir. We'll be the ending for them."

"Set your rangers and Cherokees along the banks where your cavalrymen cannot reach. Have them wait from positions of advantage. Place your horsemen in reserve and as possible pursuit units."

"Yes, sir. Eagerly, sir."

"And now, gentlemen, I think it imperative that we address the troops. Please have them gather as close as possible at the center of camp. Save the sentries, of course."

A half hour later, most of the three thousand sat on one side of the little creek facing their general. Standing before them on the lip of the opposite bank, General Jackson stared without expression for long minutes as he fingered the hilt of the saber at his side.

"Brave soldiers of Tennessee," he began as quiet descended over the men. The only other sounds were the soft run of the creek and the occasional whinny of an unhappy horse from downstream. "With the dawn, we march to meet an enemy the size of which and the fierceness of which we have not seen in other skirmishes in this wilderness. Make no error in judgment; these are vicious, blood-letting, murdering savages of top order. They have slaughtered defenseless American citizens, including women and children. They threaten your homeland and your Godly way of life. This is our best chance to destroy the strength of the Creek Nation and I have no doubt you will acquit yourselves handsomely on the field of battle."

General Jackson paused. He waited. His hard stare fixed the eyes of the soldiers farthest away, then those at the front, and finally the men seated at the middle of the slope. No one dared speak or move. He continued with a voice harder than his eyes.

"I expect many feats of courage on the morrow. But you must hear and understand, no acts of cowardice will be tolerated. Any officer or soldier who flies before the enemy without being com-pelled to do so by superior force will be called to answer before me, God, and a swift trial of your peers. You will be found guilty of cowardice and desertion and" — the final four words were spoken slowly and deliberately — "you shall suffer death."

At that, General Jackson stalked to his tent and retired for the evening. Colonel Billy Carroll stepped before the shaken army.

"Best you see to the cleaning of your weapons and the condition of your gear, and then retire for the night. We arise before dawn and march with first light. Gentlemen, this surely will be an important skirmish, vital to the settlement of this Alabama country. We fight for the future of your fellow citizens of Tennessee. Do yourselves proud; you fight for the defense of your state and your nation. Godspeed, brave soldiers!"

Virgil Tom Ottis lingered at a small campfire as most of the men broke for their bedrolls and what would be a short and probably fitful night of rest. He took out his vial of ink and the quill stub and peeled a coarse sheet of paper from the roll in his pack. He thought a minute and began to write by the dim fire light.

> Dearest Elsa—I am forced by lack of time and light to keep this letter short. I could not retire for the night without telling you again of my undying love. By the morning we will meet our enemy and will surely defeat them. I then will hurry home and back into your sweet arms. Keep warm, my love, and know that we will soon be together again. Your devoted husband, V. T.

Virgil Tom returned the ink, quill, and writing board to his pack. He held the single sheet and read it again to himself. When finished, he folded it carefully and placed it with the other letters inside the oilskin under his jacket. He then crawled into his thin bedroll to twist and squirm through a few hours of tortured rest, searching in vain for dreams of Elsa.

35

Cholocco Litabixi, the Horseshoe, March 27, 1814, seven p.m.

Smoke hung heavily over the battlefield. It would linger for days. Death hung heavier. It would haunt for centuries.

Pale coloration in the western sky was all that remained of day. Darkness had brought an eerie quiet, interrupted occasionally by a soldier's shout or the clatter of a wagon collecting bodies or the agony of a wounded man. Pine torches flickered all around the field, mixing their glow and odor with the acrid gunpowder smoke settling into the landscape. Creek women and children huddled together in the center of the village of Tohopeka, at the vertex of the bend of the horseshoe. Guarded by the guns of American militiamen, they sat silent, stoical, except for the muffled sobs of a young child. At unequal intervals of a few minutes average, they grimaced at the blast of a single musket shot, which signaled the discovery and execution of another hidden and wounded, or maybe not wounded, Red Stick warrior.

"Count every one!" General Jackson urged again to the militia details collecting the bodies of Red Sticks. "Don't miss a one. It's important."

Wagons scoured for the Indian dead and stacked them in small piles in every part of the peninsula to be burned later that night.

More dignified details gathered the American fatalities and those of the Cherokees and the friendly Lower Creeks.

"The total is forty-nine dead of our troops, more than a hundred fifty wounded," reported Colonel Carroll to General Jackson after he had tallied the counts from all unit commanders. "Some of the wounded won't survive. Colonel Williams's regulars and the Cherokees got the worst of it, I'm afraid. The Thirty-Ninth lost seventeen, the Cherokees, including our Creek turncoats, twenty-three. We only count nine dead out of all the militia."

General Jackson, at the suggestion of the Cherokee scouts, ordered the American fatalities wrapped tightly, weighted with large stones, and sunk in the middle of the river. "The Red Sticks will return when you are gone and dishonor the graves of their enemies," the Cherokees told him.

One soldier wasn't buried in the river. General Jackson, Colonel Williams, and Colonel Carroll, slightly wounded himself, stood reverently with their hats off watching two privates finish packing the dirt atop a single grave at the base of the hill facing the west side of the barricade. They smoothed the dirt and piled brush atop it to burn, thus hiding any sign of fresh digging.

"The very best and bravest soldier I've ever met," lamented Williams.

"Though we had him for too short a time," asserted Jackson, "he was truly the flower of my army. An intrepid soldier. Would that all Tennesseeans, all Americans honor his example."

Beneath the fresh Alabama soil lay Lemuel P. Montgomery, Major, Thirty-Ninth Regiment, United States Army. He had been killed leading the first frontal assault on the barricade. When a two-hour cannonade from the two artillery pieces had made but small dents in the breastworks, General Jackson had ordered the Thirty-Ninth, bayonets fixed and sabers drawn, to lead the charge. Major

Montgomery had been the first to scale to the top of the wall and fight to dislodge the Creeks behind the barricade. He caught a musket ball in the head and died almost immediately. Two other young officers of the Thirty-Ninth, Lieutenants Robert Somerville and Michael Moulton, had been mortally wounded but their bodies were disposed of in the river with the other fatalities.

A small group of regulars, officers and enlistees, stood to the side as Jackson, Williams, and Carroll turned to leave Montgomery's grave. One of the more youthful officers, an ensign, was soaked with blood.

"Are you hurt, son?" asked General Jackson. "I'd judge you've been wounded more than once."

"No, sir. I'm not hurt. But, yes sir, I took an arrow in the thigh and two musket balls in my shoulder. I'll be fine, General. Kind of you to ask."

"How old are you, son?"

"Twenty-one, sir."

"Your first action?"

"Yes, sir."

"You're a brave soldier. What's your name?"

"Houston, sir. Samuel Houston, from Virginia. Now Tennessee, sir, mountain country."

"Yes. Get your wounds tended to, ensign. Be off with you now."

General Coffee's cavalry had backed up the militia and Indian forces on the opposite bank of the river during the battle. The Cherokees in the middle, Lieutenant Jesse Bean's rangers on the island at the western extreme of the bend, and Captain Eli Hammond and his rangers on the east had prevented the Creeks from escaping by way of the river, and had killed scores making the attempt.

Lieutenant Bean and his men may have seen the most action. After occupying the island, they discovered when the fighting began that the Red Sticks considered it a principal escape route. When the Indians attempted to storm the island to regain it, Bean's sharpshooters cut them down in a virtual massacre.

The Cherokees had eventually crossed the river and attacked through the village of Tohopeka. Under the command of Colonel Gideon Morgan, whose Cherokee name was Aganstata, they became impatient after hearing two hours of firing from the vicinity of the barricade. Ignoring General Coffee's directive to stay put, some Cherokees swam the river and stole canoes, which they used to ferry across enough men for an assault on Tohopeka. That forced the Red Sticks to defend their rear at the same time they desperately fought to repel the frontal attack coming from across the barricade.

After dark, Coffee led his cavalry companies around the eastern side of the bend. They passed through the Creek village of Niuyaka, ironically named for the failed 1790 Treaty of New York, crossed the river, and rejoined the garrison on the peninsula. Coffee's horsemen had seen little action, but from his position atop the opposite bluffs, he had been one of the battle's better positioned observers.

"My officers assigned to reconnaissance," he reported to General Jackson, "estimate that at least two hundred, and perhaps three hundred Red Sticks were killed in the river, or on the bank."

"How?" Jackson didn't comprehend so large a number. "Why so many there?"

"At first they volleyed with our fellows on the other bank and we outgunned them bad. Then when the Cherokees crossed, they seemed to panic and tried to escape, or maybe some were trying to counterattack, and Bean on the island and the rangers on our side of the river had easy shooting. They didn't have a chance, General."

Two hours after dark, funeral pyres began to light the peninsula and add to the stench of an already foul mixture of odors. As the

General had ordered, careful counts of the bodies were tallied before they were burned. The number already totaled over five hundred, not counting those lost to the river.

"General Jackson," Colonel Carroll reported as the fires blazed, "the body of the main prophet Monahi has been identified. Took a load of grape shot right in the mouth. Two other prophets, possibly."

"Menawa?"

"Haven't found him yet, sir. At least, no one can identify him."

"Damn!"

At the vertex of the peninsula, a half dozen corpses lay in a heap five yards from the water. Pine straw and dry brush had already been added to the mix to start the flames. The pyre only awaited a torch.

Under the pile, something twitched. One of the bodies was alive.

Fifty yards away, three soldiers fussed over another pyre, trying to build up the fire before moving to the next one. They added pine logs into the center and stood back to watch the struggling flame catch into a roar that shot sparks and embers high into the boughs of the tall pines lining the bank of the river.

At the first pile, a leg stretched free of the heap, eliciting a reflexive, involuntary groan as the man regained consciousness. He didn't know where he was, but he felt dead. He fought to shake the stupor from his brain. He vaguely remembered a musket ball knocking him down. Did he get back up? Yes, but then he was hit again, and maybe a third time. What am I doing here, he thought, and why am I under all this debris? And what is that awful smell?

The man tried to move. Something heavy held him down. He saw to his horror that he lay beneath a corpse. He struggled to roll from under and nearly passed out again from the pain. Lying motionless and reopening his eyes, he realized that most of the mound consisted of dead bodies. He had been one of them and still felt the part. Why are we piled up so, he wondered. What is this all over me?

It was blood, some of it his, some not. It soaked his clothes and caked his skin. He painfully swiped across his face. The slipperiness there was more blood. He tried to ignore it and the nausea it provoked.

The man's eyes cleared somewhat and he looked around. A distance away, he couldn't tell how far, he saw men tending a large fire. Then he realized he lay only yards from the river. Not yet understanding what to do, he lurched when he heard a musket shot. It wasn't close, but it jarred him to reality. I must get into the water, he reasoned.

He looked again at the fire. The men walked toward him. One carried a torch; all of them carried muskets. Defying his pain, he rolled as hard as he could to the lip of the bank and eased over the edge, careful not to make a splash. The water was cold but it soothed his wounds, wounds he knew he had but still hadn't located. He eased through the water along the bank, searching for a safe haven. He found it a few feet away as he backed into a mud bank, a refuge for turtles. He didn't know if the splash he heard was caused by him or the creatures.

"Damn turtles!" cursed one of the men as they circled the heap, piling the brush a little tighter. "Have to catch one of the bastards and boil him for breakfast."

"Be the best meal we've had in weeks," said another. "Put the torch to it. Let's finish this wretched job. I'm tired of looking at and handling these damn dead savages."

"Glad they're dead, though," said a third man. "I like 'em a lot better that way."

The fire caught immediately. It needed no coaxing. The men placed logs across the top and checked around the edges to assure that every part of the heap would be burned. They watched it another minute and then walked to the next pile.

Under the lip of the river bank, the bright glare of the blaze partially lit the face of Chief Menawa, the supreme chief of the Red Stick forces at Cholocco Litabixi. Fortunately for him, the soldiers never looked his way before they moved on.

In the center of the battlefield, as the body cleanup concluded and treatment of the wounded progressed well, General Jackson and his staff made plans.

"We'll camp here overnight," Jackson decided. "Have the men bivouac where they are. Assign the Cherokees to guard the women and children prisoners and prepare to escort them away tomorrow. Collect all usable arms and secure the artillery pieces. Destroy all else; leave nothing in the field that can be turned to an advantage. Post double sentries at all key points. At first light we canvass the field one more time, set torches to the breastworks and the Indian village, and move out toward Fort Williams."

Jackson brightened. "Gentlemen, congratulations. We have won a glorious victory and thereby broken the power of a dangerous enemy. All of America will forever be proud of us."

Menawa dared not move for several hours. When a large sapling floating by nudged him awake, he reckoned by the overhead stars that it was the middle of the night. He grabbed a limb, ducked underwater, and resurfaced in the midst of the sapling's branches. He pushed as cautiously as he could for midstream to catch the current which he knew quickened as the river approached the island, rounded it, and turned to the west to continue downstream.

Two hours later, Menawa, maneuvering painfully and slowly, had cleared the island undetected, though he had spotted a dozen sentries on the near shore as he floated by. Shortly the sun would rise. He must find a safe hideaway, for the soldiers would be scouring the river. He would surely be spotted in daylight. Too, his wounds needed attention and he must rest.

A mile ahead, the river widened into an expansive shoal just below the mouth of Emuckfau Creek. He remembered a small cave, hardly more than a vine-covered indentation, just above the water line a few yards into the creek. He would rest there through the day. He thought he could barely make it by dawn.

36

Cholocco Litabixi, the Horseshoe, March 28, 1814

Streams of soldiers and wagons had marched from the field of the battle for the Horseshoe since shortly after daybreak. Patrols still scanned the peninsula for bodies and weapons that had been missed in the darkness of night. New fires burned to consume newly discovered corpses, and to destroy the tents and huts of Tohopeka. Billows of fresh smoke covered the southern half of the peninsula. The last of the wagons and soldiers of the cleanup details paraded through the breaches in the log barricade.

"Final body count, Billy?" asked General Jackson, seated on his horse and looking back on the scene.

Colonel Billy Carroll studied his notes. "Five hundred fifty-seven, sir. With the estimated two fifty to three hundred not recovered from the river, I'd easily say we got over eight hundred of 'em, probably more than nine hundred."

"How many you think escaped?"

"Surely, less than two hundred. That would bring it to the thousand we thought they had going in. I think it coulda been less than a hundred that got away, possibly."

"I want those caught, too. They'll be back on us if we don't get them. And they'll stir up trouble amongst others."

The hospital wagons crammed with wounded had been sent out first, with two companies of cavalry to accompany them and to secure the trail. Also the Red Stick women and children prisoners, guarded by half the Cherokees led by Colonel Morgan, were already on the road. The infantry regiments had been filing out for the past hour, and finally the remainder of Coffee's cavalry formed up ready to serve as the rear guard.

"All out?" queried Jackson. "Then torch the barricade."

Jackson, Carroll, Coffee, and the cavalry rear guard watched the massive log wall burn for a half hour, making certain that it was completely involved so that no remnant of the mighty Red Stick fortress would survive.

On the road back to Fort Williams, at the first pause to rest the horses, Colonel Carroll visited the hospital wagons to inquire of the wounded.

"We lost one already, sir," replied an orderly, "shortly after we left the field. Several others can't possibly survive the march. Wish we could do more for them."

Carroll pulled back the flap at the stern of one of the wagons. Several gravely wounded men, some unconscious, the others suffering, lay on pallets. Amidst moans of compatriots, one soldier near the front screamed in pain. Carroll clenched his teeth as he turned his attention to the casualty nearest him. He tenderly lifted one side of the front of the man's open jacket. The semiconscious soldier writhed in silent misery, but he tightly clutched one hand to the other side of his jacket.

The ugly wound to the soldier's abdomen repulsed Carroll. He turned his head away and spoke quietly to the orderly.

"This one looks bad."

"He is, sir. Some damn Indian chopped up his belly with an ax. Nothing we can do. I don't know how he has lived this long."

"He can't be more than nineteen or twenty. Who is he?"

"Name's Ottis, sir. Virgil Tom Ottis from near Nashville."

Carroll looked again at the fated man. "What is he holding?"

"Seems to be a bundle of papers, sir. We tried to retrieve them, but he won't let go."

Colonel Carroll started to the next wagon. "Make the poor soul as comfortable as you can. All these poor souls."

"Yes, sir."

The column pushed on but paused again at midday for a meal of field rations, and to rest and water the horses and mules. Jackson summoned Coffee and the militia infantry commanders. He had not forgotten the escaped Red Sticks.

"Form squads of mounted rangers and fan them out up and down the river, and to any other possible route of escape," he ordered. "We need to account for as many of the rotten savages as we can now, or we shall surely meet them again. They must not join other Creeks to the south on the lower Tallapoosa and Coosa."

The march continued until evening. The army made camp more than halfway back to Fort Williams. Even having to be careful with the hospital wagons, the going was much easier than the trek east had been because of already having a clear trail.

General Jackson sat writing a second report to Governor Blount in Nashville. He had written the first installment late last night after he was satisfied that the battlefield had been secured. He had included a map of the field of combat, which he titled "Battle of Tehopiska," speculating as best he could on the spelling of the Red Sticks' garrison village, since neither he nor anyone else had anything but the spoken sound as guidance.

He had described in detail the river, the landscape, the Creek opposition, and the battle itself. He now amended parts of that report and related additional observations. He made it a point to be particularly eloquent in praising the courage of his troops.

"John," Jackson addressed General Coffee at a staff briefing, "you enjoyed fine perspective on the events of the day from your position. I would like for you to submit a detailed account for Governor Blount. Your statements, I perceive, will be most valuable. And gentlemen," he added, turning to the other officers, "you, too, are invited to offer written accounts. A complete record of this event is most desirable. But, please gentlemen, I should like to read each report before it is forwarded to Nashville or to authorities in Knoxville."

Late on the afternoon of the twenty-ninth, the first of the army arrived in Fort Williams. The ferry once again sprang into fulltime operation, but now not so urgent or so hectic.

The hospital caravan had fallen woefully behind, but when they did arrive they were ushered ahead onto the ferry without delay. Four gravely wounded soldiers had died on the journey and had been buried along the trail in simple but honorable ceremonies. Others would succumb to their injuries, surgeons were certain, some to the severity of their wounds but too many to infection and inadequate medical supplies. Screams and groans of agony constantly tormented those attending the wagons.

That evening, General Jackson shared a cup of rum with his staff and command officers. He toasted the victory but voiced apprehension and shared his next strategem.

"Gentlemen, this war, I fear, is not over, though we have won the greatest victory I can imagine. We must remain diligent and take full advantage of our new position of strength."

"Our congratulations and admiration, General," hailed one of the militia generals. "What is our next adventure?"

"I think that we must march south along the Coosa without unwarranted delay. We must establish absolute control of the

Tallapoosa and the Coosa in preparation to attacking the Red Stick strongholds along the Alabama River."

"Forgive me, General," interjected one of the militia brigadiers, "but I must confess that I am somewhat puzzled. Upon our overwhelming success at the Horseshoe, I fully expected you to order the march to continue down the course of the Tallapoosa. Would that not have been the logical tactic?"

"Perhaps, General." Jackson pondered carefully. "We would have enjoyed the advantage of the enemy's disarray. They could not have possibly regrouped had we pursued in force. However, our supply lines would have been gravely stretched and our soldiers weary, and had we met another force comparable to the one at Tohopeka, we may not have had the means to prevail. A most valuable military tactic to remember, my good man, is not to forfeit a well-earned advantage in numbers. And we know there are large and formidable Creek villages along the southern runs of the Tallapoosa.

"Instead of conquering those villages by force," Jackson continued, "I propose to isolate them. The best way to do that is to win a strong position at the confluence of the rivers. Gain that and we will have little worry from the tribes of the lower Tallapoosa. In traveling down the Coosa we should meet far less resistance than we would have on the Tallapoosa. Once at the junction, we should have most of the remaining Creek hostiles trapped between us and General Claiborne's Mississippi militia. He campaigns in the south of the Alabama country.

"I trust my logic is agreeable to your own very fine instincts, gentlemen. What say you?"

"When do we leave, General?"

Jackson surveyed his officers' expressions. Each one nodded approval. He returned the gesture before answering the last question. "We'll take a few days to regroup and repair. We will send scout teams down the Coosa tomorrow. Prepare to march in less than a week. Our ranger squads in pursuit of the stragglers from the Horseshoe should have returned by then."

General Jackson lifted his rum mug in another toast. "Continued good health. And continued good hunting for us all."

As Billy Carroll stood at the doorway observing and listening to his superiors, he was interrupted.

"Colonel Carroll, sir?"

He turned to face a militia soldier. "Yes?"

"I beg your pardon, Colonel Carroll. Sir, I'm Corporal Poole, the hospital orderly you talked with on the trail. You were reviewing the wounded?"

"Yes, corporal, I remember. What can I do for you?"

Poole held out a blood soaked leather oilskin. "I think you should have this, sir."

"What is it?" asked Carroll as he fingered the soggy packet. He turned back the cover to expose a sheaf of neatly folded pages.

"It's the bundle Private Ottis was protecting under his jacket. The young soldier with the belly wound?"

"Oh, yes. A bloody mess he was. Poor man."

"He died, sir. He lived much longer than he should have with that wound. I've never seen a man fight so hard to live."

"I'm dreadfully sorry, corporal. I'm sure he was a fine young man."

"Yes, sir."

"And these papers?"

"They appear to be letters, sir. A number of them. Ottis woke up moments before he died and pushed the bundle to me. He said, 'For Elsa,' then he closed his eyes and he was gone."

"Elsa?"

"Must be his wife, sir. Or sweetheart. He hailed from near Nashville. I thought you might see that the letters are delivered to her."

"That's the least we can do for a brave soldier. Thank you, corporal. You are a kind man."

37

Because Anna had awakened restless, Soosquana walked with her in the fresh air as the sun rose. A light breeze blew under a cloudless sky, promising a gorgeous spring day. No one else had yet stirred.

"Now, now, little one," she cooed in Muskogean as she walked along the bluff and nestled Anna closely in her arms, "you usually are not so crotchety. What bothers my pretty little . . . ?"

Something amiss caught her eye and stopped her short as she scanned the river. She looked closer at the shoals and, yes, an overturned dugout log canoe straddled a large rock near the bottom of the trace. That wasn't all. A man lay wedged between two other rocks five yards above the canoe.

Soosquana ran to the cabin. "Saul!" Saul opened the door, startled, as she reached the porch. He was already dressed. "Saul, come quick! A man, a warrior, I think. He is hurt. Or maybe dead."

"Where?"

"At the river. On the rocks. Quickly!"

Saul reached back inside the door for his musket and ran for Cal's cabin. Cal and Adelin had heard Soosquana's alarm and awaited him on their porch, muskets in hand. They ran to the edge of the bluff together. Soosquana, holding Anna, hung back near the cabins.

Saul and Cal appraised the scene with one look.

"Adelin, cover us from up here!" ordered Saul. "Cal and I need to go down there. Come on, Cal!"

They ran for the path and scrambled down it, cautious that no one else lurked about. Adelin scanned in all directions from the bluff with the same concern. Saul and Cal leaped across the rocks, stepping in the water and fighting against its rapid rush where there was no foothold. They reached the man and braced themselves in the waist deep current, one on either side.

The man was indeed a Red Stick, still sporting remnants of bright red body designs that signaled war or celebrated the hunt. Blood caked in every crevice of his body that had not been cleansed by the agitation of the river. He was unconscious.

"Is he alive?" Adelin shouted from atop the bluff.

"Yeah. Barely," Saul answered. Adelin turned and relayed something to Soosquana, unintelligible to the men working frantically to examine the Indian.

"He's in bad shape," said Cal.

"Yeah. We gotta get him up the hill, but let's be careful moving him."

It took a full twenty minutes to work the man from the river and gently carry him up the trail. Adelin met them halfway to help. Gaining the top, they laid him down carefully to get a better reading on his wounds and condition.

"Good god!" exclaimed Saul. "He's been shot all over his body! He's got no call being alive."

"Knife wounds, too," observed Cal. "Or, more likely, bayonets."

"Move him to our cabin," ordered Soosquana, walking up and observing the situation. "We can best fix him up there."

The man appeared to be well into his forties, much older than the typical Red Stick warrior. The total count of his wounds was seven from gunshot, a few cuts, and dozens of gashes and scrapes from river rocks. Miraculously, none of the musket balls had apparently touched a vital organ, but he had lost much blood. He was terribly weak and his lips were swollen and parched.

"He looks as if he hasn't eaten," observed Adelin.

"Maybe not for days," Soosquana agreed. "The river and the sun have not been kind to him. We will try to get some soup in him."

While Saul and Adelin rubbed poultice into the man's wounds, Soosquana prepared a pot of thin soup and some herb tea.

"Cal," suggested Saul, "get back out there and keep a sharp eye. We need to know if there are any more of these fellows, or if there is someone chasing him."

"He doesn't seem to be bleeding anywhere now," said Adelin, "but we're going to need more bandages than we have. I'll see if I can find something to make them from."

In a short while, reacting to the salve, the warm blankets, and the cool soaks Adelin applied to his forehead, the man groaned and began moving his arms and legs.

"You better come around here, Soos," summoned Saul, as the man squirmed more vigorously and began to shake his head and blink his eyes. He groaned loudly as he felt pain. "You need to be the first one he sees."

The man became still and squeezed his eyes tightly. He grimaced and moaned again. He opened his eyes slowly and struggled to focus on the person above him. He blinked hard. He made an effort to sit up, but the pain and the person he could vaguely see forced him again to his back.

Soosquana spoke soothingly to him in Muskogean. He looked confused as he stared at her incredulously, still trying to blink the fog from his vision. She continued to talk to him and he seemed to calm slightly.

Soosquana turned to the others. "Let's try a little water first."

Startled, as the man saw the two white people for the first time, he tried to sit up, fear and surprise on his face. Soosquana wheeled, grabbed him, and coaxed him to lie back on the bed. She began to explain to him rapidly; he kept his eyes on Saul and Adelin as she talked. He clearly didn't trust them. Soosquana sensed that the man not knowing where he was made his situation even more fearsome.

Finally, Soosquana convinced him to relax again. He still eyed the strange whites. She took a dipper of water and placed it to his lips. He took a tentative sip, choked, coughed it up, then tried another sip. The second one went down. His throat thus cleared, he felt his thirst and attempted to gulp from the dipper. Soosquana prevented it.

"Not so fast; take it easy," Saul and Adelin knew she said in Muskogean. She withdrew the gourd dipper and turned to them and said in English, "Let's try some of the tea next."

Five minutes later, after a few difficult sips of warm herb tea, Soosquana decreed that her patient might be ready for soup. After three spoonfuls, he fell sound asleep while attempting the fourth.

"That helped," Soosquana sighed. "A lot. He'll sleep for a while now, and will be stronger when he awakes." She glanced at the cradle where Anna lay peacefully asleep herself. Apparently the excitement had cured her restlessness.

"What did he say?" asked Saul. "Where did he get those wounds?"

"I don't know. I didn't ask him. It was all I could do to calm him down and get him to eat something."

"Did he tell you his name?"

"No. I did not ask him that, either. We will learn more when he wakes up. Maybe he'll trust us better then."

"You girls stay with him. I'll go out and see what Cal has found."

"Did he wake up?" Cal asked as Saul approached him at the edge of the bluff.

"Yeah. He even looks like he might survive. Don't know how, though, with all that."

"Who is he?" Cal asked his first of the same questions Saul had asked of Soosquana. Saul relayed the same answers.

"He surely has been in some kind of big fight," Saul spoke the obvious. "I hope it was with other Creeks and not with soldiers."

"I'm afraid it might have been soldiers." Cal stated what Saul didn't want to say. "All his big wounds were from musket shot; none from arrows. Also the possible bayonet wounds."

"Yeah, I know. Have you seen anything?" The men turned their attention back to the river.

"No, nothing. Look." Cal pointed at the overturned canoe. "He had to have floated on that thing down the river and then ridden it over the fall. If he wasn't already unconscious, he was too weak to control it and knocked himself out on the rocks."

"I expect he was at least half out already." Saul digressed. "How do you control those clumsy boats, anyway?"

"How do they even stay afloat? They weigh about a half ton."

"Maybe we ought to get rid of the thing in case someone might be hunting this fellow. We don't want them stopping here."

Saul and Cal again scurried down the path and made their way to the log canoe. They freed it and ushered it to deep water below the shoals. They filled it with head-size boulders until it sank, then quickly reclimbed the bluff.

"He just woke up," Adelin whispered as the men came through the door. Soosquana was feeding the warrior more soup. He pushed aside her spoon and raised his head in full alert. He stared at Saul and Cal. "Soos explained who we are but I don't think he trusts us yet. I don't think he trusts her, but she's working on him."

Soosquana succeeded in directing the man's attention back to the soup. He finished the bowl and Soosquana offered him water.

He drank it down and asked for more. She then began to question him again, patiently and slowly.

"He was in a big battle with the white soldiers," Soosquana relayed to the others. "Thousands of soldiers."

"Good god!" exclaimed Saul.

The man kept talking, but in a slow murmur. Soosquana gasped. "At Cholocco Litabixi. Killed hundreds of Muskogis. Three days ago, he thinks," she continued in a choking voice, "but he isn't sure. He found the canoe and floated on the river after he got away, but he thinks he was unconscious much of the time. He didn't know how bad he was hurt or how many times he had been shot until I told him."

Soosquana desperately wished to ask the man if he knew anything of her brothers or of Pokkataw, but she resisted. She knew not to frighten him or surprise him further, and she personally feared his answer.

"Ask him his name," suggested Cal.

Soosquana and the patient had a short discussion. "He won't say," she said.

"Ask him about Pokkataw and Tolokika and Ettepti-loka," suggested Adelin. "He might know something of them, and even if he doesn't, asking about them might cause him to trust us more."

"All right. I will try." Soosquana sighed and took a heavy breath, trying to dispel the fear in her voice and in her heart. She faced the man squarely and began talking in an easy tone, pointing to herself and then to the others. She explained further and then fell silent and waited for the man to reply. He looked her in the eye and slowly began. After a few seconds, Soosquana reacted with shock and hung her head. When the man finished, she turned and looked at the three waiting anxiously. A tear lapped over from the pool in her eyes and ran down her cheek.

"He says that he saw Pokkataw fall. He died bravely. He knows my brothers but knows nothing of their fate. But he says that very few warriors escaped. He says that only by the Spirit of the Maker of Breath was he allowed to flee." She choked and sobbed.

Adelin joined Soosquana's sobs with her own. Saul and Cal tried hard to stifle their own grief.

Soosquana turned back to the man, but he had fallen asleep again. She cried over him as she tucked the blankets snuggly around him.

"I'll take the watch on the bluff," said Saul, hurrying out the door.

"I'll join you," stammered Cal.

Saul stumbled to a stop just off the porch with his face buried in one hand. "Damn! Damn, damn, damn!" he almost screamed. Cal cursed with him.

The two brothers walked to the bluff's edge without further comment. They kneeled and resumed their vigil over the river, each lost in his own thoughts.

The warrior slept through the afternoon, the pain and tension finally giving over to deep sleep. Soosquana, with a heavy burden, watched him closely while she tended to Anna and did routine household chores. Adelin looked in on her often, offering to help, but most of the day she rotated with Saul and Cal in monitoring the river. They also agreed that it was a good idea to be alert to the road from the woods and the trail from the ford.

An hour before sundown, Saul knelt at the top of the bluff, his vigilance unwavering. Sadness and grief had dominated his emotions all afternoon. Anger welled strong and continued to grow.

Something moved on the trail from the north on the opposite bank of the river. Moved slowly. At first, Saul only saw the wavering of the fresh growth of the spring foliage. Could be an animal. Then he caught a flash of skin. He saw it again, more this time. It was a man, an Indian, and he crawled on the trail. Saul studied him for minutes. Several times the man attempted to stand with a staff he carried but fell back each time, then crawled several more yards before trying again to regain his feet.

Saul hustled away from the lip of the bluff several yards. "Cal!" he urged in a loud whisper. Cal looked up and Saul gestured to him. They carefully returned to the observation spot so as not to be seen by the man across the way.

"What do you think?" asked Saul.

"He's hurt. Bad."

"He had to come from the Horseshoe. Notice how he's painted."

"Yeah. Is he armed?"

"I don't think so. Only with that cudgel."

"Well, hell, let's go get him," resolved Cal. "Might as well fix him up, too. He's gonna kill himself like that."

"Wait. We better get Soos. Let her talk to him first. Adelin can tend the cabin."

Soosquana ran to the bluff and studied the man for long seconds. Then she stood up in full view and yelled. Alarmed, the man scrambled for cover, hiding in a thicket behind a big tree. Soosquana continued to yell, telling him who she was and that she wanted to help.

"He doesn't know what to do," Soosquana told Saul and Cal in English.

"Tell 'em we're coming over to help him," Saul said. "Be sure to warn him that we are whites but are friends."

Soosquana resumed calling over to the man, trying to reassure him. He still hid behind the tree, and had said nothing.

"Keep talking to him," Saul instructed as he and Cal crept toward the path. "Don't stop talking to him, Soos."

The Indian huddled in a tight ball behind the tree, attempting to blend with the brush. He brandished his staff at Saul and Cal as they approached. Saul began talking to him in an easy voice, mixing in as many Muskogean phrases as he could conjure up. After a tense ten minutes, with Soosquana continuing to encourage him, the warrior permitted them to pick him up and support him on either side. His right ankle hung at several grotesque angles, swollen to twice normal size and apparently shattered by a musket ball. He had many bruises and minor cuts, but no other serious wounds, it seemed.

Thirty minutes later, the three struggled to the top of the path as darkness began to set in. Soosquana's urgings and the gentle handling of the two white strangers had by then gained a measure of his confidence.

"Take him to the cabin," ordered Soosquana. "We'll treat him with the other one."

Saul and Cal walked the warrior to the cabin. Adelin met them at the door, her appearance shocking the man further. Soosquana directed that they seat him in a chair next to the bed of the first patient, who still slept. The man started to sit, but then stood again, startled, fighting a stab of pain. In the dim light, he leaned over to get a better view of the sleeping man. He pointed, began babbling, became very excited and animated.

"Do you know him?" asked Soosquana in Muskogean.

He looked at her with a wild-eyed expression. "Yes!" he replied. "He is the warrior chief of the Muskogis. The leader of the Muskogi forces at Cholocco Litabixi. He is Menawa!"

38

The man's name was Hromarii. Having experienced the kindness and concern of the Murphs, and now seeing how they had cared for the great chief, Menawa, he soon opened up to Soosquana. She found that he was from the village of Ipisoga, not far downriver on the large creek flowing from the east. He was twenty-two years old.

"He says he was with a group of warriors counterattacking across the river to some island that the soldiers held," Soosquana relayed as Hromarii told his story. His lower leg soaked in a kettle filled with a strong solution of rock salt and herbs dissolved in warm water. He hungrily devoured two bowls of soup with strong black coffee. "He was shot in the leg just above the ankle and fell into the river where the current was the strongest. It took him right around the island and he was able to swim with the current. He swam for two or three hours until he came to the shoals at Emuckfau Creek."

"Did he see what happened to Pokkataw, Ettepti-lopa, and Tolotika?" asked Saul.

"He didn't," said Soosquana sadly. "I already asked him. His wound happened early in the fight."

"Why didn't he get help at Oakfuski or one of the other villages on the way down the river?"

She turned to ask him. "He says he was trying to get home to Ipisoga. Also, all the villages were on this side and he couldn't swim across after the leg got so bad." Hromarii resumed without further prompting. Soosquana tried to translate as fast as he talked. "He got out of the water at the rapids below Emuckfau Creek and was able to walk, using the stick that he found and broke down to size. He would walk a while and rest a while until last night. The leg got so infected he couldn't touch it to the ground. He was so weak he could hardly stand. He's been crawling along the trail all day today."

The other three grimaced at the warrior's ordeal.

"Shouldn't we let the poor man sleep?" reasoned Adelin. "We can't tell much about his leg until the swelling goes down."

"Yes. True," agreed Saul. "Adelin, take Soos and Anna and all of you sleep at your cabin tonight. Cal and I will sleep here."

They made Hromarii comfortable in the chair, where he quickly fell hard asleep. Menawa's condition had not changed and it was certain that he would sleep until morning and maybe longer. When they were assured that everything was well, Soosquana and Adelin took the baby and retired to the other cabin. Saul and Cal camped on the porch but they slept little. One or the other checked the patients at least each hour, and both restlessly walked the perimeter of the compound in irregular intervals until the sun appeared.

"Cal," revealed Saul at daybreak, "I thought about this all night." He looked tired, but even more worried. "If either soldiers or Red Sticks come, doesn't matter which, we're in trouble."

"Yeah, I was thinking the same thing. What do we do?"

Soosquana walked across from the other cabin. "How are the men?"

"They seem all right. Still asleep last time we checked."

"I will look at them and feed them more soup when they wake up. Adelin is tending to Anna."

While the four Murphs ate breakfast and discussed their predicament in muted voices, Hromarii awakened. Soosquana talked with him and examined his leg while Adelin prepared another kettle of soak solution. The swelling had diminished considerably but nothing could yet be determined about broken bones. He ate three more helpings of soup and drank more strong coffee, very hot.

Saul tried to plan ahead. "Soos, if anybody comes — anybody! — check the two men and make sure they stay quiet no matter what." Soosquana nodded. "Then show yourself with the rest of us so whoever it is won't think we're hiding something."

"You think we oughta challenge them?" asked Cal.

"'Cording to who it is. We'll just have to act on the situation. If somebody does come, Cal, you and Adelin cover me and I'll try to talk 'em off. All right?" Saul had an important afterthought. "Oh! Everybody, we can't let on at all that we know anything already about the fighting."

Each agreed and tried to see to daily chores, while watching every possible moment in every direction.

Before noon Menawa awakened, much stronger. Soosquana and Hromarii talked with him as Soosquana tried to get soup and tea into him. She changed his bandages and applied fresh poultice. He became upset when he realized his identity had been revealed, but abated his anger when he saw it made little difference to his hosts.

Nothing stirred until midafternoon.

"Saul!" Cal called no louder than necessary from the end of his porch, from where he could see the head of the road. Saul came running, Adelin right after him, both with muskets ready.

At the edge of the woods, a hundred yards away, stood a large group of horsemen. They weren't advancing but seemed to scan carefully the entire scene.

"Adelin, get Soos. Tell 'er to hurry over after she quiets the men." She returned in less than a minute. Short of another minute, Soosquana arrived with Anna in her arms.

The three armed Murphs walked around the corner of the porch and fifteen yards up the road. Soosquana stepped into full view around the porch but stopped at the corner.

"Who are you?" Saul called.

No answer. The horsemen started their mounts forward, very slowly, still looking to all sides. There appeared to be about twenty of them.

"Stop there, friend!" yelled Saul. They did. The leader turned and said something to the group. Then he and one other advanced again, each with a hand controlling the reins and the other gripping a musket near its trigger with the butt of the stock braced against his thigh. Both muskets were uncocked and the muzzles pointed upward. There was something familiar about the leader. The other looked to be a Cherokee Indian.

"It's that militia sergeant that was here last fall," spat Cal as he recognized him.

"Damn!" cursed Saul. He finalized his plan, speaking softly. "You two hide yourself on either side, cock your muskets and point them at that son of a bitch's head. And don't take your aim off him!"

Adelin jumped behind a wood pile on the left side of the road and Cal set up behind a large gum tree to the right. Saul searched his memory for the sergeant's name.

"That's far enough, sergeant," Saul ordered from the middle of the track. The two horsemen stopped five yards away.

"Well, looka here!" mocked the sergeant, spitting a stream of tobacco, as filthy as the Murphs remembered from before. He wiped his mouth with his sleeve. "It's good to see you squatter folks again."

Saul remembered the man's name. "It's Sergeant Barnes, ain't it? We told you not to come back here."

"Yep. Sergeant Mordecai Barnes, East Tennessee Militia, in

service to General Andrew Jackson. And I go where I please, squatter."

"I thought you hated General Jackson, sergeant. He wasn't tough enough for you, as I remember."

"Well, maybe he changed. Turns out he wanted to kill Indians more than them other generals. Them cowards went home. Not me." Saul didn't respond. He could tell that Barnes had noticed the two muskets trained on him but pretended to ignore them. Barnes continued. "I'm out hunting filthy, god damn Indians. You seen any filthy, god damn Indians around here, squatter? 'Cept for that squaw back there?" He nodded toward Soosquana.

Saul ignored the insult. "Why don't you ride on outta here, sergeant? You ain't welcome."

"Well, look at that," chided Barnes. "You done got that greasy little Indian baby, ain't you? Bet he stinks like all them other filthy, murdering Creeks, don't he?"

"Sergeant, you can't rile us with your ignorant talk." Saul's voice remained calm. "We would like you to leave. You have no business with us."

Barnes spat again. This time he let the juice run through his whiskers without wiping. He sneered. "Oh, but we do, squatter. I told you we was looking for Indians. We killed off a big mess of 'em up the river a piece, but some of 'em got away."

"You son of a bitch! Why don't you folks go home and leave these people in peace? They didn't attack you, did they?"

"Don't matter. They're in our way. We figure we got a right to defend ourselves and our country. Now, you god damn Indian lover, you hiding any of them cowardly Red Sticks that run away from us the other day?"

Saul tensed. "No! We ain't seen nobody, 'cept you guys, in a long time."

Sergeant Barnes looked at the Cherokee and sneered again. "Well, I think I'll just have a look around for myself."

"I don't think so, sergeant, unless you wanta get shot." Saul raised his musket to port arms, but didn't cock it. "You've surely noticed two muskets aimed right at your sorry nose. And I promise you, both of these good people are expert shots."

Sergeant Barnes hesitated. He looked first at Cal, then at Adelin. He looked back at Saul, standing square in the road with feet apart and staring him down, before turning to the Cherokee. He said something to him and the Indian grunted. Barnes reached over and accepted the man's reins and musket from him. The Cherokee dismounted and walked toward the cabin, ignoring Saul and meaning to walk past him. Saul stepped in front of him.

The Cherokee scowled, retreated one step, and drew back the thick, short leather whip in his right hand. Before he could unleash the stroke toward Saul, Saul's musket butt hit him solid in the face, knocking him backward off his feet. The Indian skidded on his back in the dust, blood spurting from his nose. Sergeant Barnes started to raise his musket, then realized the two weapons aimed at him had not wavered. The ranger squad back up the road made a tentative move toward their leader.

"Sergeant, keep your men away!" barked Saul. He cocked his musket and pointed it at Barnes. "If they approach, you die! Now, get this one back on his horse and get back down that road." Barnes, visibly shaken, flipped his head at the Cherokee to gesture him to remount. "And this time, don't come back! Not ever again, or we might shoot you on sight."

Barnes and the Cherokee reined their horses around and casually trotted them back to their squad. Glancing behind him, Barnes saw that all three weapons were still targeted at his head.

The group of horsemen all pulled around to ride back into the woods. Saul relaxed. Cal and Adelin stepped from their shelters. They watched the riders swallowed up into the trees, one by one.

Suddenly, an angry tirade burst from the militia squad.

Sergeant Barnes had reined around and yelled another string of curses. He steadied his horse and quickly raised his musket. The pan flashed and the muzzle spat flame and smoke in a loud report.

"What the hell?" exclaimed Saul. "Damn fool!" he shouted.

Adelin screamed. Turning around, Saul and Cal saw Soosquana sprawled on her back and Anna on the ground two yards behind her. Soosquana writhed in shock and pain, obviously hurt bad.

Saul ran to Soosquana, and Adelin to Anna, who was spattered with blood. Cal turned and fired a futile shot after the last militiaman fleeing at a gallop into the woods. He then ran to help Saul with Soosquana.

Adelin picked up Anna and hugged her. She frantically examined the crying baby to determine if she had been injured by the fall or nicked by the shot. She hadn't. The blood was Soosquana's.

Soosquana had taken the musket ball in the throat. Blood gushed in a stream from the large, ugly wound. She gurgled, looked at Saul, tried to speak, gurgled again, and collapsed.

Saul shook her as Cal tried desperately to stem the bleeding.

"Soos!" screamed Saul. "Soos! Damnit! Soos, Soos!"

"No use, Saul," said Cal, conceding defeat. "No use. She's dead."

"Oh, my god!" wailed Saul, tightly hugging the lifeless body.

Adelin, seated on the ground where she had retrieved Anna, hugged the child to her and cried. Cal stood up and walked to the nearest tree and buried his head in his arms against it.

The galloping hoofbeats through the woods had faded completely. The only sounds now heard were the constant rush of the shoals on the Tallapoosa River and the grief of a pioneering family.

39

The Tallapoosa River, March, 1815

Spring rains have filled the Tallapoosa River. Swollen waters spill in torrents over the shoals, covering most of the rocks and rushing downriver past sandbars and rapids and falls to join with other streams in a mighty network coursing to the Gulf of Mexico. Adjacent to the shoals are a worn path paralleling the river on one side and a high bluff on the other. A tall ancient oak tree peeks over the lip of the bluff.

Beneath the oak is a modest stone, marking a subtle mound with a new stand of spring clover and good grass. The mound unmistakably is a grave.

Beyond the tree rest the charred foundations of two burned cabins. A bridge that once crossed a small stream running between the destroyed cabins has also been burned. Too, a livestock shelter and a smokehouse behind the cabins. An annoyed mockingbird screeches from a low limb of the big oak. A pair of bluebirds flit about on the stone chimney of one of the cabin hulks.

New brush in every opening threatens to return the clearing to the wilderness. Shoots of pine, hickory, oak, poplar, and other tree varieties peek from hideaways among the weeds where the seeds fell at random the previous autumn. Prickly vines twist among wild flowers. Greenery and freshness abound. Nature has again painted the Tallapoosa banks and bluffs with beauty and splendor.

A horseman emerges from the woods on the weed covered road to the ruined compound. Two more riders follow, leading a mule pulling a heavily laden cart. Behind the cart walk a tethered milk cow and a goat.

The riders are two men and a redhaired woman with a small child riding on the saddle before her. They stop in the front yard of the first cabin site, dismount, look briefly and sadly at the destroyed buildings, then turn and walk to the grave.

* * *

After allowing Menawa and Hromarii another day of recovery, Saul and Cal gave them one of the Murph canoes, helped them into it, and sent them on their way to Ipisoga. All agreed that the two Creek warriors should be safer there than with the Murphs.

Anticipating further turmoil and danger in the wake of the Horseshoe battle, the Murphs had decided to flee to the Holman farm. Once there they were reluctant to return until they felt assured of their safety.

In early summer Saul and Cal left Adelin and Anna with the Holmans and journeyed to Huntsville. There they registered charges against Sergeant Barnes and his squad, though they knew the incident would never be investigated. They sought news from the region and learned that General Jackson had accepted the surrender of Chief Red Eagle, one of the principal Red Stick leaders, on behalf of most of the Upper Muskogi Nation. Red Eagle, known by his English name as William Weatherford, had marched voluntarily into Jackson's camp at the confluence of the Tallapoosa and Coosa rivers and offered himself and his warriors in exchange for mercy and aid for his starving followers. Red Eagle conceded the futility of the Red Stick cause and the unbearable stress to his Muskogi people. He petitioned Jackson for an end to the fighting.

Saul and Cal received the news with conflicting emotions. They were glad that the fighting was over; too many lives had already been lost. But they knew Jackson's victory meant an upheaval for the Muskogi community that they had grown to respect. Wonderful friends had been killed at the Horseshoe. They feared that the attitudes of those Indian friends left might forever be poisoned by bitterness.

After a week in Huntsville, the brothers returned to the Holman farm. Since it was too late to plant crops on the Tallapoosa, and also because some uncertainty remained, they decided to stay with the Holmans until the next spring.

Baby Anna did not lack for care and attention. Mrs. Holman and Bess Marie could not do enough for her. Daniel Holman regarded her as a granddaughter. Anna passed a very happy first year, oblivious to the fate of her mother.

With the coming of the spring of 1815, the Murphs loaded the cart to its limit and eagerly headed back to the Tallapoosa. They did not know what awaited them, but they knew that was where they belonged.

• • •

The Murphs linger a long time over the grave, talking softly. Finally, they drift to the edge of the bluff and survey the river below.

The child reaches down and picks up a pebble. With the awkwardness of her fourteen months she flings it toward the river. The pebble hits halfway down the slope of the bluff, bounces onto the gravel of the bank, and trickles into the water. The little girl squeals with delight at her achievement.

Water flows from the north and expends energy as it spills onto and around the treacherous rocks. A broken tree limb floats to the head of the shoals and drops through churning ripples and eddies. It escapes from each crag lurking to trap it and slides into flat water at the foot of the shoals to continue its journey down the busy but tranquil stream.

"This is still a wonderful place," observes Adelin quietly.

"Yes," agrees Cal, "as beautiful as ever. And it is home."

"Always will be," says Saul. He reaches down, picks up his daughter, and hugs her. "Let's get to work."

Epilogue

The Tallapoosa River, 1815 and beyond

The Murphs rebuilt their cabins and other structures, bigger and stronger than ever. Within a year, another family had settled a mile downriver. Shortly after, another upriver. In a few years a significant enough number of farms and hunters' cabins had grown around the Murphs for the residents to regard themselves a village, albeit a widely scattered one.

Eventually, Saul married another Muskogi woman. They had several brothers and sisters for Anna, but the family never forgot Soosquana. Those that had known her revered her memory, and those that came later honored her heritage and that of her people. Cal and Adelin soon had their first child, then several others. In a few busy years the Murph compound was transformed into a thriving community.

The Tallapoosa River basin and all other land between the Coosa and Chattahoochee still belonged to the Creeks. That vast acreage was not included in the cessions won by General Jackson in the surrender of the Red Sticks in 1814. Nevertheless, settlers came, begrudged by the Creeks but not often physically opposed. Incidents were few.

Menawa survived his wounds and lived a long and controversial life, becoming an emissary for the Muskogi Nation in continuous and losing negotiations with the United States government over Muskogi lands. He died in 1835 after forced emigration to the Oklahoma Territory.

Hromarii was never heard from again. The Murphs speculated that his leg was so badly infected that it probably had to be amputated, or that perhaps it eventually killed him.

The fate of Soosquana's brothers, Tolokika and Ettepti-lopa, and Meeskapa, Pokkataw's friend, remains uncertain. It is probable that they died among the approximately nine hundred Creek fatalities in the Battle of Horseshoe Bend, as history has named the incident. In no other fight in American lore did more native Americans fall than at Cholocco Litabixi, the Horseshoe, on March 27, 1814.

As a result of his victory over the Creeks, Andrew Jackson became an immediate hero and received the commission he coveted as a general officer of the regular United States Army. He was then awarded command of American forces in the successful defense of New Orleans against the British. Jackson's military exploits became the principal stepping stone to his eventual election to the presidency of the United States.

Through the years, enough settlers clustered around the Murph settlement to form a town. The Murphs suggested it be named Soosquana. The citizens readily adopted the name and the happy little community thrived and grew.

Throughout east central Alabama today there are dozens of place names of Muskogean origin — cities, towns, rivers, streams, landmarks. There are others with the flavor of Andrew Jackson. The city of Talladega took its name from Talatigi, where the second battle of Jackson's campaign was fought. Other towns of Indian heritage include Wetumpka, Notasulga, Tuskegee, Loachapoka, Sylacauga, Opelika, and others.

The three rivers of the region — Tallapoosa, Coosa, and Chattahoochee — have retained their Muskogi designations. So have most creeks, such as the Yufabi (Euphaupee or Uphapee), Saugahatchi, Hillabi, Emuckfau, Enitachopco, and Kailaidshi (Kowaliga), though various spellings still abound. The community of Jackson's Gap lies near the Tallapoosa River not far from Horseshoe Bend.

Montgomery County, the locale of Alabama's capital city, carries the name of the intrepid Major Lemuel P. Montgomery of the Thirty-Ninth Infantry Regiment and General Jackson's "... flower of my army." (Oddly, the city itself is named after another unrelated military hero, Revolutionary War Brigadier General Richard Montgomery.)

The State of Mississippi was admitted to the United States in 1817 and the Alabama country severed from it as the Alabama Territory.

On December 14, 1819, the State of Alabama was created. All Tallapoosa River lands remained in the official hands of the Muskogi Nation. In 1830, President Andrew Jackson, in office only a year, signed the Indian Removal Act, an order that relegated all native Americans east of the Mississippi River to the Oklahoma Territory. In 1832, the United States Congress forced the Creeks to sign over all remaining claims to their ancestral homeland.

From that time through 1838 the American government forcibly escorted tens of thousands of Creeks to their new homes in what are now Arkansas and Oklahoma. The Tallapoosa River basin was finally clear for the flood of white settlers that would follow.

A Cherokee chief, Tsunulahunski, known to whites as Junaluska, was among those compelled to move to Oklahoma Territory. He had recruited and led a large contingent of Cherokee warriors "to exterminate the Creeks," and had fought bravely at the Horseshoe. He and his Cherokee compatriots had been vital to General Coffee's charges crossing the river and attacking the Red Sticks from the rear. However, he was often heard to vow after enforcement of the Indian Removal Act, "If I had known that Jackson would drive us from our homes, I would have killed him that day at the Horseshoe."

In 1959 Congress officially established Horseshoe Bend National Military Park at the site of the battle. It is located on Alabama Highway 49 in northern Tallapoosa County. Monuments and markers explain key locations and events of that terrible day.

Major Lemuel P. Montgomery's grave lies at the placement site of the Americans' two cannon. It overlooks the field on which the Red Sticks' barricade successfully resisted the artillery barrage but could not withstand the assault of Jackson's infantry and militia.

On December 31, 1926, Alabama Power Company dedicated giant Martin Dam across the Tallapoosa River, flooding over forty thousand acres under what is now Lake Martin. Only two towns had been established on or near the banks of the river stretching from well above the Horseshoe to its union with the Coosa to form the Alabama River. One of those towns was Tallassee, located at the future site of another dam at the great falls, and named after the Upper Creek warrior village of Talisi four miles downriver.

The other town was a small farming community with a post office, bank, sawmill, gristmill, its own gold mine, and several other businesses.

It was called Susanna, and it would be flooded by the waters of Lake Martin. Not much is known about the founding and early history of that fated community, now lost forever. But its location was in the vicinity of the beautiful bluff above the Tallapoosa River that the Murphs once made their home. Susanna was actually centered just to the south of the original Murph compound a few hundred yards up Blue Creek flowing from the east.

Perhaps it is not too much to imagine, or too romantic, that the name Susanna might have been altered from its original Soosquana, and that Saul and Callister Murph's little settlement was the first non-Indian town on the majestic Tallapoosa, ancient and revered homeland of the once-mighty Muskogi Nation.

• • •